INHERITANCE

INHERITANCE

NATALIE DANFORD

St. Martin's Griffin New York

This is a work of fiction. All of the characters, organizations, and events portrayed in this novel are either products of the author's imagination or are used fictitiously.

INHERITANCE. Copyright © 2007 by Natalie Danford. All rights reserved. Printed in the United States of America. For information, address St. Martin's Press, 175 Fifth Avenue, New York, N.Y. 10010.

www.stmartins.com

Library of Congress Cataloging-in-Publication Data

Danford, Natalie.
    Inheritance / Natalie Danford.
       p. cm.
    ISBN-13: 978-0-312-37843-1
    ISBN-10: 0-312-37843-2
    1. Fathers and daughters—Fiction. 2. Family secrets—Fiction.
3. Italy—Fiction. I. Title

PS3604.A523 I54 2007
813'.6—dc22

                2006050599

♦

For Paolo

ACKNOWLEDGMENTS

I will be grateful forever to Ellen Greenfield, Allison Lynn, Moira Trachtenberg-Thielking, and Ruth Gallogly for their guidance, their patience, their company, their humor, and their willingness to read this material until they had all but memorized it. I am so reliant on them that I'm struggling to write even this single page without their input.

I'm also grateful to my eternally loyal and supportive agent, Lisa Bankoff, to her assistant, Tina Wexler, and to my editor, Dori Weintraub, who has made the publishing process a pleasure. Copy editor Carol Edwards excelled at correcting my errors and suggesting edits that were in the spirit of the original work, only better.

Pamela Erens, Ellen Miller, and Kim Dettelbach all read this manuscript at various stages (and in various states of disarray) and provided invaluable insight and feedback. Sincere thanks as well to the members of both the Danford and Pierleoni families, especially my parents.

Most of all, I want to thank Paolo Pierleoni for his moral, emotional, and financial support, for handling so many of the details of daily life while I worked on this book, for sharing an insider's view of Italy in general and Urbino in particular, for providing Italian proofreading services, close readings, and many helpful suggestions, and for simply being there for me always.

✦ 1959 ✦

In the camera store, Luigi was being choosy. He smoothed the lapels of his jacket with both hands. He was thirty-seven, and the hair on his scalp was sparse. Already the same teardrop-shaped pattern that had balanced on his father's head was emerging, a tracing of the future. In order to draw attention away from that, he'd consciously weaned himself of a habitual gesture. Rather than smoothing back his hair the way he used to, he wiped his palms down the front of his jacket, settling his clothes into place.

"I don't know," he said, weighing the lens the girl had just handed him, as though its heft might determine whether it would serve his purposes.

The girl was wearing a white dress with navy blue polka dots, which did not suit her in the least, except for one feature: It wrapped in a low V over her breasts, and every time she leaned down to locate one of the lenses in the glass case that stood between them, it loosened ever so slightly and he could see one breast, like a round rosy pomegranate. He'd had a pomegranate once, in Italy, before the war. When he'd cut it open, he'd marveled at the community of seeds living inside the gel, then slurped them down.

"Maybe my father can help you," the girl offered, straightening. Standing tall, she was just an unremarkable girl, with none of the fertility promised by that one globe of flesh. The shelves behind her were filled with camera equipment, but those around Luigi were stocked with frames and photo albums.

"Is your father here?" She was seventeen, he guessed, maybe eighteen at the most. When he was stepping off that rotting boat from Naples, she'd been in diapers. Young people, Luigi considered at thirty-seven, had no sense of history. He shifted slightly, angling his left ear, his good ear, in her direction.

"He'll be back soon," the girl said. She blinked a little too hard when she mentioned her father, so Luigi pictured a bulky man, menacing in the manner of large Americans. Speak softly and carry a big stick, he thought. He'd learned that in the history class he'd taken to pass his citizenship test. Eight weeks of squeezing himself into a high school desk in the evening, and then the test had been disappointingly simple: "Who lives in the White House?" and "How many stars are there on the flag?" But as with everything, you didn't need to know the right answer; you just needed to know the answer they wanted you to give. Luigi was certain, for example, that many, many servants lived in the White House, cleaning up after the president and his family day and night, making them cheese sandwiches at 2:00 A.M. or dusting the offices late so as not to disturb, but he had also known that wasn't the correct response. He'd done what was required, and as a result, he had a shiny blue passport. The day it arrived in the mail, he threw out his old Italian identity card with the photo so faded that it was almost white and the words *razza: italiana* still clear at the bottom.

"He should be here in a minute," the girl said. She held out her hand and he passed the lens back to her and then admired how gently she set it on the counter, so that it made no sound as it touched the glass.

"Is there anything else you'd like to see in the meantime?" she asked, indicating the crowded shelves around them with a wave of her arm.

"No." He smiled. He had been in the United States nearly a decade and a half, but he still wasn't accustomed to the blank gentility of store employees. In Italy, shopkeepers kept their stock close and safe. No one would have put up with the manhandling of goods he saw in Shaleford. In the big, anonymous grocery store one day, a woman yanked a grape from its crowded stem and popped it into her mouth. When she caught him looking at her, she tilted her head and said, "There's no way to know unless you sample." Americans took no pride in their merchandise. You could try on clothes all day and buy nothing, and American store owners would give up with a shrug.

Luigi turned away from the girl and picked up a frame from the shelves behind him. It was filled, as were all the other frames on that shelf, with a picture of a small child—lots of freckles, bowl haircut, gen-

2

der unidentifiable—hugging a puppy with floppy ears. On the shelf above, all the frames were filled with close-ups of the same smiling woman, her blond hair affecting a perfect wave across her forehead over and over.

. That afternoon, Joe Preston's blond wife had picked Joe up at work, bringing along their two-year-old son, Joe junior. Never, Luigi thought, had a boy been more perfectly named. He was a miniature of his father in all respects, except that his hair looked soft and silky, not coarse, and his tiny teeth still sat obediently in perfect rows, not overlapping like his father's. He kept his left hand shoved into his pants pocket at a sharp angle, just as his father did, and rhythmically rocked his right foot onto its outside edge, just as his father did. As Joe proudly showed him around the lab ("Can you say microscope?"), Joe junior thrust his small, creased right hand on top of everything he could reach and announced, "This is my daddy's." He'd even rested that sticky hand on Luigi's thigh and proclaimed, "This is my daddy's." Joe had laughed, and so had Luigi, but when the child took his hand away, he left a miniature print of jam or grime, which Luigi unsuccessfully tried to wipe off in the men's room. The faint shape of five fingers and a palm still staked a claim to his right leg. Children marked you, Luigi realized, in ways you didn't anticipate.

He looked over his shoulder and watched the girl as she dusted the countertop with a rag. She had a steadiness to her. She worked carefully, but she didn't seem to do things just to look busy, unlike the way he sometimes sat at the lab, pencil poised over paper, but thought of something else altogether. Then again, her family probably owned the store. Some people were just lucky that way—they got things from their families. He'd watched in amazement as Joe Preston had hoisted Joe junior to face level, where he'd covered him with a series of kisses, ending with a trumpetlike burst on the child's stomach. Then Joe lifted his son so that the boy sat on his shoulders, took his wife's hand, and left work for the day.

Now a man, who looked not at all as he'd expected, opened the camera store's door and tinkled the bell that hung over it. This man was small and dark-haired, with a thin line of mustache resting on his lip. Whereas Luigi had pictured a muscle-bound giant, here was a man who carried himself confidently but kindly. This was not someone to intimidate his daughter. Maybe the girl just had a twitch.

"This man was wondering about a camera," the girl said by way of introduction. The shopkeeper in the suit stuck out his hand and shook Luigi's vigorously. "Doug," he said. Luigi nodded, but he didn't provide his own name. The one-syllable definitiveness of the name Doug had thrown him. Luigi had never seen a man that age so energetic. He was as compact as a coiled spring. Luigi smiled, then snapped his lips together to cover his teeth. For close to five years, he'd been visiting a dentist regularly. His mouth was a construction site of caps and bridges and half solutions to the faulty dental hygiene of the Italy years. His own father cleaned his teeth in the evening by chewing on a mint leaf and then rinsing with half a glass of white wine, which was believed to work as an antiseptic.

"Yes," Luigi said. "I'd like something simple, but I want to be able to control it."

"So, no Brownie for you," the man said pleasantly. He was a born salesman. Luigi sensed that, and he pulled himself up straight, ready for the pleasure of being led down a path to just what he wanted to buy.

"No, I think not," Luigi agreed. He affected a certain tone that was almost British, a combination of the Waspy accent native to Shaleford and the inflection he'd learned off a record called *Speak American: Get Rid of Your Foreign Accent in Thirty Days or Less*. The record jacket had a cartoon figure of a woman holding a small flag. A yellow eagle perched on her shoulder, peering suspiciously at the foreign listener.

"Well, I've got just the thing." The man unlocked a glass box along the wall and pulled out a smooth brown leather case. He set that on the counter and unsnapped it, then lifted out a shiny silver camera with a black strap. "It's a fine, fine camera. Thirty-five-millimeter."

He held the camera out to Luigi, who took it cautiously. "Do you know how to work one of these things?"

Luigi paused. "There's a manual, right?" He remembered what an instructor back in New York had told him about lab equipment: "Ninety percent of what you need to know, you'll find in the manual. The other ten percent is common sense." He'd been delighted to discover that all it took to sign up for the class was cash—no *raccomandazioni*, no proof of citizenship.

"Hold it up to your eye." Doug came around behind Luigi and lifted his arms so that the camera swam near his face. "Look through the viewfinder. It's that little window in the back."

Doug's arms around him were warm and soft in the wool suit. Luigi relaxed and pressed the camera to his eye.

"I see black," he said.

Doug laughed, and it reverberated against Luigi's back. "Forgot to take the lens cap off," he said. He reached his right hand around Luigi's chest and, with a click, removed the black plastic disk. "Try again."

Luigi held the camera up to his eye. Through the window was the camera store in miniature. He swung to his left. There was the door, framed in a dotted-line rectangle. He swung to the right. There was the girl, leaning into the case with a dust rag, that one breast lolling dangerously at the top of her dress.

Eagerly, Doug reached his arms in front of Luigi and moved the ring around the lens. "This is how you focus." Luigi swung the camera around again, manipulating the ring so that his vision was fuzzy, then clear, then fuzzy. Objects came slowly in and out of focus, as if he were regaining his equilibrium after being hit in the head with a blunt, heavy object.

"If you don't mind my asking," Doug said with fake hesitancy, "what do you want such a good camera for?"

Luigi was thrown. Was he not good enough for the camera? He already loved it. Unconsciously, he ran one finger gently over the logo carved into its front.

"I want to take some pictures of Shaleford," he said. "Show my family where I live now."

"Just got here, did you?" Doug asked.

"I've been in America almost twenty years," Luigi said. Fourteen, to be exact, but like a good, if naturalized, American, he'd learned to exaggerate.

"But you're just moving to Shaleford now? I thought I knew everyone in Shaleford. Town's the size of a postage stamp."

"Right. I've bought a house on Slate Street." Luigi couldn't help smiling as he pictured his house—the clean white front of it, the fence, the green lawn. He'd changed the name on the mailbox the other day. It had taken some study, but finally he'd determined that the majority of mailboxes on the block were tagged with letters that could be purchased at the hardware store for eighteen cents apiece. "Are you sure that'll fit?" the man behind the counter had joked as he doled out the letters that spelled Bonocchio. The letters came backed with adhesive, but Luigi didn't trust them to stick, so he'd carefully penned his name on a piece of paper and taped that to the inside of the metal mailbox, where he reasoned it wouldn't suffer the effects of the weather.

"Eighteen Slate Street? The Harpers' house?"

Luigi didn't like thinking about the Harpers. Despite their American house, the couple hadn't appeared to have spent much time in it together. The first time the agent gave him a tour of the house, Luigi glimpsed through the open door of the shed a man sitting on a folding chair, drinking from a can. A baseball game played on the radio. They found Mrs. Harper at the kitchen table, an ashtray at her elbow.

Now Luigi nodded to Doug.

"Well, welcome, friend," Doug said, sticking out a hand to shake Luigi's again. "The American dream, owning that first house, eh?"

Luigi smiled. It wasn't his first house, but that wasn't a story he'd tell this man. His first house had been the Levis'. In 1940, he'd sat solemnly at the Levis' kitchen table as Ester's father signed the deed to the house and hectares of land over to him. They shook hands. The Levis couldn't dodge the laws any longer. Germans were encroaching. A lot of Jews had already left.

Ottavio Levi had treated him like a man, his equal. He had handed Luigi his own pen, with a fine quill and a shiny body. Luigi used it to sign his name to the deed. When they had finished, the notary, Vittorio Leoni, brought out a large stamp, painted it carefully with viscous ink from a glass pot, and slammed it down. It left an angry black mark on the paper.

"Ci *fidiamo*," Signor Levi said from Luigi's left. The notary blew on the ink and studied Luigi out of the corner of his eye.

"You can trust me," Luigi said. The whole thing seemed an *esagerazione* to him. Things would blow over quickly. The Jews would settle back where they had been. They'd return like a river changing direction.

"Mind if I ask where you're from?" Doug said, interrupting Luigi's thoughts.

Mind your own business, Luigi longed to say, as much to test the phrase as to rebuff the man's interest. He loved the Americanness of the phrase, the way the clean efficiency of business—as if each American had his own small steel plant or candy factory—entered into everything here.

(In Italy, his mother would chide him, *"Fa' i fatti tuoi."* The Italian—"Do your own facts"—wasn't nearly as satisfying.)

"Italy," he said instead.

"Fine country," Doug said. "It's just that . . . I thought you might be Jewish—right timing and all, coming just as the war started—and this camera here is made in Germany. You know how it is." Luigi felt a wave of warmth for the man. He was a good salesman, yes, but he was ethical. Luigi glanced at the girl to see if she appreciated her father as well. She was leaning her elbows onto the counter, her cheekbones in her hands. Luigi didn't have fond memories of Germans himself—a particular color of moss green, or the sound of certain words spoken harshly, made his stomach drop the way it did on elevators. The camera, though, was so elegant that he could almost convince himself it was Italian, or at least Swiss.

"So, should we wrap this up? Or do you want to take some snaps on the way home?" Doug asked.

Luigi paused uncomfortably. "The price?"

"The price! How could I have forgotten the most important thing?" Doug slapped his own forehead. "Memory's going, that's for sure. Let me check that for you." He scampered behind the counter and pulled out a black binder. The girl stayed where she was. After looking at a few pages and doing some figures in the air with his finger, Doug smiled at Luigi. "How's three-fifty grab you?"

Luigi set the camera down on the counter gently. "I'm afraid that's far too much." Every time he discussed price, he recalled his first purchase in the United States. He'd eaten a sandwich in a coffee shop, then tried to bargain with the cashier over the cost. He hadn't realized that the wheels of commerce here weren't greased with favors and acquaintance and respect. That was how he'd met Pasquale, who'd been eating a slice of pie at the counter. Pasquale had stepped in and shown him the ropes. Later, Luigi had gotten so accustomed to not bargaining that he'd wanted to pay the asking price for the house in Shaleford, but the agent had insisted that he negotiate, and he found he'd lost the touch.

"That includes the lens," Doug said.

Luigi shook his head and held out his hands, palms up.

"It's what the camera's worth," Doug said quietly, as if he and Luigi really were friends.

"I'm not questioning the price," Luigi said. "I cannot pay that."

Doug sighed. "I like you. I want you to have the camera."

"I want to have the camera."

"How about this?" Doug tickled his own beard-free chin with one finger. "How about if I throw in a couple rolls of film, plus developing?"

Luigi shook his head sadly. "I'm sorry to have bothered you."

"Wait, wait." Doug came around to Luigi's side of the counter and placed a hand on his arm. "Don't go anywhere. At the very least I could sell you another camera."

Luigi thought he should leave. The word *sell* was so vulgar coming from this man's mouth that he didn't think he could tolerate it. But the itch for the camera—for a *good* camera with a shiny body—for pictures to send to his family to show them that he'd done it, that he owned property of his own, fair and square, wasn't fading. He stared longingly at the Leica.

Behind the counter, the girl seemed to wake up. He hadn't noticed her eyes before. They were set deep in her head, like chestnuts hiding in their shells. They were beautiful, but the right one turned in slightly, making her look haughty. Luigi, self-conscious about his own hearing problem, tried not to focus on it.

"What if I throw in some lessons? I'll teach you personally to take great pictures with that camera. I guarantee it. Your family'll think you live in a palace. All of Italy will be talking about it!" He pronounced the name of the country as a two-syllable word.

For the first time since her father had returned, the girl spoke. "Dad, if he doesn't want to buy it, sell him something else," she said. Her voice made it clear Luigi would not get out of there without buying anything. After she had spoken, as if that single sentence had been too much effort, she sighed, then turned and went behind the curtain that led to the rear of the store.

"I suppose." Doug tickled his chin again. "Well, I can sell you a Brownie. That's reasonably priced." When he pulled aside the curtain to duck into the back, Luigi glimpsed the girl a few feet behind it, sitting daintily on a packing crate with her legs crossed and a book in her lap. The back was dark, and she squinted to see the page. Doug returned holding a box made of thin, smooth cardboard, the kind that always reminded Luigi of his mother rolling out the *sfoglia* for pasta and holding it up to the light to check whether it was close to transparent. "Won't need anyone to show you how to use it, either. Easiest thing in the world," Doug said.

Luigi opened the box and peered in at the camera. Puzzlingly, it was made of black plastic. He took it out. It was ugly and utilitarian. Still holding the Brownie, he picked up the expensive camera in his other hand. His lust for fine things would be his downfall, his mother had always predicted.

"I'll take it," Luigi said, setting the Brownie back in its box and pulling the other to his chest.

"You will?" Doug looked genuinely surprised.

Luigi was surprised, too. The purchase of the house had almost emptied his account. How many mops had he held in fourteen years to get that house? he sometimes wondered. Then again, maybe it wasn't all that many—at the hospital, they rarely replaced the mops. Maybe he'd been squeezing the same drab one in the viselike wringer the whole time. From mops to bedpans, from bedpans, finally, to beakers.

The day he'd earned his certificate in laboratory technology, he couldn't help but think of Ester, as the third question required him to give the definition of an ester. "A compound, hydrolysis of which produces organic or inorganic acid and alcohol or phenol," he wrote automatically, and a whiff of lavender seemed to rise from the trail of lead his pencil left.

He thought, too, of Pasquale, who had guided him to that first job in the hospital in New York. Even after all that time, the image of Pasquale in his white orderly's coat, asserting that Luigi would never rise above his station, burned. *Ladro.* Luigi's feet ached in the weeks and months after Pasquale disappeared with his money. He walked the streets compulsively, looking for him. His friend Franco had given up and was resigned, but Luigi kept on until November, when the first snow fell. The slush began to seep into his shoes, and he could no longer justify his search.

"He's in California by now," Franco ventured.

"Andiamo in California allora," Luigi said, but the trip would have required money, and they had none. Luigi remembered how he'd flung open the dresser drawer in their shared apartment and found what he'd suspected: Below his ledger was the key, and below that nothing, simply the wood of the dresser drawer. No bankbook for the account he shared with Pasquale. He'd pounded his fist on top of the dresser, and the mirror shook.

After making the down payment on the house, Luigi's balance was almost back to zero. But he deserved this camera, as a reward, as a birthday present, as a memento of the moment when he'd changed, again. It hadn't been so hard to reinvent himself the first time, he reasoned, why should the second time be any harder? In this incarnation, he wanted to be a man with a fine camera.

"With the lessons and the film and the developing," Luigi said.

"Of course. Of course. It will be a pleasure." Doug was already ringing up the camera on the cash register, working quickly, as if he were afraid Luigi might change his mind.

"Take your time," Luigi said. And then he remembered an expression he loved, something he'd gleaned from the accent-reduction record, then had double-checked in the little printed booklet that accompanied it. "Take your time," he repeated. "I am a man of my word."

EVERY WEDNESDAY AT FIVE WHEN HE FINISHED AT THE LAB, LUIGI GOT INTO his car and drove to the camera store, where Doug taught him to take pictures. His first photos were simple, almost embarrassing: cars in the parking lot, lined up in rows like fish slapped onto a table at the market, and Doug's face, his thin mustache and full eyebrows dividing the frame horizontally into thirds. That first evening, Luigi took two rolls of film, and when he returned the next week, they were waiting for him. The developed photos were sticky and smelled like unripe fruit.

"You'll get tired of taking pictures of this ugly mug pretty quick," Doug told him as Luigi leafed through the pile and saw photos of Doug smiling, frowning, pointing a finger near his forehead in a mock salute. He'd been in the army during the war, he'd told Luigi casually, but the farthest he'd gotten was Tennessee. "Foreign enough for my taste," he'd reported. Like most Americans, Luigi noted, Doug believed that where he was and the way he was were the best place and way to be. Luigi had tasted a little of that security himself one night about a month after he'd moved into the Shaleford house. He sat at his kitchen table and ate a plate of pasta that he had cooked, and he felt something. It was an unfamiliar feeling, one he groped to put a finger on. And then he identified it: contentment.

"No, it's fine," Luigi said.

"Well, why not take some pictures of Diane here?" Doug suggested, pointing to his daughter. The first day of Luigi's photo lessons, she'd been wearing a different outfit, a simple white shirt and dark skirt, but today the polka-dot dress was making another appearance. She blushed at her father's suggestion, and Luigi could see the reddish color traveling down from her neck and disappearing into the V of her dress like spilled wine spreading over a white tablecloth.

"Dad," Diane said warningly.

"You're a prettier subject than I am," Doug insisted. "Come on around from behind that counter."

Diane stayed where she was.

"She's just a little shy," Doug told Luigi. He tapped twice on the counter and pointed to the door of the store, and Diane slowly closed her book and stood.

Outside, it was still light, which was a good thing, because Luigi could hardly afford the camera, let alone the flash he would have needed to take pictures after dark. In the two weeks since he'd bought it, he'd eaten macaroni with an onion browned in butter for dinner every night, and he'd taken his lunch to work—salami sandwiches on soft supermarket bread, which were damp and squashed by lunchtime, the white chunks of fat like pliable lumps of tissue. He and Doug had agreed that he'd pay in five installments, one every two weeks.

Now only two cars, Luigi's and Doug's, were parked on the metered strip outside the camera store. The owners of the surrounding stores—a pharmacy, a beauty parlor, the brick post office, and a men's clothing store staid and obsolete enough to sell lederhosen with a straight face—had all turned out their lights. A diner called Bill's Boxcar sat at the end of the block, an apron of parking lot spread in front of it. The clinking of cups on saucers jumped through its open windows and into the night like sparks. A neon sign in the shape of a hot dog nestled in a bun buzzed in the window, although Luigi was pretty sure they served hamburgers and excellent milk shakes, but no hot dogs.

Diane stood primly in front of her father's black Oldsmobile, which was parked directly in front of the store. Luigi noticed that the meter had run out of money and the arrow now rested in the red zone. Doug was a man who could charm the police, Luigi was sure. Only later did he learn that as a store owner, Doug was entitled to park without paying—no bribing or cajoling necessary. Diane pulled her back straight, a serious expression on her face. She looked like someone who had her picture taken frequently but had never learned to like the attention. Luigi took a step back from her, and then a step forward. He centered her. "You want to fill the frame," Doug had explained to him several times the week before. "Most people get their pictures back, and what they were looking at is just a tiny dot in the distance." Luigi moved in closer, so that the crown of Diane's head brushed the top of the viewfinder rectangle and her toes rested gently on the bottom. He inhaled and held his breath, as Doug had taught him, bracing his arms against his chest to keep the image stable. Diane blinked and her bad eye straightened, looking forward against its will. And then, at the last second, just as Luigi clicked the button, she grasped the flared skirt of her dress in both hands and pulled it into a wide fan against the hot black metal.

SIX MONTHS LATER, AT NOON SHARP ON MARCH 12, 1960, DIANE'S MOTHER, Rita (although she'd insist moments later that Luigi call her "Mom," and he would comply), sprinkled a dozen or so grains of rice over Luigi's head.

"Congratulations," she cried out, clapping her hands at her own cleverness. She'd secreted the rice in her pocket, and Luigi realized that throughout the quick ceremony in the judge's chambers, when he'd thought she was anxiously rubbing her fingers together, she'd really been playing with the white pellets, getting ready to spring her surprise. He should have known. Rita and Doug weren't nervous people, at least not in any visible way. Not like his own mother, who sat at the kitchen table and anxiously rubbed her forehead, or took to bed with unexplained *crisi*, mental episodes that had no cause and therefore no solution. At least that was what she'd been doing when he left. He was unable to picture his parents fifteen years older, so he quickly put them out of his mind. The fact that his parents had never met Diane, didn't even know her name, made the whole occasion feel unreal.

"Say cheese!" Doug shouted cheerily, and he snapped a picture. Light danced in front of Luigi's eyes, then faded.

"Dad," Diane said warningly. Her hand was moist in Luigi's.

Doug said, "Someday you'll be glad I did that." A few weeks later, Luigi would help himself to the photo and place it in an envelope, noteless, to send to his family. In it, he and Diane, their eyes wide with shock, their hands clasped, looked as though they were about to plunge into a swimming hole where they didn't know the depth.

"Aren't you a sight." Rita beamed. They were walking down the somber hall of the Shaleford courthouse, Rita just ahead of them, and she kept turning to stare at her daughter, and Luigi, too. Diane walked purposefully, with none of the slow shuffle of a bride. Her one concession to tradition had been a brooch of her mother's in the shape of a bird with a sapphire chip for an eye. It was old and borrowed and blue—Luigi had had to have the rhyme explained to him as they sat in the anteroom to the judge's chambers, and just as he'd started to ask about the something new, his name was called, and the four of them rose together. And Rita replied, "A new husband, of course."

He was somebody's husband. He could already imagine Diane using the word as she picked up his suit at the cleaners ("My husband's suit, please") or took their car to the garage in town to be serviced ("How long until my husband's car will be ready?"). They would sleep together in a queen-size bed with a new mattress that he'd purchased two weeks earlier. There'd been little touching during the quick work of courting Diane—they'd spent most of that time with her parents—but the moments when he had been permitted to fix his hands on her were so fleeting and exquisite that they were carved into Luigi's memory. At will, he could call up the feel of the deep hollow at the base of Diane's neck where her pulse fluttered like the unsteady heartbeat of a lab mouse lifted from its cage, or the soft moaning breath when she said "Lou," which was what she called him, the night his hand finally dared to reach into the V of her dress and grasp one of those perfect breasts.

He supposed they could have insisted on going out alone, without her parents. He might have taken her to a drive-in or to Bill's Boxcar for a sundae. But the nights he treated himself to a grilled cheese at Bill's, he sat apart from the young kids in felt jackets with leather sleeves who shouted and played tricks with sugar packets and saltshakers. The waitresses always shooed him down to the end, where men with T-shirts peeking out from under their button-down shirts stirred their coffee dreamily. It would have been awkward for Diane, he feared, to sit with the old people.

He didn't mind spending time with Doug and Rita, either. He couldn't help measuring them against his own parents. Doug and Rita had no angry silences. They didn't object to their daughter marrying a man sixteen years her senior. (Diane was older than he'd first thought, twenty-one.) "You're a little more mature. That'll do her good," Doug had confided when Luigi asked him for permission, even though he and Diane had already decided. Doug and Rita never mentioned that he was foreign. In fact, they delighted in introducing him to their country. Luigi didn't point out that he'd already tasted numerous apple pies and seen the Fourth of July come and go fifteen times. He didn't mention that as a citizen he'd had to study the history of their country, and so the name George Washington was not a strange one that he needed spelled out. They enjoyed being the Americans for him, and he could see no harm in that.

After the wedding, Doug drove the four of them two towns over, to the closest Chinese restaurant in the area. They sat around a table covered with a red cloth, which snagged on Luigi's rough palms. Gilt dragons danced on the walls, breathing stunted flames. Doug ordered, then sported a wide smile as he watched Luigi eat sweet-and-sour pork and beef chow mein. The waiter left a slender set of chopsticks next to each plate, but they all used forks, to Luigi's relief. He was wearing a new suit for the occasion and didn't want to risk staining it with the sweet brown sauce that was the hallmark of Chinese cuisine.

"Can't be American until you get a taste of Chinese food," Doug decreed when Luigi admitted that he rarely went out to restaurants, aside from the occasional grilled cheese at Bill's.

As cheerful and gung ho (another expression picked up from the accent-reduction record) as Diane's parents were, she herself was introverted. On those evenings when the four of them sat in the living room (Luigi had called it a "salon" one night, and Rita's laughter tinkled merrily, then died down, but bobbed back up to the surface each time she remembered), Diane often pulled out a book and started reading. She looked beautiful in the lamplight—her bad eye followed her good one when she read, and her hair tumbled down into her face. "Something half-hidden is more interesting than something revealed," Doug had taught him during the photography lessons. Luigi had once spotted a perfect photograph: just one of Diane's slender calves and ankles poking out from behind the curtain that divided the public part of the store from the private. He hadn't taken the picture, though, for fear that when Doug developed it, he'd see what Luigi had been thinking.

On those evenings at Doug and Rita's house, Luigi cast furtive glances Diane's way as he tried to keep up a conversation with her parents about their backyard or the camera store, which defined their universe. Doug was, as Luigi had sensed upon meeting him, the consummate salesman. Twice a week, he went to Kathleen's Beauty Salon for a manicure so that his nails would be buffed and neat as he highlighted the features of cameras for his customers. He reread Norman Vincent Peale's *The Power of Positive Thinking* every year, he'd informed Luigi, and each time he did, he picked up a new trick. When he told a story, he introduced it by announcing that it would be the funniest (or occasionally the saddest) story Luigi had ever heard. He had a knack, as did Rita, though to a lesser extent, for putting people at ease, and he used it on Luigi, oiling his insertion into their family.

Luigi only noticed later how he'd been manipulated. When Doug was leaning over the counter of the camera store and showing him that first set of pictures of Diane, complimenting him on how much he'd improved, and then saying with a sigh, "She's a sight, isn't she?" Luigi could only nod and agree. When Doug told him to forget the last installment on the camera, that it would be a crime to take money from such a fine man, Luigi congratulated himself on having made a friend in Shaleford. His happiness only increased when Doug insisted on having him for dinner once the photography lessons were over.

After dinner that first night (a casserole of broken spaghetti, ground meat, and onions, he was horrified to see when they sat at the round wooden table), Diane walked him out to the street where his car was parked. That was when he knew that it was for Diane that he was there. He was flattered, and at the same time disappointed. He'd believed he was wanted for his company, but clearly there was a more concrete motive at hand. How had it come about? he wondered. Had Diane confided in her father that she was interested in Luigi? Was it Doug who considered him appropriate for his daughter?

During his first week in New York City, when a woman in a shiny short skirt approached him and asked if he wanted a date, Pasquale had had to explain to him that she was a *puttana*. Later, he'd looked up the word *date* in his dictionary, its well-thumbed edges already as soft as a woman's thighs, and found the fruit, *dattero*, listed first, then *data*, and then *appuntamento*. There had been no mention of sex for pay. How had Pasquale known? he wondered.

Luigi had been to prostitutes in New York, their mattresses as dank as the one he'd slept on in that first apartment, smelling as his own shared bed did of somebody else. He'd even gone on a date with a nurse named Sarah, who took him back to her efficiency, where everything gleamed white. She unzipped his pants, gave him a *sega*, then handed him a clean dish towel and sent him on his way as briskly as if she'd pulled a tooth or lanced a mole for him. After that, when he saw her in the hospital corridors, she looked at her unscuffed white shoes and kept walking.

But there would only be one woman, a girl, really, he would ever love. In his mind's eye, Ester was always fifteen, her skirt spread around her to cover her knees, like a lily turned upside down, the stalk of her body rising out of it, green and fresh and untouched. Captured in that pose, she held still and immaculate as the cake decoration of a bride and groom that Rita placed on top of four stale fortune cookies the day he and Diane were married. Afterward, they'd cracked open the cardboardlike cookies and let the silly pieces of paper drift onto the plate. "A man makes his own fortune," Doug insisted after reading out loud the stock sentiment printed on his: YOUR LIFE IS FULL OF PASSION. "Attitudes are more important than facts." Rita picked up the decoration and snapped off the groom's cunning pink hand, which looked like a mouse's paw. She placed it between her teeth, and then she must have noticed Luigi's horrified expression.

"Sugar," she explained, holding the curved fingers between her front teeth so he could see them. Then she bit down hard. Luigi looked again at the fortune in his hand. It said BE CAREFUL WHAT YOU WISH FOR. He displayed it to Diane with a questioning look on his face, and she read it thoughtfully.

"It means you might want something a lot, but in the end it could disappoint you," she explained. Already the security he'd sought—an American wife to interpret for him—was paying off.

When Diane walked him to his car the first night he'd gone to her parents' for dinner, she leaned in and kissed his cheek. "Well, see you around," she said, suddenly girlish, her hands clasped in front of her. She ran from him across the lawn, her pumps making scrubbing noises in the grass. She disappeared for a moment in the dark, then reappeared in the light cast on the front step. He stood and watched her go, but she didn't turn to wave.

AFTER THEY WERE MARRIED, DIANE MOVED HER THINGS INTO LUIGI'S HOUSE gradually. She went to see her parents every day, and she returned from each trip with a satchel or a suitcase, and once with an electric contraption for drying her hair, a clear plastic bubble attached to a pink base. Without asking him, she arranged these things where she wanted. My husband won't mind, he imagined her thinking. He heard her refer to him only once though, on a morning when he woke with a headache so bad, it nauseated him. She called the lab to report that he'd be taking a sick day. "Mr. Bonocchio won't be coming in today," she said, as though she were his secretary. One day, he returned from the lab and discovered that his underwear and socks had been relegated to a single drawer, his T-shirts to another. The remaining four drawers in his dresser were filled with Diane's things—camisoles and swishy underwear and bras. Her dresses hung in his closet already.

They hadn't taken a honeymoon. Rita had counseled against it, suggesting that they go away together in a year or two, when they'd be more comfortable with each other.

"Not that I'm the type of mother-in-law to meddle," she assured Luigi.

Rita had squeezed Diane's hand when she said this, and Luigi could see that rather than squeezing back, his soon-to-be wife let her hand hang limp and boneless.

"Of course not," he said.

Diane stopped working at the camera store and began to stay home. A few times, her father called in the evening to inquire whether she might come in the next day, and she sighed and dutifully did as he asked. But if he didn't ask, the days were hers. Luigi wondered how she filled her time. She cooked dinner, he knew, because the results were on the table every night when he returned. (He was relieved to discover that she was less experimental with food than her mother. Most nights, they sat down to identical plates of pork chops—cooked in a contraption she called an electric frying pan—mashed potatoes, and string beans, with steaks replacing the chops on Fridays.) And she went to the library. Stacks of library books, their inner leaves bearing flaps of paper stamped with black numbers, piled up on her side of the bed. Women could look sexy when they read, Luigi knew, but Diane looked troubled, as though she could never take in the words fast enough.

"She's practically jailbait," one of the other analysts at the lab had cried out in mock horror when Luigi let slip that his fiancée would turn twenty-two just before the wedding. He hadn't heard the word before, but he knew immediately what it meant. After that, there was no stopping the teasing.

"Does she still suck her thumb?"

"Going to bring a game of Chutes and Ladders on your honeymoon?"

"Didn't her parents teach her not to take candy from strangers?"

From there, they sank further into jokes about his lollipop and his Sugar Daddy, which Luigi knew was a caramel on a stick that could yank out most of his dental work with one chew. He might have been insulted for Diane, but their image of a girlish kitten in baby-doll pajamas was so far from her bookish distance that he wasn't. She was ageless, he often thought, defined more by her persistent seriousness and her dedication to books than by some number.

Once they were married, she got into bed each night and picked up a book from the stack, turned on her right side, rested her head on her right hand, and opened the cover. If he stroked her hip over the sheet (she wore long, soft nightgowns that covered her from neck to ankles and that he found strangely arousing), she placed her left hand over his, but he could see in the soft light of her bedside lamp that she didn't move her eyes from the page.

Twice a week, after turning off the light, she rolled over. Luigi had never been quick to fall asleep; even if Diane read for an hour or more, he was still awake, curled on his side, away from her. He could feel the gentle rocking motion of the mattress as she arranged herself on her back, and that was his signal.

Sex between the two of them was cold and unexpectedly difficult. Diane had been a virgin, and the first few times he'd entered her, she'd whimpered. Now she lay stoically on her back for him. "Are you okay?" he asked as he hovered over her. He tried to be gentle, but it never seemed to make any difference. She threw her arms up, so that her hands were by her ears, and turned her head to one side. "Uh-huh, fine," she replied, with the same tone she used to respond to the milkman when he inquired whether she'd like her usual order. When he was done and sagged onto her, she kissed him chastely on the forehead, as though he were a child who had finished his chores. Luigi tried to imagine what Rita had told her daughter about sex—that it was something to be endured, to judge from the evidence. He would have liked to peer into Diane's vagina, to study up close the lips folding around her clitoris like a fuzzy green fava pod split with a thumbnail to reveal a single bean. But he didn't know how to ask for that, and Diane didn't offer.

When they'd been married for two months, she announced over dinner that the last of her things were moved in. "I'm all here."

Luigi smiled. He'd already learned the blank acquiescence of marriage, even in the face of an absurd statement. She was as absent as he was. He slurped tomato soup from his spoon. He tried mightily to detect the flavor of tomato, but he could taste only salt. A glistening grilled cheese sandwich cut into triangles sat at his right elbow. He'd stood and watched as Diane prepared it, using the flat back of the spatula to sizzle it in the electric frying pan. Initially, when he realized that Diane would be only what she was, that her reserve wasn't shyness that would melt away, but her actual personality, he'd felt duped into the marriage. They'd pulled one over on the immigrant. They'd convinced him to marry the Brooklyn Bridge, to buy the broken bride.

But as the weeks went by, he adjusted his expectations. As long as he didn't picture the empty spiral of the future, he found their quiet evenings comfortable.

Luigi bit into the grilled cheese sandwich. His wife cooked with a cheese called Velveeta. The first time he'd seen a rectangular block of it sliding out of its yellow sleeve of a box, he'd figured that anything with such a brilliant orange color must also have a strong taste, but he'd been wrong.

"You're all here," he repeated back to Diane.

Sometimes, when they sat like this, he tried to trace how they'd come to be here, together, married. What had he done to bring her here? Why had she wanted to come? Her parents, he realized at the weekly Tuesday-night dinners at their house, were pleased with the match. Initially, he'd been heartened that they didn't object to him, but since he and Diane had married, Luigi had changed the way he interpreted Doug and Rita's relief. He'd recognized that they'd thought Diane would never get married, that she'd sat home reading too many nights to be somebody's choice, that the way her eye danced toward her nose was too much damage for a boy her own age to ignore. "Half a loaf is better than none," Rita was fond of saying in disappointing moments—often when a culinary creation didn't pan out. Luigi could imagine that she'd said the same of him once.

Even married, on Tuesdays and Fridays, Diane took a book along to her parents' house, and as Doug and Rita and Luigi enjoyed coffee and cookies—and once a cake constructed out of canned whipped cream and chocolate wafers, which Luigi liked in spite of himself—she read. She read through discussions of her cousins out west, offering the occasional nod or grunt. She read through Doug's tales of the camera store and the big customers he thought he might get. She read until about two minutes before they were to leave, when she shut her book, thanked Doug and Rita, and asked Luigi to get her coat from the rack in the front hall. While he busied himself with that, she packed in a night's worth of conversation with her parents. From the hall, he could hear her low tone, but not her words.

"Do you want more soup?" Diane asked, gesturing to the pot on the burner, its contents occasionally burbling and spitting up a red splotch onto the stovetop.

"No, thank you." But the joke was on them, as the faceless American on his record would have put it. It didn't bother Luigi that Diane was quiet. And he didn't mind that she had secrets from him. He had stories of his own that he didn't want to tell. He'd adjusted to Diane. He didn't feel suckered the way he had back in New York, with Pasquale. He still felt ill when he thought of Pasquale running off with his and Franco's money. His stomach had seized then at the realization, once again, that a protector might take from those he sheltered the only thing that mattered.

Instead, he felt that he and Diane benefited equally from their mutual silence. She never asked about Italy, and he never talked about his family in Urbino. He continued to send photographs. He thought of the Levis less and less frequently. They were receding, finally. He had trouble recalling their pale faces, almost phosphorescent in the darkness. He remembered Ester, though, and tried sometimes to picture her in Shaleford, living with him. That didn't make any sense, of course. If she'd lived, he wouldn't have left. Diane never asked why he couldn't bear to go into the crawl space, or why he avoided the attic. When he suggested that they knock down the shed in the backyard, though, she protested, as the house had no basement to speak of, just a small room filled almost completely by the furnace. He didn't like small spaces, he told her. Claustrophobic. She wasn't fond of the closeness herself, she replied.

The one thing he missed, and it had nothing to do with being married, but, instead, with living in Shaleford, was speaking Italian. His speech in English was better—he could feel his accent trickling away almost daily and noticed that strangers had less trouble understanding him than before. Being married to Diane was an immersion course, better than any record. She never seemed to notice that he had an accent, and she certainly made no attempt to speak slowly for him, all good as far as he was concerned. But while he didn't miss Franco or Guglielmo and couldn't imagine them visiting Shaleford in their white orderly uniforms, he missed the ease of speaking Italian, the way it spilled off his tongue.

"Lou, I've been thinking," Diane said.

"Yes?" Luigi brushed the last of the sandwich crumbs from his fingertips onto the plate. The cheese had left a slick film on the roof of his mouth.

"I've been thinking about babies."

Luigi froze, his greasy fingers poised above the plate, as though he were about to launch into a piece of piano music.

"Are you?" He indicated Diane's waist with his chin.

"No, no." She blushed. "The diaphragm's still working." She blushed again.

"Diaphragm?" Luigi wiped his hands on his paper napkin, shredding it in parts. On their first night together, when Diane had worn a mint green nightgown with lace ruffling the neck, he'd nervously pulled a condom out of the drawer of his nightstand, and she'd rested a hand on his wrist and shaken her head. He'd thought she'd taken care of it with a *spirale* or some American device he hadn't heard of, but then, when he couldn't enter her and he ended the evening by giving himself a quick jerky *sega* in the bathroom once Diane's breathing grew regular, he'd changed his mind and thought maybe somehow she knew that there wouldn't be any danger. Since then, he hadn't given birth control much thought at all. It seemed impossible that a baby could arise out of the dry, joyless act.

"Don't make me repeat it," Diane whispered. He cocked his left ear toward her.

"So, babies," Luigi said, prompting her. He couldn't stand to see her so uncomfortable. They'd never discussed children. Luigi had never known anyone married who didn't have children—several of them, in fact. He'd simply assumed she'd want them eventually. Men had work and cars and money, but besides children, what else was there for women? Luigi brushed his hands down the front of his shirt, adjusting nonexistent lapels.

"So, throw out the diaphragm," he said expansively. He vaguely remembered, during a trip through the medicine cabinet as he searched for aspirin, seeing a case that, when he popped it open, revealed a beige rubber dome. He'd taken it for a piece of plumbing equipment, a drain cap.

Diane glanced at him shyly.

"Really?" she said. "You think we can?"

Luigi had a vision of himself with a young dark-eyed boy. The boy's moist hand would fit into his. He remembered Joe Preston, Jr., at the lab, watching out for his father. *Babbo*, this imaginary child said in a high, firm voice, and he held his arms out to Luigi to be picked up. A son would be a companion, someone he could form not just in his own image but better than he was. An American boy who spoke Italian, who both played baseball and loved his father unconditionally. Someone to take care of him as he aged. *Figli maschi* went the old toast—"May you have male children." Luigi looked at Diane. As it did when she was excited, her eye had straightened.

"Yes, we can," he said, failing to realize that he was quoting Doug quoting Norman Vincent Peale, "and we will."

22

✦ SATURDAY ✦

The road to Urbino was steep and winding. At each curve, the bus stopped and sighed patiently before the driver sharply spun the wheel and swung the vehicle onto the next portion of asphalt. Olivia found the rocking-cradle motion comforting. With her forehead pressed against the window, she closed her eyes, but even though she was jet-lagged and travel-weary, she couldn't have slept, not now that she was this close. Anticipation fluttered in her stomach, and the key from her father's nightstand prodded from her back pocket. She'd taken to carrying it everywhere. Warmed by her own body heat, it reminded her of the sun-bleached skeleton of a fragile bird.

The bus purred louder as the driver changed gears, and Olivia opened her eyes and gazed up. Above her, perched on the hill and looking as inevitable a part of the landscape as a plastic figurine of a bride and groom atop a wedding cake, sat the city where her father had been born. At least, he'd always called it a city, *una città*, but now she saw that it was smaller, more accurately a town. The buildings, all the reddish gray color of bisqued brown clay with no glaze, stood shoulder-to-shoulder, so that the cluster appeared a single enormous dwelling intended to house thousands. Two turrets, which she recognized as the towers of the famous ducal palace, extended above the rest.

Sun glinted off windows here and there, giving Urbino the look of a mirage glimpsed through shimmering heat, but this was far from dry desert. The surrounding countryside consisted of lush green fields dotted with the occasional farmhouse. She recognized the scenery as the background from Piero della Francesca's portrait of the duke of Urbino, staring stone-faced at his wife in the other half of the diptych. A framed poster of the duke in his red mushroom hat had always hung on the wall in her father's living room. When, in an art history class in college, the regular click and whir of the slide projector had thrown the image onto the screen, she'd smiled in the dark with both recognition and disorientation, feeling like a third grader encountering her teacher in the grocery store.

The sweet, silky smell of a flower she couldn't identify drifted lazily through the open windows of the bus. Around her, the other passengers murmured in Italian in low voices that blended with the engine's soothing white noise. Olivia was pleased to find that she understood their discussions of whether they'd have time to hang the *panni* on the line before the sun set, or what they planned to eat at *cena*. She was surprised, however, that they kept talking and didn't stare upward as she did. They didn't seem to notice that something beautiful hovered over them.

Could you grow so accustomed to the awesome sight of a five-hundred-year-old city planted on an isolated hill that you stopped noticing it? Olivia smiled, but then she thought of her father, the last year, and what it had proved: You could get used to anything. The bus turned, following the brick wall that cosseted the city, and the town dipped out of sight. It was right above the road, but so close that it became invisible. Then the bus pulled into a parking lot, and suddenly the palace reappeared, towering directly overhead.

Olivia stumbled off the bus with the other passengers. The airline had lost her suitcase, so she had only a small carry-on bag, outfitted with a spare pair of underwear and her toothbrush and toothpaste. In front of her was a tall brick wall, and above that the arcaded balconies of the ducal palace, slung between the two turrets. Behind her and up a steep slope stood a grove of pine trees, to her left a grand arch with a white stone eagle balanced at the top, observing closely as passengers from the bus walked beneath it in groups of two and three. The road they'd arrived on stretched to the right and wrapped tenderly around the town before tumbling into the green countryside.

Olivia opened the side pocket of her bag and felt for the paper she'd found in her father's nightstand after he died. Without pulling it out, she gently caressed the thick folds. Then she withdrew her hand and zipped shut the pocket.

She walked under the gate, below the watchful eyes of the stone eagle, and started up the cobblestoned hill that led to the town center. How could he have left a place so beautiful for the generic suburb of Shaleford? she wondered. The sharply sloped street was wide enough for cars, but jutting off to each side, like capillaries stemming from a fatter vein, were tiny alleyways, some fretted with stairs, that burrowed deeper into the city. Looking down these side streets, she spotted wooden doors and low windows, most of them with their shutters closed. They looked like cozy miniature houses for mythical creatures—trolls or fairies. Tentatively, she touched the key in her back pocket. Might it open one of those cunning doors?

On one of the *vicoli*, a gray-haired woman leaned out a third-story window and lowered a basket on a rope. A stout man standing below packed the basket with a bunch of greens, two tomatoes, and a plastic bottle of mineral water. *"Tira su!"* he shouted, indicating for her to pull it up. The whole scene felt staged for her, as if she were strolling through a Hollywood set for a movie about Italy, rather than having just made the journey—flight, bus, train, and then bus again—to Urbino.

Olivia, her breathing quickened from the climb, topped the crest of the hill and found herself in the piazza. Urbino's main piazza was not one of the famous ones immortalized in art history slides; it lacked the seashell shape of Siena's or the ornate statuary of Rome's. But it had the charm and comfort of a public space that was alive. There were four cafés around its perimeter, and a large building with a plaque announcing the presence of government offices. To one side stood a pharmacy, its glowing red plus sign an out-of-place touch of modernity on the ancient stone building. Facing the pharmacy was a Benetton with headless mannequins and handwritten cards indicating the prices of the skirts and jeans and T-shirts in the window. Stretched over one of the two streets that led upward, out of the piazza, a banner crowed URBINO: 50 ANNI DI LIBERTÀ, 28/08/44–28/08/94.

Instinctively, Olivia scanned the piazza for anyone resembling her father. She herself took after her mother's side of the family, with her high forehead and thin hair. There was a man in the corner, talking loudly with another, who had her father's eyes, peering out of deep sockets. A relative? There was another man with the same eyes, and a third. Exiting the pharmacy was a mother, holding a child's hand in hers, who was pursing her lips in thought, a common expression for Olivia's father. Descending one of the hills was an older woman, smartly dressed in linen, whose gray hair came to a point between her eyebrows, just as Olivia's father's hair had. And all around her were foreheads marked with the regularly spaced wrinkles that always reminded Olivia of a comb through clay. All these people moved slowly but with certainty, as if their paths were laid out on the ground for them to follow. Olivia felt their eyes pass over her, and she imagined their surprise in finding out that she was not the outsider she appeared.

She did have relatives here—that much she knew. Olivia's father had told her of a younger sister, although he'd never spoken the sister's name. Olivia had sent an announcement of her father's death to the address listed under the name Bonocchio in his address book and received shortly afterward an unsigned piece of paper with *"Condoglianze"* in handwriting that looked like someone spelling out words with sticks, along with a shiny prayer card.

When she was little, Olivia had run her finger over that address under *B* and wondered what her relatives might be like. She'd dreamed of a huge family gathered around a table on Sundays, a warm, earthy grandmother dishing out pasta and urging her and a multitude of cousins to eat. Typical only-child fantasy, she chided herself as she got older. In her teens, she'd pictured a more orderly clan of thin characters out of a neorealist film. Now she wondered which of the two she'd find—the grandmother who would press Olivia's long-lost face to her cushiony bosom, or the cousins and aunts and uncles who would welcome her with concern. They were certain to be curious, but would they resent her father for leaving and, in turn, resent her? Or would she be a conquering hero?

There was another possibility, as well: Her relatives might not be there at all. She hadn't told them she was coming. She'd thought of writing about her arrival, but she hadn't known what to say—not the Italian, but the proper expression. Besides, she wanted time to gather her thoughts. She'd contact them after she'd been in the city a day or two, she'd figured.

Having arrived, she wondered now if perhaps she should have given notice. She might have been caught in a warm embrace, rather than standing here in the piazza, trying to pick out familiar features.

Olivia followed a sign with an arrow to her hotel. The woman behind the desk in the nondescript lobby took her passport without looking up and, in exchange, handed her a key attached to a strange Saturn-like key ring. It was a large copper-colored globe bigger than a golf ball, with a rubber strip hugging its middle.

In front of the door with the matching 38, Olivia struggled briefly with the key. It was old-fashioned—not so different from the one from her father's nightstand that still rested in her back pocket. When she tried to open the door, the gap-toothed end of the key jammed sideways. With careful determination, Olivia straightened it and pulled it out. She took a deep breath, then rearranged the key and turned it. It caught neatly in the lock, and the door swung open.

OLIVIA WOKE TO A SHARP KNOCK. THE HOTEL ROOM WAS DARK, ALTHOUGH through the window she could see a patch of still-light sky that framed a church's bell tower. She'd been dreaming that she was back in her father's house in Shaleford. In the twilight between sleeping and wakefulness, she was convinced she felt the warm weight of Smudgy, the cat she'd had as a child, holding down the blanket by her feet. Eighteen years earlier, as her father was leaving for work, Smudgy had darted out the door and never returned. The cat headed into the woods, he told Olivia as she cried, the way sick animals did when they sensed they were dying, the way years later she'd wish her father had the instinct to do himself.

And then today came back to her—the long trip, her thrill at the first sight of Urbino, and the way she'd fallen into a heavy sleep as soon as she lay down on the squeaky hotel bed. She hadn't even removed her shoes. Awake now, Olivia reached for the wall switch, but the overhead bulb gave off light so faint that it made her think of a field trip she'd chaperoned to the planetarium, where they'd learned that light from the stars was traveling billions of miles and thousands of years to reach them. As she rose from the bed, she again felt the key in her back pocket, its beak pecking her.

There was another short rap on the door.

"*Un attimo,*" Olivia called out. A muffled female voice came from the other side, but she couldn't make out what it said. Maybe it was a hotel employee with her suitcase.

Olivia swung open the door, and in the hall stood a woman about her own age, holding a lighted cigarette down by her hips. She was wearing a white V-necked shirt that dipped between her breasts to make room for three gold chains, one with a crucifix, and jeans that hung low on her hips, exposing a strip of very tan, very taut skin with a belly button as perfectly round as the perforations made by the three-hole punch Olivia had at school.

"Olivia," the woman said decisively, throwing one arm around her while keeping the other up in the air to stop the cigarette from coming into contact with skin. She kissed Olivia's cheeks—right, then left, then right again—and Olivia rushed to keep up.

"It doesn't bother you, does it?" the woman asked in Italian, indicating the cigarette with her chin. "I know in America you're all crazy with the *antifumo.* It's okay, I understand." She took a long drag on the cigarette but showed no sign of putting it out.

Exhaling, the woman took a step back and studied Olivia, then shook her head and looked away. She drew greedily on her cigarette again, as if to assuage her disappointment at what she'd seen. Olivia still hadn't spoken, but already she felt defensive. I just got off a plane. They lost my luggage. This isn't really what I look like. Self-consciously, she pulled at the T-shirt she'd worn for more than twenty-four hours and slept in twice.

"Excuse me," Olivia said finally, "*ma tu chi sei?*" "Who are you?" was an expression her father had used with her when she was acting up, his version of "Who do you think you are?" Olivia spoke the words with the same offended inflection.

"O *santo Dio!*" The woman laughed. "Of course. We've never met, but I recognize you from the photos. I'm Claudia." She pronounced it *Cloud-ee-ah*.

"Claudia . . ."

"*Tua cugina,*" the woman continued. "Claudia. Giuseppina's daughter." The names meant nothing to Olivia.

"Giuseppina?"

Claudia laughed, a short, sharp snap of surprise. "Giuseppina was your aunt, your father's sister. You mean he never talked about us? *Mai?*"

Claudia was eyeing her, clearly wondering what kind of Bonocchio she could be.

"My father didn't talk much about Italy," Olivia said apologetically.

"Really?" Claudia raised one eyebrow and sucked on her cigarette. "He sent us a photograph every month. I have them all at home if you want to see."

Now it was Olivia's turn to be surprised. "Really?"

"I loved looking at those photos. *La casa, la macchina.* Everything so big."

Olivia felt embarrassed, as though in addition to the house in Shale-ford and her father's car, Claudia had glimpsed inside of her and spotted something unwieldy. And then she was touched that her father, never sentimental, had been emitting images of her to the family he'd left behind. Had he missed them? He never said.

"Everyone used to tease me that I had a real *zio d'America*," Claudia was saying.

"*Scusa?*" Olivia half-smiled, perplexed.

"*Uno zio d'America,*" Claudia repeated, more slowly this time. "You know, like the expression. When we get money unexpectedly, we say, 'Oh, my *zio d'America* died.' " Claudia stopped abruptly and turned away. She coughed into her fist, then took another drag off the cigarette.

"Are you okay?" Olivia asked.

"I'm sorry. I said something stupid." Claudia placed a rough hand on Olivia's arm. "I was making a joke, but my American uncle really did die." Her fingernails were long and polished, but Olivia could feel a callus on her palm.

Her cousin was afraid of hurting her feelings, Olivia realized.

"That's okay," she said, waving away both the thought and the smoke, which was beginning to make her eyes feel beady and red like a gerbil's.

"My mother is dead, too, but for a long time now," Claudia said.

"I'm okay." Olivia had been only five when her own mother died of cancer, and she remembered little about the aftermath—only that their neighbor Mrs. Teitel had brought over an apple cake, and Olivia and her father had consumed it in a single sitting, one moist piece after another. They'd started by cutting it with a knife, but then they began to use their hands, grabbing off chunks and sprinkling crumbs on the table and floor. She'd wondered if that was how it would be without a mother—their house a place of no table manners and no limits.

Her father's death had been completely different. It was a relief. She knew it was unseemly to say that, but she refused to deny it. She'd felt mournful when he was alive, but with his death, she'd experienced the buoyant release that came when a long-lasting fever broke. She was excited to be back in the world. "When did he expire?" they'd asked at the funeral home, and she thought that wording was all too appropriate, as he hadn't ended in a moment so much as he'd turned, like a carton of yogurt past its sell-by date.

"Anyway, we are family," Claudia said inexplicably. She stubbed out her cigarette in the ashtray that sat on the night table, dangerously enticing hotel guests to smoke in bed. She quickly lighted another.

"How many *parenti* do we have in Urbino?" Olivia asked. Maybe she'd discover the big family of her childhood fantasies.

"Not many," Claudia said sadly. She shook her head, then brightened. "One more now. Our *nonni* have been dead a long time. My mother went ten years ago. Her lungs."

Olivia wondered if her father had known his sister was dead. "Do you have brothers and sisters?"

Claudia looked uncomfortable. "My mother was older when I was born. She married *tardi*. I'm the only child."

"Like me."

Claudia flicked ash onto the floor and nodded.

"How did you know I was here?" Olivia asked.

"*Madonna mia*, what an Urbino accent you have."

Olivia nodded. "My father's the only one I ever spoke Italian with." And he'd spoken Italian to her always. As a child, she thought of it as their secret language, a grown-up pig latin.

"You can really hear that you're from Urbino."

"How did you know I was here?" Olivia asked again.

"Giovanni," Claudia said. "But you don't have to stay in a hotel. We could make room for you at home."

"Giovanni?"

"Giovanni, my husband. Giovanni works in the hotel sometimes." She stubbed out the second cigarette next to the first. The filter was rimmed with lipstick.

"He was here when I came in?" Olivia could have sworn it had been a woman who checked her passport.

"No, not at the reception," Claudia said. She pronounced the English word *reception* with excruciating enunciation. "He works in the hotel, but not today, just sometimes."

"So how did he know I was here?"

Claudia waved her hand as if shooing a fly. "They told him."

"So the hotel called him?"

"They called him; he called me," said Claudia.

"It's just strange," Olivia said.

"Strange?"

"I've only been here a couple hours." She glanced at her watch on the table next to the bed. Could it have stopped? Was it Sunday rather than Saturday?

Claudia laughed. She pulled a pack of cigarettes from the back pocket of her jeans and toyed with one, almost taking it out all the way, then letting it slip back through her fingers. She returned the Marlboros to her pocket.

"I forgot it's your first time in Urbino," Claudia said. "Everybody here knows everything about everybody else." '

"I know about small towns. I grew up in a small town." "Pitifully small" was how Olivia described Shaleford to everyone she met.

Claudia nodded. "You'll see."

"I mean, in Shaleford, too, everybody knew all about their neighbors." Not exactly true—she and her father had nodded hello to the Teitels next door, but they couldn't have been said to know one another. And her father's house had been situated on a corner, so the other side faced the street. A familiar microcosm like Urbino sounded appealing—a place where someone was always watching over you.

Claudia gave in and took another cigarette from the pack. From the cellophane encasing the cigarette box, she slipped her hot-pink translucent plastic lighter. Olivia could see the lighter fluid sloshing ever so slightly as Claudia lifted the lighter to the cigarette, flicked her thumb, and sucked hard. She exhaled the smoke with pleasure.

"Not like this," she said. "Not like Urbino. You'll see."

IN THE SECOND-FLOOR APARTMENT ON THE GIRO DEI DEBITORI (THE APARTMENT where her father had grown up, Claudia explained offhandedly), Olivia's cousin wouldn't let her set the table. Instead, Olivia sat in a creaky wooden chair and watched as Claudia put out plates—mass-produced china with faded ivy crawling around the perimeter—and glasses. Then she expertly spritzed a huge salad with oil and vinegar and tossed it. When Claudia used the vinegar, Olivia noticed, she placed a finger over the mouth of the bottle, like someone warning against spilling secrets.

Claudia took the lid off of a pot, under which she'd ignited a flame as soon as they entered the apartment. She picked up a cardboard tray filled with tiny pieces of pasta, each about the size of a fingertip.

"You like *cappelletti in brodo*, right?" she asked Olivia.

"I've never had them." Claudia's face fell. Had she been rude? "They look delicious."

"Your father didn't make egg pasta for you?"

Olivia shook her head. He'd been a good cook, but he'd used dried pasta: spaghetti, penne, gemelli, with its two strands that clung together.

"I'm happy to make your first cappelletti, then."

Claudia picked up a yellow ring of egg pasta and held it out to Olivia, placing it delicately between her lips. The dough was soft, even uncooked, and wrapped around a slightly salty mixture. Olivia nodded her approval, and Claudia turned back to the stove and tilted the remaining pasta into the pot of boiling broth. There were dozens of little pieces. It must have taken her cousin all afternoon to prepare them, she realized. Olivia's heart flared with gratitude. This welcome was better than she'd imagined—Claudia was as loving as her fantasy grandmother, but Olivia's own age as well, so they could relate.

"*Butto giù!*" Claudia announced toward the back of the apartment. "I'm throwing it down" was what Olivia's father had always said, too, as the pasta entered the pot—a notice that dinner was on its way.

"So, you have come to see the *patria*?" Claudia asked.

Olivia hadn't told her cousin about the deed. In fact, Olivia still hadn't decided what to make of the deed herself. It had been the last thing she'd found in the dark interior of her father's nightstand—the last gasp in cleaning out his house for the estate sale. First she'd pulled out a manicure set in a red leather case. Next came a half-empty packet of tissues, a handful of presumably dead batteries in various sizes, a rusty thimble, a cash register receipt in faded purple ink for $3.69, and a raffia coaster from a long-gone set.

When she reached in again, her hand landed on a book—the dictionary he'd consulted for the Italian meaning of English words. Olivia leaned back on her heels. He'd relied on the dictionary constantly, but he had left no mark except the softened edges of pages that his fingers had rubbed too many times. Once, when she was in high school, she'd caught him staring at a page. By then she was as accustomed to anticipating his queries as she was to speaking to his left ear, not the impaired right one. She raised her eyebrows to prompt him, and he ran one white-tipped fingernail under the word *manure* and asked, "It's really spelled like that? Horse shit?"

Next she extracted a shiny white cardboard tie box. In it were a small perfume bottle and a funny old-fashioned key. She assumed the perfume had been her mother's—lavender water, according to the label. The key, she didn't know about, but she loved its old-fashioned length, with a few jagged teeth at the bottom and the loop at the top. It was nothing like the prosaic keys to their house, but long and thin, like a jailer's key in a cartoon. Something this heavy should open an important lock, she thought. Maybe on a solid, creaking wooden door or a treasure chest or Pandora's box. She began to set it aside, but then she changed her mind and slipped the key into the pocket of her shorts. She liked the way it tugged at the material and didn't let her forget its presence. The bottle of lavender water was scummy and odorless, its contents having all but evaporated. She dropped it into a garbage bag.

Only then did Olivia notice the folded paper in the bottom of the tie box. The paper looked as if it had been through hard times. It had turned nicotine yellow and soft with age. It was covered in a linty coating of fuzz. Carefully, not wanting to do damage, she unfolded it. It was handwritten, generated in a time before computers.

ATTO, it said across the top. There were stamps and seals around the page, a decorative border. And then the words came into focus. She reached for her father's dictionary without looking away from the paper. An *atto* was a deed. The rest she could understand without help. Here in the name of her father, Luigi Bonocchio, who had just died without leaving enough money to cover his own funeral, was proof of a piece of property. A house at Via del Rinascimento 2, it said, had been transferred to the ownership of Luigi Bonocchio. It was dated 1940.

A deed to a house in Italy.

She ran her thumb thoughtfully over the raised seal and considered it. Nineteen forty. It had probably been sold since then. This was 1994. A deed couldn't be good for more than fifty years, could it? Why would he have kept an old paper like that? It wasn't a memento, like a photograph; it had to mean something.

Impulsively, she decided to skip the ten-day bike trip through California wine country that she was planning to take with her best friend, Claire, and go to Urbino instead. Yet even now that she was here, she was unable to picture a house for her father other than the one where she'd found the deed—the square white box in the suburbs of New York City where she herself had grown up. The place where four weeks and four days ago he'd mumbled his last addled words. Her plan, if the deed proved to be good, was to sell the property in Italy and use the money to pay off the bills for around-the-clock nursing, which had been the price of allowing him to die at home. It was an excuse, too, to come to Italy. His past rattled tantalizingly out of her grasp, like a few coins dropped long ago into a ceramic piggy bank—coins that could be retrieved only by shattering their container.

But the deed would probably turn out to be a fluke, she reasoned, a meaningless document her father had lost in the back of a drawer and forgotten about, just as he'd forgotten so much. Something told her not to involve Claudia or anyone else.

"*Sì,*" she said now to Claudia. "I've come to see the *patria.*"

"Do you have the ashes?" Claudia asked casually.

"No, he was buried," Olivia said.

"He didn't want to be buried here, in Urbino?" From the oven Claudia withdrew a platter loaded with roasted zucchini, tomatoes, and eggplant, all cut down the middle and sprinkled with bread crumbs.

"He'd been away almost fifty years."

Claudia looked startled. "Forty-nine. And a lot of people come back to be buried, even after they've been away for decades."

"He didn't say what he wanted. He couldn't say what he wanted. He wasn't *cosciente* at the end."

Claudia nodded and lighted the burner under a pan. "My mother had *un malaccio*. A tumor in her lungs. *Che brutta morte.*"

Claudia began cracking eggs into a bowl and whipping them forcefully. From the refrigerator she withdrew a package wrapped in butcher's paper. She pulled out six chicken breasts, arranged them side by side on the brown paper, folded the remaining paper over them, and then pounded them mercilessly with the heel of her hand. She emptied a bottle of murky green olive oil into the pan, dipped two chicken breasts first in egg and then in bread crumbs, and slipped them into the pan.

"With my father, it was his mind," Olivia said.

Claudia paused for a moment to push some hair off her forehead. The kitchen was warm and close. Each time she turned around, the light glinted off sweat on the triangle of breastbone framed by her shirt. She took a large loaf of bread from a cupboard and sliced it up against herself, as if she were wrestling it into submission, then placed the slices at different spots on the tablecloth.

"I hope this will be enough," she said.

Olivia would have laughed, but she was afraid she'd burst a button. When she'd mentioned losing her suitcase, Claudia had insisted on lending her a pair of stiff cropped pants and a shirt that reminded her of a popped gum bubble, it was so stuck to her and so sheer. The pants were tight, too. Her father's key was thrown into relief inside the pocket, like scar tissue.

"We're exactly the same size," Claudia had crowed when she threw open the doors to the wardrobe in her bedroom, and it was true, but their taste couldn't have been more different. To Coleman, the private school where she taught art, Olivia wore black or gray pants—she had about ten different pairs—and shirts in the same spectrum. On weekends, she liked baggy jeans and sweatshirts. Claudia had clothes that wrapped a V around her breasts. She had clothes that clung. She had clothes that were red and purple, sometimes in combination.

Olivia had giggled when she caught a glimpse of herself in the mirror in Claudia's wardrobe, but then she'd stopped and examined herself seriously from all sides. The face was hers. Her short dark hair protected her skull like a helmet; wide brown eyes stared at her. But her nipples pointed accusingly through the sheer fabric of the shirt, and the pants—made of a material not found in nature—hugged and lifted her cheeks. Was this who she would be if her father had stayed in Italy? Claudia had left the room while she changed, and Olivia walked back and forth in front of the mirror with a swagger. Did she look sexy or cheap? She couldn't decide.

She ran her hands over her stomach and hips, and her dry, ragged cuticles snagged on the cheaply made shirt. *"Le mani screpolate,"* her father would mutter, shaking his head at the rough skin she'd earned since she began throwing pottery. A few days from the end, he'd held her hand and examined it, openmouthed, as if it were something completely separate from both of them—a chunk of lava or a souvenir piece of the Berlin Wall.

Sitting in the kitchen, watching Claudia perform, all she knew was that she was not feeling like herself here. When she spoke Italian, she sounded instantly younger. It wasn't just that linguistic uncertainty shot her voice into a higher register but also that Italian was the language of her youth, because she'd spoken it with her father. Suddenly, she was no longer thirty-three, but five again, eating a crumbled handful of Mrs. Teitel's apple cake. She was twelve, asking permission to go to the mall with friends. She was fifteen and shy and intimidated by boys, but fascinated by them, too, and avoiding the whole question by hiding out in the garden shed she'd converted to a studio, throwing pots.

As if she'd conjured him with her own imagination, a lanky boy about fifteen wearing flood-high Levi's and a polo shirt wandered into Claudia's kitchen and folded himself into another of the chairs around the table.

"Ciao, Ma," he said. He unscrewed the top from a plastic bottle of mineral water and poured some into his glass, then drained it.

"Alex!" Claudia shouted, turning away from the stove. "Say hello to my *cugina* from America."

Alex blushed. *"Scusami."* He got up and went over to Olivia's chair, kissed her quickly on each cheek, leaving a trace of floral cologne, then sat down again. He stretched out his legs and rested them on the rung of the chair next to him and slowly tipped his own chair backward, an action that drove Olivia to distraction at school. She could never shake the thought of a student landing on her back, cracking her skull on the tile, permanently marking the art room floor and likely causing Olivia's dismissal.

"*Ciao,*" Olivia said to Alex.

With a slotted spatula, Claudia transferred the chicken breasts to a platter lined with several layers of paper towel. Without spilling a drop, she ladled the broth into three bowls, then set the bowls on the table.

"There's more if that's not enough," she said.

Alex rolled his eyes and brought the legs of his chair to the floor with a smack. Without a word, he picked up a piece of bread, wet it in the broth, and stuffed the whole thing into his mouth.

"*Esagerato!*" Claudia said warningly.

It was an expression Olivia had heard many times growing up—the person, rather than the thing, was termed *exaggerated*. She was exaggerated when she pouted dramatically, or threw a tantrum, or complained about having to clean her room. Alex was exaggerated for eating too much at once.

"Olivia?" Claudia said expectantly. Olivia raised her spoon and took two cappelletti—swollen now that they were cooked. She wouldn't have thought to eat soup on such a warm day, but the broth was restorative, the pasta tender.

"*Buono.*"

Claudia smiled, satisfied, and picked up her own spoon. Claudia's fingers were long and tapered. Her hands would have looked like Olivia's hands, except that Claudia's nails were filed and shaped, her cuticles pushed back to reveal even half-moons. They were covered in shiny clear polish. Olivia glanced down at her own nails, cut to the quick so that they wouldn't nick her pottery. She'd sat in the bathroom at her father's house and sliced them off with his clippers, letting the ragged shreds fall directly into the toilet.

What had happened to her handprint in plaster? she wondered suddenly. She didn't remember taking it from her father's house. He'd kept it on his bedroom wall all those years, suspended from the paper-clip hook her kindergarten teacher had cleverly stuck in the back. In college, in

Olivia's first-ever art education class, the professor had stood at the front of the room and opened by saying, "Whatever you do, whatever you come up with, please, please, no more handprints in plaster." Olivia had obeyed dutifully, but she loved her own handprint. When she was standing by her father's bed, she liked to place her adult hand over it, as if she were holding her own hand to comfort herself.

"*È molto buono*," Olivia said sincerely to Claudia. It *was* good, and not only because she was hungry.

"*Non è McDonald's,*" Alex said, smiling.

"Alex wishes there were a fast-food in Urbino," Claudia explained.

"Really?" Olivia asked.

Alex nodded.

"We didn't have a McDonald's in Shaleford," Olivia offered. She pronounced the name of the chain the way they had, with a crisp *c* and no *s* on the end. "There was a diner. *Lo sai cos'è un diner?*" she asked. When she was little, her father let her have french fries and a milk shake at Bill's once a month. On those nights, he ate a grilled cheese and tomato sandwich with apparent distaste.

Claudia shook her head, but Alex perked up.

"Oppy dice!" he shouted, almost rising out of his chair.

"*Cosa?*" Olivia couldn't help smiling at his enthusiasm, although she had no idea what he was saying.

Alex took a breath and pronounced slowly, "*Il telefilm americano. Fonzie. Ricky. La signora C.*"

Olivia burst out laughing. "*Happy Days?*"

"*Come si dice?*" Alex asked, then twisted up his mouth and tried to imitate her.

Olivia didn't ask about Claudia's husband, but she assumed the fourth table setting was for him. Through the steam rising from her bowl, she studied Claudia, who was spooning grated cheese onto her broth. Claudia, they'd discovered earlier that afternoon, was only eleven months older than Olivia. Olivia felt as if she'd been allowed two lives running side by side, like abutting lanes on a highway. The Italian life didn't look bad, she decided. Alex was pleasant enough—he'd launched into a long story about a friend who'd skidded and almost fallen riding his moped that afternoon—and Claudia seemed content. Olivia credited some of Claudia's mood to the smoking. Although the smell and fear of disease had always kept Olivia away from cigarettes, sometimes she wondered if they wouldn't make her calmer.

Olivia glanced up, to find Claudia smiling at her.

"You're a Bonocchio," she said. "Look at the way you're sitting."

It was true, Olivia saw that she and Claudia were mirroring each other exactly, their shoulders not hunched, but angled forward over their plates. Each held a piece of bread between the middle finger and thumb of her left hand to wipe out her bowl, and each rested her left elbow lightly on the edge.

"Was your mother very stubborn?" Olivia asked. "My father was so *testardo.*"

"*È la razza,*" said Claudia.

"And he would never talk about anything. So *chiuso.*"

"*Tipo?*" Claudia asked, obviously intrigued by stories of an uncle she'd never known.

"Such as his family. I didn't know your mother's name. What life was like here."

Claudia placed her spoon on the table and leaned back.

"Can you say what life was like for your father in the United States?"

Olivia was silent. "Life was good, I think."

"So your father was happy?"

Olivia thought of her father wrapped in his routines. She'd often worried that he was isolated, especially after she left home, but she thought he'd been happy, or at least not sad.

"Yes," she said. "Until he got sick, he was happy."

"*Beato lui,*" said Claudia. "And lucky you, too. My mother was never happy. *Crisi dopo crisi.*"

"What was wrong?"

Claudia shrugged. "*Chissà?*"

"Did you ask her?"

Claudia took a sip of water. "There's the idea here that family don't need to ask questions. They can always count on one another."

Olivia pictured her father and her aunt sitting at the same table, eating their dinner. Her aunt she saw as a female version of her father—the wrinkled forehead curtained by long hair. Her grandparents she couldn't imagine at all, though.

The front door opened, and the atmosphere in the room changed. Alex sat up straighter. Claudia jumped from her chair and pulled a cardboard container of wine from the refrigerator. Following their lead, Olivia brushed some crumbs from the tablecloth into her hand and deposited them onto her plate.

"We started already," Claudia was saying as she poured wine and water into the same glass.

The burly man who came around the corner didn't reply. He stood for a moment behind his chair, his hands resting on the knobs atop the back. He wore his curly black hair in a style Claire had dubbed "the Julius Caesar," not a comb-over but a comb-forward. He stared at Olivia but didn't speak. Then he picked up his glass and, like a man making a toast at a wedding, said, *"Benvenuta, Olivia."* He walked around to her side of the table and kissed her once on each cheek. "Giovanni," he said, pointing to his own chest, as though she were a member of a lost tribe who could not be expected to understand his language.

"She speaks Italian perfectly. No, not even Italian, but *urbinate*," Claudia said proudly.

As Giovanni settled into his chair, he smiled at Olivia and revealed an extra tooth protruding from his gums. She thought of the cancer that had migrated from her mother's breast to other parts of her body. Could a tooth move about of its own accord?

Claudia smoothly slid a fourth bowl of broth in front of her husband. He took a long sip of the wine and water mixture in his glass and swiftly emptied the bowl of broth and pasta. He wiped up the dewy moisture left behind with bread and ate that, too. He helped himself to another long drink, draining the glass. He picked up the plastic bottle of water in one hand and the wine in the other and poured more of both. His sleeves were rolled up, revealing thick forearms covered as if with brushstrokes in coarse dark hair.

As soon as Giovanni's plate was empty, Claudia jumped from her seat and transported the rest of the meal to the table. Without asking, she speared a crusty brown chicken breast and shook it onto Olivia's plate.

She piled some salad alongside it. She did the same for Giovanni, then Alex, and finally herself.

"Why are you staying at the hotel?" Giovanni asked. "There's plenty of room here."

Had she insulted them by taking a hotel room? The apartment didn't seem very large—two bedrooms and a single bathroom—and the hotel had been so inexpensive.

Claudia jumped in. "Maybe tomorrow she'll come stay here."

"At least I could have gotten you a *sconto*," Giovanni said.

"A what?"

"*Uno sconto*," he repeated. He looked searchingly at Claudia and Alex.

"It costs less," Claudia explained. Alex bolted from his chair and disappeared for a second, then returned bearing a hardcover Italian-English dictionary. He leafed through, then found the word.

"Discount," he pronounced carefully.

"Oh." Olivia nodded. "*Sconto*," she repeated, practicing.

Giovanni smiled, and the tip of the extra tooth lifted his lip into a funny grin.

They tucked into their food and grew quiet. At home, with just her father, silence had always felt depressing—a gap Olivia should be filling. Here, though, with four of them gathered around the table, it felt companionable. It wasn't the family she'd fantasized about, but it was sweet all the same.

After they'd eaten fruit and Olivia had declined three offers of coffee, Claudia gathered the tablecloth and took it to the terrace. Looking through the half-open French doors, Olivia could see her unfurling it to scatter the crumbs into the garden below. Claudia came in and folded it into a thick square, sponged off the table, then disappeared into the back of the apartment. She returned with a large wooden box and lifted the lid to reveal an interior lined in burgundy velvet and containing hundreds of photographs.

The first one Olivia focused on was her eighth-grade class picture, her teeth sparkling with braces, her hair pulled back, tight and shiny, with a large plastic barrette. She picked it up, then dropped it. Underneath was a photograph of her mother that she'd never seen. Her mother held a book open on her lap, and her face pointed into the distance, away from the photographer. Her hair was gathered in a bun at the top of her neck and it looked ready to come undone. In another, her mother stood in front of a black car with the skirt of her dress held up to form a semicircle. She stared into the camera. Olivia thought her mother looked like a straight shooter, the sort of woman who didn't make compromises.

There were dozens of shots of the house in Shaleford, in both black and white and color. It was a jolt to see the familiar front door with its metal knocker. There were various versions—the fence more or less painted, different cars in the driveway. And there were dozens of her: Olivia, just a blur on a new bicycle, circa 1967; sitting on the couch with Smudgy, smiling warily at the cat, who clearly wanted to escape her hold; at the kitchen table in a pair of shorts, newly long legs spread before her and crossed at the ankles. Every year, she posed in front of a sky blue backdrop, and sometimes a wagon wheel, as her breasts grew and her face shed baby fat. Flipping through the photos was like watching a sped-up movie of her life that ended, suddenly and bluntly, with the beginning of her father's illness. It was as if someone had granted her access to her father's mind, during the times when it still functioned. Here, in black and white and in color, was how her father had seen her. Olivia's eyes filled with tears.

"I told you," Claudia said.

Olivia picked up a clump of photographs, then let them dribble between her fingers like sand. They made shushing noises as they fell into the wooden box and brushed against the other photos. The last photograph that remained in her hand showed the house in Shaleford, a straight-on shot no different from the one the real estate agent had run in the newspaper ad. And then Olivia realized that soon her father's house would be sold, and that she had no images of it. Claudia had turned away from her and was attacking a water stain on the stovetop with a sponge. Olivia started to slip the photograph into her pocket, but then she guiltily changed her mind and dropped it back into the box. What sort of person would steal from a cousin? Especially one this kind?

Olivia dug in again. There was not a single picture of her father, unless you counted the occasionally blurry piece of thumb in the upper right-hand corner. She turned a few photographs over and checked their backs for written notes. He hadn't bothered to date any of them, nor had he provided captions. Olivia shook the box in her hands the way she might have shuffled the letter tiles before a game of Scrabble. Although the faces in the photographs were invariably smiling, or at least content, tossed together that way, Olivia found them unbearably sad. Jumbled and out of order, they were reminiscent of her father's mind at the end. She reached for the lid and covered the box.

⋆ 1990 ⋆

Mrs. Teitel—*Eve*, Luigi could hear her correcting him—was coming for dinner. Mrs. Teitel had joked the night before that they ought to dig a tunnel between their houses so they could go back and forth freely, maybe carve a deep channel the way a dog would under the fence that separated their two backyards. He'd tilted his head back and bayed at the mention of a dog. That was what he felt like now, with her—an animal who could simply do as he liked. He sniffed around her body, wanting to know all its odors. He pawed at her to get her attention. If he'd had a dog's agility, he would have licked his own balls.

In the twenty-four years since his wife had died—the doctors claimed it was cancer, but Luigi saw her illness and then her failure to fight as a slow, sneaky form of *suicidio*—there'd been no one. Alone on their queen-size mattress, he'd satisfied himself, hopping up quickly to go to the bathroom he shared with Olivia to wipe off afterward. When she was younger, she had pleaded to climb into his bed on Sunday mornings, so he laundered the sheets on Saturday and never touched himself on Saturday night or Sunday morning, just like when he was a kid and keeping clean for church.

Smoothly, he slid on his turn signal and pulled out of the lab parking lot. In ten minutes, he'd be on the highway. In another twenty, he'd be at the grocery store, buying lemons and capers. He'd promised to make dinner if Mrs. Teitel would bring the dessert. Desserts were her specialty. She smelled of cinnamon but tasted of something else altogether. At first, he'd wondered if everything about her was Jewish. In Urbino, Jews had been halfway to witchcraft with their refusal to believe in Jesus. He himself didn't buy any of the religious thinking and hadn't been to church since he'd left Italy, but that didn't stop him wondering: Was her smell a Jewish smell? Her taste a Jewish taste? As a boy, he'd kissed a Jewish girl, and she smelled like lavender and books, but not cinnamon. Or was every woman's taste and smell and feel as individual as a plot of soil? He hadn't been with enough to know.

And what could she tell about him? Did she know that her Jewishness made him slightly uncomfortable? Could she sense that he thought if a Jewish woman loved him, it would be his salvation? That was how he'd come to think of it—that her presence in his house, in his bed, was a kind of forgiveness after all the years of penance. It was a release that had been a long time in coming.

Her comment about the tunnel had unnerved him, though. The thought of a dark, earthy passageway with worms pulsing through the dirt disgusted him. Maybe it had been a hint that they ought to move in together. He didn't think so, but the only person he could have asked, his source for all things American and many things female, was Olivia, and that was impossible. He hadn't told Olivia that he'd been with Mrs. Teitel. What would he call it? They certainly weren't dating. They'd never been anywhere in public together, unless sitting in the backyard looking at the stars and drinking a glass of wine—Mrs. Teitel insisted on spritzers, even though he'd told her they were an abomination—counted as public. The neighborhood wasn't a neighborhood anymore. Families came and went, single people, too. Two ugly large condominium buildings had gone up on the next block, with identical kidney-shaped swimming pools out back that reminded Luigi of a couple of small children curled up and sleeping. There was nobody left to talk to. If Olivia were more observant, or came home more often—Mrs. Teitel's son, Jared, was equally absent—she might have noticed how frequently his attention strayed over the fence, might have sensed that his greetings to Mrs. Teitel in the morning as they both leaned out of their front doors to retrieve their newspapers from their identical stoops were more intimate, but now, after years of inviting his daughter home on the weekends, he'd stopped asking. She seemed relieved, rather than curious, about his reasons.

So he was left to consider Mrs. Teitel alone. He saw her as an experiment, a study in American women. Diane had died only six years into their marriage—and she hadn't been typical, he'd realized almost as soon as they had married, either as a woman or as an American, with her long, sad silences and incessant reading. Olivia was too close to him for proper study; it would be like trying to get the whole picture of an organism by staring at one cell through the microscope. So now, at the late age of sixty-eight, he had set out to try to understand women.

What he'd found had surprised him. Mrs. Teitel had come across as shallow at first, with her talk about tennis and the way she waved away her husband's death with one hand, as though decades with the same man were pollen that she needed to distance from her sensitive nose. But ultimately, he'd found her good company. As much as she talked, she also listened. She knew when to rest a hand on his arm and when to lean back and study him inquisitively. She knew the rhythm of his sentences, but she let him complete them on his own schedule. And the sex between them was hot and mucky. Once, after they'd finished, she'd thrown her head back on one of his pillows, sighed, and said, "Fabulous." He'd replayed that in his mind for days. The vision of her skin shining pink in the dim light that darted through the gaps on either side of the window shades kept intruding when he should have been recording data or calculating pH values at work.

At the start of the highway on-ramp, he hesitated, then let a truck pass. His reflexes weren't what they used to be. At least he recognized that. He'd decided that was the key to aging happily—being able to admit you just weren't up to certain tasks anymore. That had been Mr. Teitel's problem, apparently, that he hadn't accepted his own decline. He'd fallen off the roof six years earlier while trying to restaple a loose shingle. "Even in his youth, he was no Mr. Fix-It," Mrs. Teitel once said ruefully. He recovered from his fall, but it set off a chain reaction of physical problems—first a soreness in his back that never quite went away, then a bad hip that was replaced but didn't feel right, and finally what the doctors simply termed "unmanageable pain." ("They might as well have written 'crazy' across his chart," she said. "We could all see they thought he was imagining it. And maybe he was.") He fell deeper and deeper into depression, took more and more pills.

Finally, one early evening while Mrs. Teitel was in the kitchen spearing kabobs and her son, Jared, home from law school, sat at the kitchen table and told her about his classes, Mr. Teitel rigged a noose over a beam in the garden shed out back. Their houses were identical, and so were their garden sheds, although the Teitels kept tools in theirs, while Luigi's belonged to Olivia by then. Jared found his father when he went to call him in for dinner. Luigi didn't know that at the time, of course. He did see a small bulldozer in the Teitels' backyard the day after the funeral, and he watched as it knocked down the shed in a matter of minutes, then scooped up the remaining detritus and dumped it into the back of a truck, leaving only the cement foundation, a gray square that now sat at the edge of the backyard.

He angled into the right-hand lane and then off the highway. Behind him, a car beeped in surprise. He turned to glare at the driver, and when he faced forward again, the front of his car was dangerously close to the guardrail. He swerved to bring himself back to the center of the off-ramp. YIELD, a sign admonished him sternly, and he did, bringing the car almost to a complete stop, just the barest rolling forward, as he wiped his brow with the back of one hand. Olivia was right: He ought to be more careful.

His daughter drove just as her mother had—with serious intent. "I never forget that a car can be a deadly weapon," Diane once told him gravely as he lifted his right hand from the wheel to fiddle with a radio button. In the car, he heard her as if from far away, because she sat to the side of his bad ear. She drove the way she lived. She was the kind of girl, strangely enough, that his mother would have picked for him if he'd stayed in Urbino. His mother would have taken Diane's quiet demeanor for industry and determination, although Diane's incessant reading would have confused his mother.

Luigi sat up straighter behind the wheel and pulled into the grocery store parking lot. It was a chain store, part of a shopping center that included a large pharmacy, a dry cleaner, a liquor store, and a nursery that displayed thick-leafed rubber trees and bags of potting soil out on the sidewalk. The automatic doors whooshed open and sucked him into the carefully cooled space, which smelled of nothing, even though its shelves were packed with any food imaginable and both a butcher's counter and a bakery sat in the back.

Mrs. Teitel's smell had been at the base of it all. He'd forgotten what a house smelled like with a woman in it. Olivia didn't count, not only because she was seventeen when she left and not yet a woman—she still wasn't a woman to him now at twenty-nine—but because she was his daughter and he could never smell her that way. Even before he'd lost the hearing in his right ear, he'd relied on smell: the crisp blank of a clean lab coat; the almost overwhelmingly human scent of Olivia the first time he tentatively held her, afraid he might crush her soft skull. And the odor of Mrs. Teitel when she'd come over that first time, two years earlier. Her husband had been dead four years by then; Luigi's wife had been dead forever. Mrs. Teitel brought some cookies, but that was an excuse. He knew it from the way she lowered her eyes as she handed over the plate. She stood, nibbling her lower lip, while he bit into one. It was too sweet for him. Chocolate chip with no nuts to break the wave of sugar. He smiled anyway and made approving noises, and she smiled back and said, "When you're finished, bring me the plate. You know where to find me, right?"

"Thank you, Mrs. Teitel," he said like a schoolboy.

"Eve," she said, correcting him. He imagined the fine, hot mist that syllable would make on his cheek if he leaned in close. She smelled of cinnamon, but also something tangy and slightly rank, like an oozy cheese. The smell had drawn him in, was still drawing him in. He only wanted to locate its source.

He hadn't known her first name, but he'd seen her all those years. From the second floor of the house, from his bedroom or Olivia's, he could view her backyard. In the seventies, she'd sunbathed with a foil reflector around her chin. In the early eighties, she'd thrown a couple of barbecues. Mr. Teitel, hands hanging uselessly at his sides, hovered by the house's sliding doors on those occasions. Later, Luigi saw the foundation of the shed. One early morning, before the cookies, he got up to go to the bathroom and spotted a shape through the shade. He tugged the shade up, and there was Mrs. Teitel, standing near the shed's cement footprint. She leaned in, as though she were reading an inscription on a tombstone, and then he could have sworn that she spit at it.

It was a Jewish tradition, he figured. Early on in Shaleford, he'd realized that the neighbors with German names were Jews. There was no other way to tell. He tried to recall how everyone in Urbino had known

Ester and the Levis were Jewish. The way that everyone knew everything, he concluded: information passed down in whispers and hand gestures and silences that said more than words. Jews buried their *defunti* quickly and named new children after dead relatives instead of saints or themselves. They didn't put pictures on headstones, and they didn't bring flowers, either. The cemetery in Urbino was awash with blossoms; several men made a living stocking graves with fresh ones. But the patch of Jewish cemetery he walked by on his way to the Levis' was gray and forlorn, with small armies of pebbles on some of the stones.

The first time with Mrs. Teitel, he took back the cookie plate, and she thanked him and invited him in for coffee and a piece of pie.

"How do you stay so thin when you bake so much? Do you give cookies and cakes to half the neighborhood?" he asked.

"Oh no." She smiled. "Only to a select few."

Luigi closed his eyes for a moment when she said this. Even so many years after her death, his sex dreams centered on his wife. Diane had been quiet and lived in a world that resembled his but was slightly different—the way he'd discovered Toronto to be so like and not like the United States the one time he'd visited. In his dreams, though, his wife was sexually vicious. In some dreams, she attacked him and gave him a *bocchino* and then scraped his sensitive skin with her teeth, drawing blood. In others, she simply rode him to exhaustion. He woke from those dreams sticky and breathing hard. He woke sad, not just because he was alone but also because he felt sorry for her in her desperation.

Coffee and pie with Mrs. Teitel had stretched into dinner (if you could call a giant green salad and a few bottled olives dinner—Luigi understood then how she stayed so thin). Afterward, they sat at the table, and Mrs. Teitel swung her leg, letting the hem of her pants brush the hem of his pants. *Swish, swish.*

"Have you seen the rest of the house?" she asked suddenly.

Luigi shook his head.

. Her upstairs was identical to his, although the furniture was all misplaced. In the doorway of her bedroom—the bed covered in a blanket the almost black red of blood in test tubes—she kissed him. He knew he would have to decide now. He looked at Mrs. Teitel. Her lipstick was eaten away at the corners. Up close, her face was gray and tired, but so was his, he supposed. An erection strained against his fly. Maybe Mrs. Teitel would redeem him.

Mrs. Teitel murmured in his right ear. He could only feel her breath.

"I don't hear with that ear," he told her.

She shifted to his other side. "Let's get undressed," she repeated. Her breath was still sweet with pie. He moved a hand to his belt buckle.

Afterward had been the nicest part. They stayed in bed. He talked about his work, Olivia.

"She's twenty-seven," he said, shaking his head. "It does not seem possible to me." He'd been twenty-seven himself not that long ago.

"I know," Mrs. Teitel said, her arm across his chest. He thrilled to her familiarity. "One day, Jared came home when I wasn't expecting him, and I thought, Who's that man at the door? For a moment, I was a little afraid, the way I would be of a stranger."

She'd already confessed to him that she'd been relieved to have a son rather than a daughter, because girls fell out of love with their mothers in a way boys never did. "The Oedipal thing," she'd said, and laughed. Back home, Luigi would have a hell of a time locating that word in the dictionary. He'd find *edible* but know it was wrong. And then he'd be horrified at what he read under O.

"Sometimes I look at Olivia and think for a moment that she is her mother," Luigi said. Then he wondered whether it was polite to talk about his wife in this situation, no matter how long she'd been gone. She, his wife, had been so *permalosa*, so touchy, that saying anything to her was like cutting into a tomato and then trying to keep the seeds and pulp from leaking onto the counter, but Mrs. Teitel didn't appear bothered.

She said, "Thinking he's a stranger is better, at least, than those times I look at him and see his father."

She was absentmindedly pinching Luigi's foreskin. It had elicited a curious gleeful cry when she first spotted it, and now she was drawing the sides together to cover the top of his still-slick penis and then letting it slowly separate and slide down again.

"What was your husband like?" Luigi asked. He could remember the man's grim face from across the fence, but they'd hardly ever spoken. The closest they'd gotten was waving occasionally when each was mowing his own lawn.

"His parents were very religious," Mrs. Teitel said. "It messed him up."

"And you? Are you very religious?"

Mrs. Teitel laughed. "I wouldn't be in bed in the middle of the afternoon with a goy, would I?"

Luigi smiled. He didn't know the word, but he had a feeling it wasn't a compliment.

"I'm a modern Jew. I did things for his sake, but when he died, I stopped. I used to do the whole schtick—the candles on Friday night, two sets of dishes."

Luigi raised his eyebrows but remained silent.

"Now all I do is the *yahrzeit*," she said.

"The what?"

"It's a candle—well, a little electric bulb. You light it on the anniversary of someone's death. I figure it's the least I can do for him."

Later, when they went to bed together repeatedly, she usually came to Luigi's house ("Your den of iniquity," she called it, and he had to look up *iniquity* after she left), but on the few occasions that he was at her house, he searched for things familiar from the Levis'. The Teitels' bookshelves were inhabited mainly by knickknacks, however, with the occasional detective novel here and there, and the furniture was the very opposite of the heavy wooden pieces the Levis had favored. The Teitels' furniture was modern, circa 1978—Lucite side tables like small, transparent, headless deer and a bright living room rug marked with a large red circle and a green triangle.

That first afternoon, when the tender conversation had ended, Luigi found he was suddenly embarrassed to be naked in front of her. He moved to dress, sliding under the covers, as close to the edge of the bed as he could get, so that when he leaned down to pick up his pants, she'd see only a flash of skin, but he moved over too far and failed to account for the nightstand flush against the bed, and the right side of his skull met its sharp corner with a loud crack.

"Oh my god," Mrs. Teitel said, forgetting her own nakedness and sitting up straight. Her breasts were small flaps of skin.

Luigi raised a hand to his head and felt the sticky presence of blood. He lowered his hand and stared at it. Mrs. Teitel was in the bathroom, noisily going through a drawer.

"I've got gauze," she yelled to him. Tenderly, he touched the spot and felt for bone, but the cut was shallow. He wouldn't need stitches.

"I'll be okay in a minute," he told her. She emerged with a plastic first-aid kit in one hand. Something about his own voice sounded funny, but he couldn't identify it yet.

"I'll tape on some gauze," she said softly, "but I can't stand to look at blood, so you'll have to help me."

"I'm fine," he reassured her.

She stood over him and moved his legs back up onto the bed so that he was in a reclining position. Absentmindedly, she opened and closed the scissors in her hand a few times. "You'll be okay," she said.

"Repeat that?" Luigi was realizing why everything sounded strange, clear.

"You'll be okay," she said, her voice not breaking this time.

"Whisper it in this ear," he instructed her, pointing to his right side. She closed her eyes so she wouldn't see the blood and leaned down.

"You'll be okay," she whispered throatily. They were the first words he'd heard with that ear in fifty years.

IN THE GROCERY STORE, LOST IN THE KIND OF TRANCE OF HABIT THAT CAME over him every morning as he hung up his coat at work and put on a white lab smock, Luigi extracted a cart from the long interlocking chain of them by the door and wheeled it down the first aisle. Frozen foods flashed by behind their glass doors, each box and bag robed in milky frost. He turned down the next aisle, paper goods, and flicked past plastic cups and forks and knives, paper towels with psychedelic logos, napkins with clever sayings, or drawings, or blank. At the end of the aisle was the children's birthday party section, with cone-shaped hats and balloons in bright colors. After her mother died, Olivia organized her own parties.

He was no longer shopping, but taking an automated stroll up and down each aisle. Breakfast cereal was the product he loved to look at best—silly yellow-and-red boxes printed with chipper cartoon characters. He'd even tried one of them, but discovered that its false crunch promised substance and delivered only air. He paused for a moment to study the toucan on the boxes of Froot Loops, then the wily leprechaun on Lucky Charms.

Luigi noted with approval that the boxes were lined up neatly at the edge of the shelf. Order was a passion. He liked to visit the towel section at the nearest department store, just to stare at the rows and rows of colors, the fabric plush and perfectly folded, the hues muting from cherry to brick to rose. There had been no such towels in Italy. In the early days, alone in New York, he'd stood outside stores and felt his mouth watering. Not food stores (food was his greatest disappointment in America— uniformly brown and white and tasting nothing like what his mother cooked at home), but stores selling clothing, and bedsheets, and stationery. Americans hurried past, not even stopping to look at the wonderful *things*. More than glass kept him out—he lived hand to mouth then on what he made mopping floors at the hospital. He couldn't have afforded these stores, even if he'd had the courage to go inside. Still, he was amazed to see others walk by without any sign of desire.

Now, Luigi wheeled his cart to the end of the aisle. His eye fell on an orange box with two letters, but they made no sense. He stopped his cart, and his mouth fell open slightly. The alphabet was gone, cut from his brain with a swift, terrifying excision. He could no longer remember how to use the cart, either. He experienced the sudden and heart-pounding fear of a dream. It was like the first time he'd picked up a newspaper written in English, or the first time he'd watched a baseball game, only it was the world now that was the unintelligible language, the unknown rules. He could not process it. For two minutes, maybe more, he stood at the end of the cereal aisle motionless, his hands curled around the plastic bar of the cart, his feet in midstep, one a few inches ahead of the other.

"Excuse me," a woman murmured behind him, and then more loudly: "Excuse me."

Luigi turned and looked at her but didn't speak.

"I said 'excuse me.' That means you're supposed to move." She was wearing flip-flops and a T-shirt two sizes too small for her stocky frame, so her belly button stared at him like a third eye, and when he failed again to answer, she shoved past him, the wire bars on her cart's cage clanging against his.

"Sorry," Luigi said. He was returning, slowly, to the world. It was seeping through his blotter paper. He moved his feet, like an athlete getting ready to take the field. The motion came back to him. Tentatively, he pushed the cart and it rolled a few inches. He caught up to it, put his hands on the bar, and returned to walking around the grocery store. If he scanned the shelves long enough, something would jar his memory.

His body was functioning again, but his mind was focused on one thought, far, far away from the grocery store. It had been buried, but now it blared in his head like a giant subtitle to a foreign film: The girl is dead. *La ragazza è morta*. It flashed like the colors that played fireworks behind his eyelids on the nights he couldn't sleep, when he'd press his fists hard into the sockets, willing himself to drop off. First in Italian, then in English. *La ragazza è morta*. The girl is dead.

Luigi shook his head again and inhaled deeply. No smell at all. That brought him back to the grocery store. Slowly, he rolled his cart. He saw a woman grab the arm of a girl perched in a cart, legs swinging. The girl laughed uncertainly. When he reached the produce aisle, he went straight for the slick bright yellow lemons. He started to squeeze them one by one, then changed his mind and snagged a net bag filled with a dozen and dropped it into the cart. He picked up a few oranges and a grapefruit for good measure and threw those in next to the lemons. He palmed three kiwis in each hand and let them fall into the cart. Then he helped himself to a head of lettuce—deposited carefully into a plastic bag—and a bunch of scallions. He took two waxy tomatoes and four potatoes, their eyes sprouting, and an avocado. By the time he had finished ravishing the produce aisle, he was back into his routine, rolling the cart, staring at the colors, wondering at the brightly lighted abundance of the modern supermarket.

He slid smoothly into the checkout line behind a woman buying several gallons of milk, a bag of potato chips that advertised itself as GARGANTOSIZED, and three loaves of packaged bread. Luigi smiled to himself at the image that these items inspired: a house full of kids, rangy and with a new goatlike smell in their adolescence. He'd seen such boys roaming down the street in unthreatening packs, their shirts untucked and their hair too long. The woman turned and smiled at him as she set down the rubber bar that kept people's groceries from running together into one giant nutritional mass. Luigi returned the smile and began to transfer his fruits and vegetables to the belt.

AT THE HOUSE THAT EVENING, LUIGI DIDN'T MENTION THE EPISODE TO MRS. Teitel. He didn't even know what he would have called it. At first, frozen there in the aisle, he'd been afraid he was having a stroke, or an aneurysm, but there was no pain, only that terrible blankness, as if all his years of experience—not just in the grocery store but also as a citizen of the world—had drained away. There was a commercial he'd seen for juice. Smiling children poked their straws into a series of boxes with apples or grapes or oranges on the side, then sucked on them, and he thought, later, that it was as though someone had popped his skull with a straw and inhaled his brain. In the commercial, though, the children gulped the juice and smiled beatifically. Whatever had begun to drink his brain had changed its mind and let it spill back down through the straw. He felt grateful that he'd gotten away with something, although he couldn't have said what it was.

And then there had been that one thought he couldn't wipe off. That memory from forty-plus years ago that had seemed, just for a moment, more real than the grocery store, more urgent than shopping.

That evening, when Mrs. Teitel ducked into his refrigerator to store some cream (to be whipped later at the last minute and then plopped onto the dense chocolate cake she'd brought), she laughed.

"Looks like somebody went a little fruit crazy," she said, extracting the bowl from the top shelf and showing it to him. "You don't even like kiwis."

"I don't know what came over me," Luigi said truthfully.

She put the bowl back on the shelf. "Must be a full moon."

Luigi grunted but didn't agree. This was the same logic his mother had employed: Cutting children's nails on Tuesdays and Thursdays made them grow up to be thieves; drinking hot milk after a meal formed ricotta in your stomach; strong wind caused pain in the liver. For years, his mother had attributed his father's bad humor to poor digestion. Luigi believed in science. He believed in squirming single-cell organisms glimpsed through a microscope. He believed in platelets and iron counts and pulse rates. He did not believe in superstitions of the body.

He filled a large pot of water and placed it over a high flame. How many times had he made that motion in his life? How many times had he flicked on the gas, waited for bubbles to break the surface, tossed in salt and pasta, then yelled up the stairs to Olivia, *"Butto giù!"* The first week she'd been in college, he'd caught himself trotting over to the stairs anyway, ready to alert her that dinner was eight minutes away. When she'd come home over Columbus Day weekend and tucked into a dish of *spaghetti al pomodoro* and moaned with pleasure, he'd been horrified to hear her admit that she hadn't eaten pasta since she'd left home. "It's cooked in advance and then kept on a steam table, Ba," she complained. "I'd rather eat salad." He gasped. It had been a great concern for him when he'd come from Italy, and he remembered his relief at finding macaroni on the grocery store shelf, his horror at his first glimpse of spaghetti with glistening brown meatballs resting on top rather than served separately as a second course.

"You don't miss it?" he'd asked.

Olivia had smiled condescendingly. "Not everyone eats pasta every day, you know."

"But it's good for you. It fills you up," he'd said.

"I guess salad fills me up." Olivia had rested her fork on the plate with its lacy design of tomato sauce, then reached for a piece of bread to mop it up. "I'd rather eat salad that's okay than pasta that's terrible."

"Bad pasta is an insult."

"I know," Olivia had growled. "That's why I eat the salad."

Luigi heard that the water in the pot was boiling before he saw it. He lifted the lid and tossed in a handful of coarse salt. Mrs. Teitel had been horrified at how much salt he used, so now when he added it, he shielded the stove from her view. He did the same with olive oil.

Mrs. Teitel was talking about the town tennis courts. It had been proposed that they be changed to asphalt, as the clay was too difficult to care for. Someone from the Parks Department had to go over twice a day in the summer and smooth it with a gigantic roller. Mrs. Teitel played tennis on Tuesdays and Thursdays with a group of three friends. She recognized that asphalt was more practical, but she much preferred clay, for both its bounce and its color.

"It just feels more sporting," she said.

Luigi wondered whether his wife, had she lived, would have been friends with Mrs. Teitel, who moved in just months before Diane's death. He thought not. Diane was not a tennis player, nor a drinker of spritzers. (Even the word was disgusting, like someone talking too close and spitting.) She was a reader only. Before Olivia was born, he'd come home and find her stretched out on the couch like a corpse, her skirt covering her legs demurely. The sound of his key in the lock didn't even disturb her.

Luigi tossed in the linguine. He thrust a small paring knife up the back of each shrimp, snapping off their shells and digging out their black intestinal strips with one motion. He'd forgotten capers, he realized, but Mrs. Teitel would never notice. When the pasta was almost ready, he'd toss the shrimp in a hot pan and sear them. He loved the way they transformed so quickly from gelatinous gray to firm pink. It was like watching evolution in a sped-up movie, from amoebas to crustaceans in seconds. Back in high school, when evolution was in question, he'd argued for it. He knew that animals had lost their hairiness and begun walking upright and looked around and realized they were men. And since then, Luigi had seen evolution in reverse—the way people could become like animals again. The way the will of the pack could assert itself.

La ragazza è morta, he heard again, and he shook his head as though stung sharply by an insect.

In a small bowl, he whisked together a generous amount of olive oil and a little lemon juice. It would need to be emulsified again before he drizzled it over the pasta. The acidic juice and the smooth oil would flee each other as soon as he set it down.

"Don't you think?" Mrs. Teitel was saying.

"Absolutely," Luigi agreed, nodding. She was easy that way, satisfied with one-word answers. He thought again of Diane stretched on the couch, nothing moving but her eyes as they raced over the lines. "Let me finish this chapter," she'd say without looking up.

"I mean, pasta salad should be served room temperature. Everyone knows that," Mrs. Teitel said.

"Horrible," Luigi said sincerely.

"I like pasta salad," she said.

"It's terrible."

"What?"

"Pasta salad, any pasta salad," Luigi said.

"What's wrong with it?"

"Cold pasta? Never." He picked up the wooden spoon and stirred the linguine, bending them so that they sank into the boiling water.

"Pasta salad is perfectly delicious," said Mrs. Teitel.

"It is not," he said.

"What, is it an American invention, so it can't be good?" Mrs. Teitel asked.

Luigi shook his head. "It is not American." He knew Mrs. Teitel was laughing at him. She'd heard his tirades about spaghetti and meatballs and shrimp parmigiano and wine spritzers. He'd had to explain to her how to eat long pasta, like the linguine he was cooking now. The first time he'd served it to her, she'd cut it into pieces, like clumps of hair that littered the floor of a barbershop. Then she'd asked for a spoon. She still had trouble with what to him was a natural motion: tilting the fork against the side of the bowl at a forty-five-degree angle, a few strands trapped between the tines, then twirling the fork so that just those pieces wound into a neat skein. Occasionally, she ended up with the contents of a whole bowl snarled into a huge knot.

Mrs. Teitel leaned back in her chair and sipped at her spritzer. "So it's Italian?" she asked.

"It's—" Luigi stopped himself in time. In Urbino, the Levis' closest neighbor reported that on Saturdays they asked him to do things for them, strange things. They weren't allowed to light the fire or run water. It had to do with religion. They ate room-temperature pasta cooked the afternoon before. Of, course, it wasn't pasta salad. It was tossed with oil and vegetables and left to sit, but it wasn't refrigerated or turned to glop with Italian dressing flecked red with something dried and tasteless. They ate fish robed in onions. They smelled of garlic and paper and stillness on those days, Luigi imagined.

"It's not Italian," he said. "It's a Jewish dish. Italian Jews."

"Italian Jews?" Mrs. Teitel looked skeptical. "I was Jewish," she'd told Luigi once, "but after Frank died, I went back to being nothing."

"There were Jews in Italy," he said.

"Of course there were some." Mrs. Teitel leaned back in her chair and sipped her spritzer. "I just never knew they had their own food."

"You learn something new every day," Luigi said. It was one of his favorite expressions. Although it was a cliché, he also thought it was true. He wondered, would she be horrified if she learned about him?

"You certainly do," Mrs. Teitel agreed. She scooted her chair closer to the stove and reached out a hand to his back. Her touch settled him. When she touched him, he felt lucky. When he and Diane had had sex, she'd lain still, as if she were reading a book. Sometimes he'd glanced over his own shoulder at the ceiling, just to see what she was staring at up there.

All the passion he and Diane were missing, he felt for his house. Once he owned that house, he knew he was American, with his picket fence and green lawn. It was the distillation of a vision that had sustained him on the boat and through the lean years in New York: a house full of things that were his. A house in his own name, to erase the other one. A house in his own name that was not marred by anything unclean, unless he counted the ugly shed that sat like a pimple in the backyard. He'd planned to knock it down, but he couldn't stand to go near it, and Diane's father told him it added to the value of the house—especially since it had running water and electricity—and he'd be a fool to remove it. The shed stunk of rot, as though the gray boards were being eaten away from the inside, even if the exterminator he called pronounced it clean. On hot nights when they ate on the patio, the odor drifted to the table and hung there. Diane, and later Olivia, claimed not to smell a thing.

Luigi plucked a strand of linguine from the pot and dangled it in the air to cool. He tasted one end, then offered the other half to Mrs. Teitel. She bit.

"It's a little hard, isn't it?" she asked.

"Two more minutes," Luigi said, and he glanced at his watch.

She slurped in the rest of the strand, then smiled. There were moments when she thought she was charming and he did not, but he pretended to anyway, because it was so obvious that that was what she wanted. He smiled back. Would she be willing to make the same sort of allowance for him? Her face was flushed with the heat of the kitchen. She popped up from her seat and opened a drawer and took out two place mats, then opened another and took out two forks, two knives, and two napkins. She knew his house almost as well as her own, and she used an easy motion, one that Diane had never mustered in that kitchen. The familiarity touched him. She was a good person.

"Something strange happened to me in the grocery store today," he said.

"Really?" She gently put the place mats on the table, then smoothed the napkins on top.

"There was a girl, in Italy," he began.

He turned back to the stove and stirred the pasta. The strands gave easily under the spoon. He knew without tasting that it was ready. He turned on the burner under the pan in which he'd cook the shrimp.

"I bet there were lots of girls in Italy," Mrs. Teitel said.

"This was different."

Luigi reached for two pot holders, and in one motion he turned off the gas and lifted the pot from the burner. He poured the pasta into the colander and shook it gently, then transferred it to the serving bowl that had been a wedding present from Diane's aunt. Her few relatives had disappeared right after she did. Her mother and father were both gone within a year of Diane's death, of a heart attack and a stroke, respectively.

"Hold that thought," Eve said. "I'm just going to run and wash my hands."

Luigi drizzled some olive oil into the pan and sizzled the shrimp, turning them quickly with tongs. He sprinkled the cooked shrimp with minced garlic and parsley, then flicked them onto the linguine. He whisked the lemon juice and olive oil he'd prepared earlier and poured that over the pasta, and with two forks he began mixing vigorously.

Eve came back from the bathroom and slid into her seat. "You started to tell me something. You were telling me about your girl."

He'd half-told her already. In one of those easy moments in bed together, she'd talked about her family—how her mother was always envious of her youth, how her father coddled her so when she was young that, as an adult, no man could measure up. In return, he'd recounted for her the terror of living with his father, the drop in his gut in response to the rhythmic thump of his father's cane on the stairs, the story of how he'd lost his hearing. She'd been so sympathetic that he felt the need to give her something afterward, and, awkwardly, he reached over to the nightstand next to his bed and opened the cabinet. He didn't extend his hand through to the back, where the box sat. First, his fingers landed on an abandoned coaster, then a manicure set, then a small, hollow, off-white ceramic oval Olivia had made. "A closed form," she'd called it. He pulled that out and presented it to Mrs. Teitel with great ceremony, and she accepted it seriously and rubbed the smooth surface against her cheek.

Now he placed an avocado-colored soup bowl of pasta in front of her. *"Buon appetito."*

She sniffed and rolled her eyes appreciatively, then sighed deeply. Luigi had never told her that she made the same sounds when she ate something good as she did in bed. He thought it might embarrass her, and he liked those sounds—on both occasions—and wanted to continue hearing them. It was better, he decided in that moment, not to reveal too much. Look at how Eve had reacted to her own husband's problems. She didn't appreciate weakness. She wouldn't want to know his shame. She might turn from him in disgust.

"You said there was a girl in Italy."

He shrugged. "I don't remember. Sorry."

"It was only a couple minutes ago. You've forgotten already?" She shook her head. "You're getting old." He was thirteen years older than she was, but Mr. Teitel had been even older than Luigi, and Diane had been much younger than Luigi, so they were both used to the difference. Still, she teased about it. She ran her hand through the silver hairs on his chest and called him "a gray-breasted Italian bird," or asked if she was going to give him a heart attack. She dyed the hair on her own head; age and unhappiness had chiseled lines from the corners of her mouth down to her chin. Luigi knew enough not to tease back.

As he placed a second bowl on his own place mat and pulled out the chair, he thought of her husband slipping on those shingles, the way it would feel for the very thing he was relying on to give way. That had happened to Luigi, too—his own slip, the world he knew not there to catch him.

He made a bargain with himself. If she managed the pasta properly, it would be a sign. But if she couldn't do it, if the strands snarled and pulled one another in, or if the whole clump slid off her fork and back into her bowl, he'd know not to tell her. It was as reliable an indicator as any of the superstitions that had governed his mother. More scientific, really. If Mrs. Teitel was adjusting to his way of doing things physically, wasn't that a sign that she would understand what was inside his head?

"Maybe it'll come back to me."

She picked up her fork and he did the same, but he was too focused on her actions to eat. She sunk the fork deep into the pasta and angled it against the sloped side of the bowl. A few strands of linguine slithered back to the bottom, and four or five remained entangled with the tines. Slowly and regularly, she began to turn the fork handle. The linguine wound around the metal. She smiled at him, unhurried, anticipating. When the pasta had formed a neat bite-size bundle, she lifted the fork. The tail of one piece of linguine waved in the air, but she caught it gracefully between her lips and withdrew the fork, clean. Already, he felt lighter.

"This is fabulous," she said after she'd swallowed. "Even if I didn't like you so much, I'd stay with you for your cooking."

"I remember what I was going to tell you before."

"See? If it's important, you always hold on to it," she said. She stabbed a whole shrimp, curled as if to protect itself now that it was naked of its shell. She opened her mouth wide and plucked it off her fork with her teeth and chewed.

✦ MONDAY ✦

Olivia walked out of the dark alley where her hotel was located and into the glaring sun. It had been unbearably hot for the three days she'd been in Urbino so far. Sweat made her neck so damp, she felt as if she'd just stepped out of the shower, an American shower, she amended, since the shower in her hotel room trickled when it gave up any water at all. *La dolce vita*, she smiled wryly to herself, quickly putting on her sunglasses to protect against the intense light.

On Sunday, the people who clustered in the piazza had been burnished to a glow in their perfectly ironed clothing. Today, they looked dustier, more worn. An old man wearing a light blue hat stood in the cool shade cast by the arches in one corner; a group of kids in high-water belted jeans and T-shirts sat in another corner, on the steps leading up to a stationery store. She could see them, as if in a series of time-lapse photos, moving around the piazza year by year, from the youth section to the geriatric.

Back in Shaleford when she was little, Sunday meant simply sitting out the last drops of the weekend before starting school again. On Sundays, her father did laundry (except for the sheets, which he washed on Saturdays—a Catholic thing, she'd always figured) and worked in the yard; he vacuumed the house and removed the dishes from the cabinets and rewiped each one with a soft old dish towel—marked with red checks faded to the faintest pink—that he reserved for that purpose.

The day before, she'd realized Sunday was a true holiday in Italy. Stores were closed. Church bells roused Olivia early. Claudia and Giovanni and Alex picked her up in the piazza and drove her to Giovanni's sister's out in the country for lunch. The house, reached over miles of un-paved road, was a restructured farmhouse surrounded by fields. Gio-vanni's sister, Francesca, had a son, a two-year-old, who toddled after Alex everywhere he went. She also had three large dogs, and apparently she adopted stray cats, because on the portico outside the door sat a row of plastic bowls containing milk and leftovers, and after lunch she piled a piece of newspaper with strings of prosciutto fat and bits of uneaten salad and other scraps and set it on the stone floor, and a flock of cats ap-peared out of the trees and set to eating.

Francesca's husband, Marco, asked Olivia questions about New York. Was the Bronx as dangerous as it was depicted in the movie *The Warriors*? Was it safe to take the subway alone? Did she own her own home? What did it cost to rent an apartment? Was it true that anyone willing could find work? Did she drive hours in a car to get to her job? Had she ever met any famous people? Was it true that squirrels filled the parks and people ate from garbage cans? What were her feelings on the Palestinian situation? If you had no health insurance and were injured, would you be left to die like a dog in the hospital parking lot?

Olivia had tried her best to answer, although it made her realize how little she knew about her own city, her own country. She was reminded of the awful questions her father was forced to answer when she took him to the doctor: "What were your parents' names?" "Who's the president of the United States?" (He'd pleased her there by replying, "What does it matter? They're all the same.") "What year is it?" "Can you draw the face of a clock?" In response to most of them, he'd sat silently, palms up in front of him. As a teacher, she'd learned that asking a question when you already had a specific answer in mind could only lead to disappointment, but her father's doctor seemed not to have gotten that message.

"These are incredible," Olivia said as her fork cracked through layers of baked *millefoglie* pasta.

Francesca waved a hand at her. "I didn't make them," she said.

Marco laughed. "The women of our generation don't know how to do any of that anymore. They buy it all at the *pasta fresca*."

"But you made the *cappelletti* last night, right?" Olivia asked Claudia.

Claudia shook her head. "What gave you that idea?"

Olivia was certain her cousin had claimed to have made them. As Claudia had dumped them into the broth, she'd said so. Maybe she'd misunderstood.

Now, standing in the piazza on Monday, Olivia spotted Claudia in the distance, heading up the hill in the direction of the university, where she worked as a *bidella*. As far as Olivia could grasp from Claudia's explanation, that meant her cousin made photocopies. Then again, it might have been any number of other women walking to work. The women of Urbino appeared to have agreed on a single style of dress, the way groups of Coleman students would call each other the night before the first day of school and establish a uniform. The town's women looked alike, too, with their deep-set brown eyes and long hair.

And Olivia, except for her cropped hair and her inability to look pert in the oppressive heat, might have mingled with the women of Urbino as well, since she was still wearing Claudia's things—although maybe her discomfort marked her. Before Olivia left after dinner Saturday night, Claudia had loaded her arms with clothing. Her cousin had also loaned Olivia a threadbare towel and a thong. Giovanni gave her a ride to the hotel in a beat-up car so small that her head almost bumped the ceiling.

She felt a pang of nostalgia for her father's boatlike station wagon, traded in for a small sum. Even as he seemed to shrink with age, he always sat up straight when he drove. One of the last times she'd been in the car with him, he'd attempted to parallel park, and each time he swung out from the space and pulled back in, the tires screeched in protest as they met the curb. His sudden inability had disturbed her. Finally, he drove a little farther up the block and found a space in the ten-car lot reserved for customers of the dry cleaner. They were going to Bill's for a sandwich, but her father was distracted, pointing out to her—as if she didn't already know—the store that had once been her grandfather's, now a liquor store squeezed between a florist and a hardware store. When it came time to finish the story, though, her father stopped, his lips still pursed.

"He sold those things, you know," he said. He looked distracted.

"Cameras," Olivia reminded him. "Photography equipment."

Her father nodded in relief. Lately, he'd come to rely on her to fill in the simplest facts. Those were the days when he still believed her, before he grew angry, then detached. Later, when it got worse, she heard him ask a nurse conspiratorially, "Is that really my daughter?"

On Monday, Olivia noticed for the first time that the walls on all sides of the piazza were papered with white posters with black type and black borders. At first, she took them for public notices, like the ones pasted to lampposts in New York, announcing that local restaurants had applied for permission to seat patrons on the sidewalk. With closer inspection, she realized they were death announcements, checkering the stone walls with the news that beloved so-and-so had gone on to a different and better world. Maybe Claudia had arranged posters for her father. Maybe that was why even the woman cleaning the hotel lobby this morning had known he was dead.

When Olivia had approached the woman about the water problem, she'd laughed and raised her hands. *"Manca l'acqua."*

The water was missing?

"There's no water?" Olivia asked.

The woman shook her head. "Not at this time of day. It's the heat. It dries up."

"But in the afternoon there's water?" Olivia checked her watch. It was 10:30.

"Morning, from five until about eight." The woman turned back to her dusting.

"Just in the hotel?"

"Everywhere." The woman shook her head. "Urbino. Every year they spend money to fix the water system, and every summer there's no water. *La politica.*"

"Also, my suitcase should have arrived. Do you know where it is?"

The woman shook her head. "Look back there," she suggested, indicating the reception desk with her chin.

Olivia peered behind the desk and into the small office through the door behind it, but there was no sign of her suitcase anywhere. The office smelled of coffee and ink. Her stomach rumbled.

Olivia had changed a few hundred dollars into lire before leaving New York, and she had the money in a tight bundle in her pocket. She'd go for breakfast, she decided. A cappuccino, maybe a pastry. After that, she'd buy underwear and call about her suitcase. Already she could imagine the feel of cool, clean cotton just out of the package. She turned away from the front desk and started to leave.

"*Sei l'americana, vero?*" the cleaning woman asked her suddenly. "*Sei la Bonocchio.*"

"*Sì,*" Olivia responded slowly.

"I knew your father," the woman said abruptly. And then she repeated it. "*Lo conoscevo.*"

"He died this summer," Olivia said. She didn't even look like her father, so how did this woman know who she was?

"I know. I heard. It's a shame what happened to him." The woman spritzed the glass coffee table with cleaning liquid, then smoothed the surface with a rag.

"It's a terrible disease," Olivia agreed.

"*È un peccato,*" the woman repeated. She smiled, and her teeth were uneven and gray.

"*Sì,*" Olivia said again.

The woman vigorously rubbed the rag up and down the stem of a table lamp. "He didn't deserve what happened to him," she said.

"He forgot everything at the end. He didn't recognize me."

The woman looked at her strangely.

"I'm not talking about the end. I'm talking about the beginning."

Olivia held her head to the side. "The beginning of what?"

The woman opened her mouth, then hugged the rag to her chest and hurried away, her shoes squeaking on the tiled floor. She went into the office behind the unmanned reception desk and closed the door.

Olivia could mark the beginning of her father's Alzheimer's, at least for her. He'd called her at three o'clock in the morning.

"Hello?" Her voice had been groggy and scratchy, but her heart pounded furiously. No good news arrived this time of night.

"Olivia? *Pronto?*" came through the receiver. She glanced over at Ivan, her then boyfriend, who mumbled something in his sleep and turned over.

"Babbo, what's wrong?" Was he in the hospital? He was well enough to speak. In fact, he didn't sound upset or even mildly disturbed.

"Wrong?" he asked. "Wrong? Why does something have to be wrong for me to call you?"

"Because it's three o'clock in the morning," she whispered. She'd been out to Shaleford to see her father a few weeks earlier. He'd been disappointed to hear that she wasn't staying the night.

"So?" he asked.

"Why aren't you asleep, Babbo?" She was awake now, and although she couldn't put a name to it, she knew that something very, very strange was happening with her father.

"Oh, that's right. I forget how young you are," he said. He laughed quietly. "I'll go now." Olivia was left with just the gnat-annoying buzz of the dial tone in her ear. For a moment, she stared at the phone, as if it might answer some of her questions; then she fought the urge to call him back and placed the receiver in the cradle. In the morning, he claimed not to know what she was talking about. Later, he took a wrong turn in the night and pissed in the linen closet. He rubbed his face with a dry washcloth and then told her it was broken. A shirt on a hanger was a soldier. The man on television was looking at him funny. Olivia should not go outside, he said, as she might be followed. But it was that first phone call that frightened her most, because it was so normal, except for the part that wasn't.

Now, in Urbino, Olivia's thighs clenched as she started up steep Via Veneto. After lunch on Sunday, she'd begged Giovanni and Claudia to drop her at the hotel so she could nap, but she'd found herself unable to sleep. Instead, she'd paced the room restlessly, opening and shutting empty drawers. In the nightstand of her hotel room she'd discovered a faded brochure that said the name Urbino came from the Latin *urbs bina*, or two hills. Indeed, to one side stretched Via Raffaello, and to the other Via Veneto, and the streets met in the middle of town like two fists clasped in a strong handshake. The brochure had included an English translation claiming that "the duke of Urbino was a potent man of the Renaissance and his palace the most important erection of Italy of the epoch."

The ducal palace *was* extraordinary, deserving of all its art history accolades. She'd stood awestruck in back of it for some time on Sunday evening, interrupting the long walk she took to counter the enormous meal they'd eaten at Francesca's house. The *torricini*, the two turrets, peeked over the top from there, like the two fingers inevitably held behind the head of a quiet girl in Coleman's annual all-school photo. At one time, the photographer had used a camera that swiveled slowly on a wooden tripod to produce a long horizontal strip. In those pictures, which hung on the wall around the trophy case, there was always a blur and the same smiling visage on either end, since an enterprising girl could be counted on to run faster than the camera in order to show up twice.

The back was the public side of the palace, the faded brochure announced, the facade designed for the duke's subjects. The front, with its turrets and the initials FC carefully carved into the white stone and the triple arcaded balconies, was the one meant to make an impression on arriving outsiders. Mission accomplished, Olivia thought when she read that.

Olivia entered a café across the street from the palace and ordered a coffee, then grabbed a napkin from the metal dispenser, as she'd seen others do, and clutched a cream puff. The pastry shell was topped with a squirt of whipped cream and a single candied coffee bean that looked like the pupil in an eyeball. It was sweet, the cream rich and dense. She closed her eyes in pleasure.

"*Pronto il caffè!*" the bartender called out, although he was standing directly in front of Olivia. She looked dubiously at the shiny sugar container he'd pushed her way. Pulling on the spoon raised the lid on a hinge. Before dumping in a spoonful, she lifted it a few times, studying the ingenious mechanism, something her father would have enjoyed. Something her father would have enjoyed years ago, she corrected herself, before his brain ate itself. A memory came: her father on the other end of the phone, and herself, unable to explain to him in words how to use the knife he said he held in one hand to spread jam on the slice of bread he held in the other. "This knife doesn't work," he kept insisting, but he couldn't answer when she asked why.

"Dip it in the jar," she repeated. "Dip it in the jar of *marmellata.*"

"*Non funziona,*" he answered sadly.

Finally, she conceded. "Just eat the bread plain if you're hungry, Ba," she said. "*Mangia il pane senza niente.*" By then she was repeating herself in both languages, hoping that one would get through.

"*Ma non ho fame,*" he'd replied, puzzled. "But I'm not hungry."

She'd laughed, tears leaking, at the "Who's on first" impossibility of it all. That night, a Friday, she'd taken the train out to Shaleford, expecting to find a piece of stale bread on the counter, a knife bloodied with raspberry jam on the table. But the kitchen was in perfect order. Her father looked surprised to see her. "I wish you'd call," he said. "I never hear from you anymore."

Now she watched the sugar sink into the thick coffee, then gave it a quick stir with the miniature spoon. Demitasse clutched firmly between her thumb and forefinger, Olivia turned from the bar and eyed the men standing around her. They were her age and older, spiffily dressed, with soft leather briefcases under their arms or at their feet. All of them wore jackets and ties; none seemed bothered by the heat.

Her plan was to approach one of the offices marked AVVOCATO that lined Via Raffaello and were concentrated around the Palazzo di Giustizia and show the deed—now wrinkled and tired-looking after its long trip—to a lawyer in order to get a professional opinion. She didn't have any idea what a lawyer might cost in Urbino, or how to go about finding a real estate lawyer in particular. In fact, now that she was here, the whole trip seemed a folly. Sunday night, alone in her hotel room, she'd pulled the deed out of her book bag, unfolded it, and considered dropping the whole thing. She could remain in Urbino one week, as she'd planned, get to know Claudia, explore her father's birthplace, then go home. School would be starting soon afterward, and Claudia had already warned her that she was wise not to stay past August 15, Ferragosto, when Italy shut down firmly for two weeks. Claudia, Giovanni, and Alex had already reserved an apartment at the shore in Fano, as they did every year.

She wished she had a traveling companion to share the disorientation, that she'd roped Claire into skipping the California bike trip and coming with her. Claire would have enjoyed the architecture and the new experiences with Olivia. On the other hand, the excruciatingly slow pace would have done in her friend. Olivia had seen her rage build once when a movie started twenty minutes late because of projector problems. Olivia was perfectly happy sitting in the dim theater, talking, but Claire had gotten up four times to check with the manager and was suggesting that they get their money back and leave, but just then the lights went down all the way and the screen lighted up. She wouldn't have reacted well at the bus or in the bar, where masses of people squirmed like impatient fourth graders and shoved their way to the front.

Ten minutes later Olivia stood before a door with several plaques sporting engraved names. AVV. FUCILI sat on top. She started to press the buzzer, but then thought better of it. *Fucili* were rifles—a terrible name for a lawyer. She rang the bell on the second, marked AVV. BATTELLI. The bell reverberated inside the building like a swarm of angry bees, but there was no response. She tried AVV. SPERANDIO and AVV. ANGELINI, although she wrinkled her nose at the pious sound of the latter surname that meant "little angels." There was no reaction.

She reached for the last panel, marked AVV. DIOTALLEVI, then hesitated. Was she crazy? She'd asked herself that question a lot since her father got sick. Every time she searched for her keys or stood blankly in one spot in her apartment, unable to recall what she'd been about to do, she wondered whether she'd recognize Alzheimer's if it came knocking for her. Deciding to take off to Italy and investigate this deed seemed the act of an imbalanced person. Her father had never come back, and he'd discouraged her, too, insisting that if it was art she wanted to see, she'd be better off in Paris. Italy, he'd warned her, was *complicata*.

She finally pressed the bell for Diotallevi, but there was no response. Did lawyers play golf on Monday mornings in Italy, the way doctors did on Wednesday afternoons at home? She was turning to go when someone buzzed back, popping open the door. Inside, the dark hallway smelled like Coleman and had a floor with the same gridlike arrangement of tiles— these terra-cotta, those at school a matte white. A door at the end of the hallway sprang open, and a man's head popped out.

"*Chi è?*" he called in a nasal voice.

Olivia moved closer. She could see nothing in the dark. "I'm looking for a lawyer," she began in Italian, then stopped. She didn't know what more to say.

The man cleared his throat but didn't answer.

"I'm looking for a lawyer," she repeated. Suddenly, doubt took over. She glanced around and saw that on several doors there were signs that announced CHIUSO PER FERIE, which she understood to mean they were closed for vacation. As her eyes adjusted from the bright outdoor light, she got a better look at the man, who came into focus like someone rising out of the water. He had curly dark hair and wore a lightweight jacket and a tie. Up closer, she saw he wasn't the elderly agent of justice she'd anticipated, but someone near to her own age. His hair fell in almost perfect ringlets, like the curls of clay that spiraled off when she trimmed a pot. With a puff of his cheeks and a loud exhalation, he ran his hands over the top of his head, pushing his hair tightly off his forehead. Before the curls had a chance to spring back into place, she glimpsed something odd—the top of his left ear was missing, as if the cartilage had been sliced away cleanly with a knife.

"Gianfranco Diotallevi," he said, dropping his hand from his head and extending it to her. She squeezed it and let it go. An attack of shivers came over her. After the blazing sun outside, the hallway was dark and cool. "Never trust a man with two first names," Claire was fond of saying. She wondered if a compound name like Gianfranco counted.

"Olivia Bonocchio," she answered.

"Bonocchio?" He looked interested. Without saying another word, he opened the door and waved her in.

Gianfranco Diotallevi led her past a reception desk covered in dust. He opened a wooden door with a glass window and motioned for her to enter. The setup reminded her of a 1940s mystery movie, the film noir quarters of a private dick. As she passed by him into the office, he touched the small of her back with his fingertips.

"You are American?" he asked in English as they settled into their respective chairs.

Olivia nodded. Her accent gave her away, she supposed.

"But you speak Italian?"

Olivia sighed. How many times would she repeat this? "I spoke Italian with my father, Luigi Bonocchio. He was from Urbino."

"Of course, of course." The lawyer frantically moved around some papers on his desk. Then he relaxed, holding up a pen. "I lose my head if it is not tied on," he said.

Olivia smiled. "Where did you learn English?"

"In school, and then I studied in England for a year. I try to keep it, but it is difficult."

She hadn't realized how stressed she had been by speaking Italian constantly until the chance to speak English presented itself. The words felt easy, good, like water from a faucet.

"I was lucky, I guess," Olivia said. She'd burned with shame when she brought friends home and her father spoke Italian in front of them. As she thought of it now, she blushed. No Italian in public, she'd insisted. In the grocery store, her father had yelled to her once across the aisle, *"Non dimenticare i limoni."* A few Shaleford women had looked up in surprise. Olivia purposely picked out lemons with bruised spots, and one with a fuzzy white birthmark of mold on its cheek. "English please," she said in a surly tone as she dropped them into the cart. Lucky.

"Allora," the lawyer said, switching to Italian. "What do you need a lawyer for?"

"I found this paper." Olivia pulled the deed from her pocket. The folds were turning fuzzy; the paper was as soft as an old pair of jeans. Gently, she handed it over, and as she leaned toward him, the key in her pocket poked her backside.

He looked at the paper briefly, then set his pen on the desk.

"Mi dispiace," he said sternly, not sounding sorry at all. "I can do nothing for you." He folded the paper and dropped it on her side of the desk as if it were contaminated.

"Why not? Does this house still exist? Is it my father's?" In her confusion, Olivia had slipped back into English, and the attorney followed her.

"Do you think you are the hair ace?" he asked.

"What?" Olivia had no idea what he meant.

"Do you hope to get the money, a—how do you say it?—an inheritance?" He pushed the word off his tongue as if it were a piece of gristle he was spitting into a napkin.

Olivia shrugged. "If the house were his, I guess I'd sell it."

"So you think you are the hair ace?"

This time she got it. "Heir," she said, correcting him. "Nobody uses heiress anymore, and you don't pronounce the *h*." She softened, remembering a time when she was a teenager that her father had left the door to their shared bathroom ajar. She'd walked in and caught him pronouncing *h* words in the mirror, near enough that his breath formed little clouds that evaporated immediately. "Hair," he whispered. "Hair, hear."

"Okay, hair ace," he repeated, still mangling the word and adding a hiss to the end. "That is not the question. The question is another."

"What's the question, then, Signor Diotallevi?"

He smiled slightly. "Please, *dammi del tu.*"

"*Va bene*," Olivia said. "*Ti chiedo di nuovo*. What's the question?"

He looked uncomfortable. "Your father is the last owner in the registry."

"So the deed is good?"

"Yes," he said. "Yes, the deed is good, but for a very short time still."

"So, really I own the house," she said.

"In theory."

"Why just in theory?"

"What do you know about your father?" he asked. "I mean, here, what do you know?"

"He left Urbino after the war, in 1945."

"Yes. And this year is 1994, so how many years?"

"Forty-nine." Olivia remembered Claudia's quick correction, then the banner outside commemorating fifty years of freedom. She hadn't made the connection to the end of the war when she'd first seen it.

"The law in Italy is that after fifty years if they cannot find the owner and he is no longer a resident of this *comune* and has not registered a change of address so they cannot reach him, the property goes back to the *comune*."

"But I'm here now. I'm his"—she smiled—"heir. So it's mine, right?"

Gianfranco didn't smile in return. "You know about your father after the war. Do you know about your father during the war?"

Olivia shook her head.

"Do you know who the Levis were? A family here in Urbino. Did your father ever talk of them?"

Olivia shook her head again. She'd seen the name Levi on the deed. An Ottavio Levi had sold the house to her father. Had the sale been unfair somehow?

"Do they want the house back?"

"They do not exist," Gianfranco shot back. "They are all died."

"I'm sorry."

Gianfranco looked at her more kindly now. "He did not want that you should know. I do not want to say you. I respect your father that he did not want this."

"I'm tough," Olivia said. Gianfranco looked at her questioningly. "Strong," she said. But was she? What had her father kept from her?

"Fine." Gianfranco gave up with a sigh. He rose from his seat so quickly that he startled her. He snatched a linen jacket off the coat tree that stood in the corner and dug into the pocket. A set of keys jangled in his hand. "We go."

"Go where?" Olivia asked.

"You want to know about this house? You want to know about your father?"

"Yes."

"We go, then." He bounced the keys up and down.

Olivia stood. They were the same height. She could smell his minty breath. His eyes were warm, but his corkscrew curls were as disheveled as the papers that littered his desk. She looked down at the keys in his hand. One was a car key with black rubber covering its head, like an executioner's mask. Maybe she should ask Claudia about this Gianfranco, if he was okay. Maybe she'd look for another lawyer. He couldn't be the only one in town.

As if he'd read her thoughts, Gianfranco said, "You were very lucky to find me. Everyone else is on holiday."

"Everyone?" Olivia raised a skeptical New York eyebrow at him.

"It's August. Everything is closed," he said.

"My hotel's open."

He waved a hand impatiently. "Everything not for tourists."

"I just remembered," Olivia said, blushing again at how fake she sounded. "I have another appointment this morning." She reached for the office door. Gianfranco stopped bouncing the keys. Could he tell she was lying? Or were the nuances of truth lost in translation?

"Tomorrow, then," he said. He reached an arm over her head and nudged the door open. Up close, she noticed his shirt. It was made of a featherweight material, a thin cotton or whispery silk. The color matched his hazel eyes.

"*A domani allora,*" he said. Then he switched back to English. "You come at ten o'clock?"

"Ten o'clock," she said. Now she felt silly for being afraid of him. But it was too late to take back her excuse.

"Tomorrow I will take you to see the very ugly part of Urbino," he said.

Olivia giggled nervously. How could anyone find Urbino ugly?

"*A domani,*" he repeated, and he reached out and shook her hand again, but she wasn't ready and hadn't formed her own hand into a stiff block that he could hold in a businesslike way. Instead, their fingers intertwined, mingling. She extracted hers first.

"I can't wait," she said, and then she slunk out the door as if she were guilty of something and he were defending her.

✦ 1976 ✦

Luigi picked up Smudgy by her skinny middle and carried her outside to the patio. Row after row of ribs pressed into his palms, reminding him of the pickets of the fence around the house, which, in turn, caused him to remember that the fence needed paint. He could begin that evening. When spring arrived and the light lingered long, he had time for outdoor chores after work. Fifteen-year-old Olivia wouldn't show her face to the sun—she'd learned in school that sunlight was bad for you, although he couldn't imagine what *cretino* teacher would spread such a rumor. Afternoons after school, she huddled in the shed.

Olivia had grown her hair long and it looked greasy, he thought, like the glass in the back door, which was permanently smeared with Smudgy's nose marks. That was how Olivia had chosen the cat's name. The first day they brought her home—a month after Olivia's mother died—the tiny black kitten stood on her hind legs to peer out the door to the backyard, and when a bird flew down and began pecking at the grass, she pressed her nose to the pane, trying to reach it, and applied a small pockmark.

That was ten years ago, though, and recently Smudgy showed no interest in anything. Over the last six months, she'd gotten scrawnier, and now the cat no longer let Olivia's head rest on her furry middle, but instead squirmed if the girl tried to use her as a pillow.

At times, Luigi had been jealous of the cat. He knew that was ridiculous. Olivia was his daughter, after all, and she couldn't even choose her own mother over him, since Diane was dead, but he knew she didn't find the same comfort in him that she did in Smudgy. Smudgy slept on her bed at night, right next to Olivia's mouth, smelling her breath. He had the sense, too, that Olivia told Smudgy much more than she did her own father. The cat couldn't smile or frown, of course, but sometimes, when it peered up at him through slit eyes from a reclining position and let its long black tail pound the floor once, twice, three times, he felt that it was judging him.

Smudgy lifted her head for a moment and looked around. She wasn't an outdoor cat. Previously, on her annual trips to the vet, she'd crouched in a corner of the carrier and meowed lustily until they reached the house. Now they were bringing her in almost every week, and she just slumped on her side, resigned.

"Do something," Olivia had begged him in the car on the way home after the vet told them in a serious voice that Smudgy was suffering. The cat had cancer. The vet guided Luigi's fingers to feel a few nodes under the skin. He pulled his hand away. Cancer again. Luigi wasn't a religious man, but sometimes he feared he was being punished.

La ragazza è morta.

"There is nothing to do" was his answer to his daughter's pleas. Privately, the vet had pulled him aside and suggested that putting Smudgy to sleep would be the kindest thing, and Luigi agreed, but how would he break the news to Olivia? She'd gotten the cat as consolation for her mother's death. Olivia and Smudgy had a welded bond. When his daughter was younger and slept with her bedroom door open, he'd always take a last look at her before he went to bed himself, and he'd noticed that she and Smudgy breathed in unison, a deep up-and-down motion that lifted even heavy winter blankets as if they were made of parachute silk. On cold mornings, Smudgy burrowed under the covers and slept by Olivia's feet. Luigi couldn't stand to see the lump the cat formed under the skin of the blanket. It reminded him of the malignancy in his wife's breast.

On the patio, he was surprised at how docile Smudgy was, leaning into his hands complicitly. For a moment, he regretted his decision. Maybe he should let the vet do it. But to pay the vet for that seemed ridiculous. To be an American, he'd had to learn to be wasteful, and he'd succeeded in some ways. In New York City, he'd seen office lights left on overnight and marveled at the lack of thrift. He'd been careful to turn off the lights in the doctors' offices he mopped down at the end of the day. But he'd adjusted. He now cleaned out the refrigerator on Sunday nights and threw away food that looked questionable—cheese with mold where it wasn't meant to grow and carrots that hung as limp as wind socks when he picked them up. Occasionally, he went for a drive, burning gasoline just for the pleasure of it, navigating his car off the highway and down unknown streets in the adjoining suburbs. When Olivia was afraid of the dark, before she began shutting him out by closing the door to her room, he'd agreed to leave the hall light on until morning, and he'd stuck to his promise, even on nights when he lay awake in his bed, itching to get rid of that seam of yellow under his door. This, though, was too much—paying for something nature should have taken care of anyway.

Luigi placed Smudgy on a patch of dirt that showed through the scrubby grass of the lawn. Near the patio, grass refused to grow. He knew the topography of his lawn the way he'd known the streets of Urbino, with no need to look where he was going. The circle of grass directly over the septic tank was a bright, lush green; waste was a secret that refused to stay underground. In the corner of the lawn farthest from the house was a little ditch where his mower always sank and he had to stop and push it out. And scratchy dead brown grass formed a moat around Olivia's pottery shed, no matter how often he fertilized it.

The shed had only recently been emptied of its single snow shovel and rake and lawn mower (these things now resided in the garage). It had become Olivia's a few months earlier. She'd taken a pottery class at the Y last winter with a friend from school. The friend had dropped out almost immediately—"A boy," Olivia had said, sighing, and Luigi hadn't inquired further—but Olivia had remained enthusiastic, looking drunk after her lessons as she explained what she'd learned.

Afterward, she had come up with the idea for the shed. She bought a used wheel from her teacher at the Y (a white-haired English woman, whose accent he had trouble understanding) and somehow knew to purchase plastic trash cans and a set of shelves. And that was it. As surely as if she'd married, Olivia moved out of his house. Smudgy wandered around forlornly in the afternoons, meowing at the rose wallpaper in her empty room and her vacant spot on the couch, and for once Luigi related to the animal. Olivia stayed inside in the evenings to do her homework, as he'd insisted. Her mind was out back, though, whizzing around in a circle the way Smudgy's head did when Luigi made a halfhearted show of playing with her and swung a piece of string like a lasso. Inside, Olivia sighed impatiently at him.

Luigi had never expected a girl. Throughout Diane's pregnancy, as his wife's ankles swelled until her legs were as straight up and down as test tubes, he'd pictured a boy. A son. When his son was born, Luigi would finally write to his parents, a letter, not more wordless photographs. He'd sit down with his best pen and compose a letter about his life, how well it had turned out, and, best of all, that he had someone to leave it to. He wouldn't say straight out that he was a superior father to his own, but they'd read it. He might even exaggerate a little. He could give the house a few more rooms (even with five, it was enormous by Urbino standards), make Diane prettier. In his letter, she'd be a perfect mother, not the nervous, quiet one he feared she'd turn into. In his letter, he'd be, finally, a man with his own family. He'd be wiped as clean and untainted by the past as the beakers in the lab were when they emerged from the sterilizer.

And then he was sitting on a hard plastic chair in the hospital waiting room with Diane's parents, Doug and Rita. Well, he and Rita were sitting while Doug paced around the perimeter of the room, seemingly measuring it with his shoes. Finally, the double doors swung open and a nurse emerged and announced, "It's a girl."

She turned efficiently and went back through the swinging doors—like the saloon doors in a Western, Luigi thought, and then wondered why he couldn't stop strange ideas from coming into his head today. Luigi looked at Rita.

"Excuse me?" he said.

Rita and Doug were hugging, though, and then she hugged Luigi, and Doug hit him on the back, hard, with an open palm.

"What did she say?" he asked again.

"That's what we say in America," Rita told him helpfully.

"She said you've got a daughter," Doug said.

Luigi tried to digest the idea that he'd come to the hospital to pick up a boy and instead would be taking home a girl. The girl would hang around her mother, just as his own sister had. She'd learn to cook from Diane—pork chops and damp dark green string beans—and wear dresses and never explain baseball to him, as it wouldn't interest her in the least. It was the way things worked: Girls belonged to the mother and boys to the father. He tried to erase the feeling that something had been stolen from him as Rita took him by the hand and led him to another floor, where they pressed their noses against the glass and stared at what he and Diane had made.

LUIGI CROUCHED OVER SMUDGY ON THE LAWN, THINKING THAT PERHAPS HE should be doing this in the privacy of his house. Out here, someone could spot him. It was nine o'clock; he'd already called the lab and said he'd be an hour or so late. That was how long he thought it would take him to knock out the poor creature. He hadn't wanted to do it in the house. He knew that sometimes, at the end, animals lost control of their insides. He wanted this to be clean and neat, and he didn't want to stain the carpet.

Luigi lifted his hands from the cat and fished in his pocket for the syringe. He pulled off the plastic cap and squirted the liquid into the air. The tip glinted in the morning sun. He found the fat jugular in the cat's neck and rolled it between his fingers. He pulled back the plunger, sank the needle, pressed with his thumb. He'd envisioned a struggle, the cat coming alive like a cougar to fight. The will to live, he knew, was a powerful force. He'd felt it himself, propelling him out of Italy. But Smudgy lay limp as a pelt.

The cat's eyes rolled back and only the whites showed, and then the third eyelids rolled in from the corners like window shades blocking the sun. It closed its eyes with a sigh, as if it were channeling Olivia, although his daughter would more than sigh if she could see what he was doing. She'd rage. She'd hate him, something he could never tolerate. He thought how she'd looked getting onto the bus that morning, her legs encased in the tight jeans he'd forbidden her to buy. She'd bought them anyway, with baby-sitting money, and when she came down to breakfast wearing them defiantly, he'd said nothing. He was like the House of Savoy these days—all his power had been stripped. He had been left a mere figurehead.

The animal went limp in his hands. The fluttering pulse stopped. He withdrew the syringe and lowered Smudgy's head to the grass. The plastic chairs on the patio were black with mold, he noticed. All those years spent planning to buy a house, and he'd never once considered how much work it would be. There was always something to be fixed; it never happened that everything was in place at once.

Instinctively, he turned and glanced at the shed, where the coiled hose hung off a hook on the outer wall like a hoop earring. Olivia had begged to get her ears pierced and he'd said no—only *zingari* and *puttane* had pierced ears—and then she'd done it to herself anyway, icing the lobe and making a hole in the soft flesh with a sewing needle. Her right ear grew red and puffy a few days later, and he had to take her to a doctor, who swabbed it with antibiotic ointment and told Luigi sternly that the infection might have traveled to her brain and killed her.

Upon hearing this, Luigi had reflexively touched his own right ear. He'd so long ago learned to compensate for the loss of hearing there that he rarely thought about it anymore. It was easy to lean into a conversation with interest, to turn his head to the left corner of the television screen and raise the volume.

He'd been unable to hear with that ear since 1940, the day he turned eighteen. He remembered waking that morning, going into the kitchen of his parents' apartment, and sawing off two ragged pieces of prosciutto with his mother's longest knife. He slapped two thick pieces of bread around the prosciutto. But could that be true? Would they have had an entire hock of prosciutto during the war? He thought so, and anyway, he was sure about what had come next. He took a stained napkin from the drawer and spread it over the kitchen table. His mother would give him hell for eating without a tablecloth, but he didn't care. He bit the sandwich, wrenching off a small, chewy piece, and smiled with his mouth full and his jaw working. Let her scream, he thought. Now that he was eighteen years old, he could be drafted into the *esercito*. Soon he might be marching around in one of those clay-colored uniforms. He felt nervous about the prospect, but excited, as well. He might finally have a purpose, and for the first time he felt like a man.

When eighteen-year-old Luigi crouched in the dark coffinlike confessional, there was one thing he couldn't admit: He was better than his family. Was it a sin of pride? He thought it was just a statement of fact. His mother cleaned floors; his father was a *muratore* with grit lodged in the soles of his boots. Granted, his father had the ability to look up at the sky and know what the weather would be the next day. There was, he supposed, skill in the way his sister flirted with boys, daring them to come closer and then pushing them away, but never out of her orbit. His mother's ability to make food, day after day, even during the war, when there was so little, represented a certain aptitude. But none of them knew what he knew. None of them knew the periodic table, which he had memorized, or even what the periodic table was. To his mother, a table was something to be filled with dishes; to his sister, something to clean; to his father, something to build out of slabs of wood and a few long nails. They did not live in the abstract as he did.

He got up to make himself another sandwich and switched on the gas. Today, like every day, he'd go to school. He didn't mind. He loved science the way some of his peers loved girls. The surge of a Bunsen burner, the fizz of a chemical reaction were stronger than his hormones, more powerful than the erections he made short work of in the bathroom once the key was turned firmly in the lock.

There were no girls in his high school anyway. It was a school for scientists, and the female brain wasn't capable of complex thought. Girls went to the *magistrale* next door to learn to work as teachers or, more often, stayed home with their mothers and trained to iron clothing and make pasta. His own sister, who cleaned houses with his mother, was fourteen and already had the reddened hands and jagged nails of an old woman, he'd noticed with disgust and then guilt the night before.

The only girl who interested him was Ester. The day before, he'd gone to her house, sat on the grass with her and her aging grandfather. Her grandfather was close to death, Ester had told him days earlier. He might go anytime. At night, she reported, wrinkling her nose in distaste, he wet the bed like a child. Ester didn't go to school at all now, not since the introduction of the *leggi razziali* two years earlier. The laws were followed haphazardly in Urbino—Jewish children didn't go to school, and the Jews gave up their maids, but the laws about how much property Jews could own were ignored. No one was really going to take away the home of a man just because it was over the property limit for Jews. Urbino wasn't Rome, after all; Mussolini would never have to know. And the *urbinati* had always tolerated their own *ebrei*. They were strange with their rituals, and they clung together, but they did no real harm that anyone could see.

The coffee bubbled and he stirred it and poured it into a cup, then drank it without sugar while standing by the sink. He shook his head with satisfaction at the bitter jolt and burped.

"O *santo Dio!*" his mother said. Luigi turned and smiled at her.

"This is how you eat?" she asked, indicating the table with crumbs scattered over its surface. "Like a *vagabondo*?" She shot out a hand and grabbed the broom from the corner.

"I was going to clean it up," he said, suddenly ashamed and young again.

"When? When?" She slapped the broom against the scarred legs of the table. "I suffer and work so you can go to school, and instead you want to live like an animal?" She sighed and pushed her hair off her forehead, then swiped his napkin from the table and opened the door to the terrace. She sprinkled the crumbs into the garden. When she came back in, already folding the napkin precisely along its ironed lines, she slammed the door.

Luigi didn't react. He was used to it. His mother seemed angry at him, at his sister, at inanimate objects. He'd learned in school that actions built momentum, so when she got angry, he tried to stay still. When he was younger, he'd memorized the periodic table in order, and he ran through it in his head whenever he had trouble falling asleep at night. He began it now. One, hydrogen. Two, helium. Three, lithium. By the time he got to oxygen in the eighth position, his mother had wandered away. He could hear her mumbling in the *salotto* about *maiali* and the sacrifices she made that no one appreciated.

Luigi's father entered the kitchen, listing and leaning on his walking stick, and sat at the table. He wasn't old yet, but he already had the habits of an old man—the reliance on a walking stick, the grunt as he settled into a chair.

"*Auguri,*" he said.

"*Grazie,*" Luigi said, surprised his father had remembered his birthday. His father's work never necessitated a glance at the calendar, so he rarely knew the date. Without asking, Luigi poured his father a cup of coffee the way he liked it—black and bitter. His breath always smelled of either wine or coffee, along with some intangible manly mix of wet hay and rubber. In the mornings, his tongue was coated a dull yellow.

His father tossed the coffee down his throat in a single gulp. Luigi had tried to do that once, and he'd scorched his tender epiglottis so badly, he couldn't swallow without wincing for a week. Luigi lifted his father's empty cup and saucer from the table and carried them over to the sink, where he rinsed them and placed them on the drain board. He walked toward his father again on his way out of the room. His father scraped his chair back from the table and then rose to his feet, so that they stood facing each other for a moment, without saying anything, which wasn't unusual. The older man stood and began to move away ahead of Luigi, resting lightly on his ever-present walking stick. He'd found it out in the woods years earlier, when he was hunting, and now it was such an appendage that he used it not only to climb leaf-strewn hills when sighting down small birds but to get around in the house, as well. He took three steps, and then without warning, he turned and bashed the right side of Luigi's head with the stick. Luigi, astonished, sank to the floor.

IN HIS BACKYARD, LUIGI WAS STILL CROUCHED OVER THE CAT, HIS HAND RESTing on its throat, when it flinched. He looked down, and the animal began dancing crazily on the grass. Its eyes were still closed, but its body twitched and jittered. He'd seen a young man in a flannel shirt have a seizure once, in a hospital emergency room when Luigi passed through to deliver some results by hand. "Drugs," the woman behind the desk had whispered confidentially when she'd caught him staring. "They'll put anything into their bodies, these kids."

He held the cat's head still. Drool trickled out of its mouth and wet his palm. One small tooth pinched his skin, as if now the cat were injecting *him* with something. Luigi placed his hands around the cat's neck, knowing that with one gentle jerk he could take care of it. The cat's fur was hot from the sun. Its tongue poked out of its mouth and the rough surface brushed his hand. This wasn't the quick death he'd expected to inflict. He had to look away.

His first thought had been to drown the poor cat. That was the closest they'd come to animal control back in Italy. (How Luigi loved the luxury of a town dogcatcher—a man paid a salary to chase after strays, as if wandering, unowned animals weren't an inevitable part of the landscape.)

The cat that lived in his parents' garden had a litter of kittens every spring, a hot, mewling mess. Eventually, they were placed in a bag with a few heavy rocks and taken to the river. It got so that when Luigi saw the cat growing each year, her abdomen lumpy and strange, he dreaded what was to come. There was no river in Shaleford, however. He eyed the hose again. Olivia had buckets in the shed.

That shed. He hated it. Olivia's pottery was fine—slender vases with bulbous middles and delicate bowls he feared he'd chip, so instead of using them, he kept them on display, locked away safely in a cabinet behind glass. She was capable, he recognized. He knew nothing about art, but he thought she might even be good, although he wasn't sure it was right for a girl her age to spend so much time locked up in a shed. Was it normal? Shouldn't she want to spend time with other children? Boys? It wasn't a subject he could discuss with her.

He thought often of that first night after her mother's death, he and Olivia in the house alone together. Of course, they'd been alone together for a while, since Diane went into the hospital, but their attention had been focused there. Afternoons, Rita came by and stayed with Olivia while he visited Diane. Olivia had a sharpness to her already at the age of five. She possessed her mother's seriousness, but she also cut through to the truth in a way that pleased Luigi. When Diane died, it was Doug who called. Luigi was home with Rita and Olivia, having just come from seeing Diane in the hospital, where the doctors told him she wouldn't last more than a couple of days. The phone rang as Rita was pulling on her modest wool coat. She picked up the receiver, nodded, said, "I'll be home soon," and put it back down. Then Rita turned to Luigi. She was grim, dazed. Her lips were parted slightly, but she seemed to have forgotten to breathe.

"She's gone," he said before she could explain. *La ragazza è morta.*

Rita nodded and her bloodshot eyes—she'd insisted on overnights at the hospital, although Diane had told her it wasn't necessary—filled with tears.

They turned to Olivia, who was sitting at the kitchen table with a coloring book and crayons.

Rita approached the child and gently patted her long hair, running her fingers all the way to the ends. Olivia looked up.

"Mommy's gone to sleep," Rita said.

Olivia looked from her grandmother to her father and said nothing.

"Do you understand?" Rita asked. "Mommy went to sleep and she'll be asleep forever."

Luigi pictured Olivia in her bed at night. He envied her strong sleep, the deep breaths. She snored slightly. Was Rita right in comparing death to sleep? Was Diane as peaceful as Olivia looked on those nights?

Now she stared at Rita, looking as serious as she could with the two pouchy cheeks that hung from each side of her face. When people asked, in earlier, easier times, whom she looked like, Luigi struggled to identify a resemblance. Who could tell under all that flesh?

"She died?" Olivia asked innocently. For a moment, his daughter's unwillingness to be lied to pleased him, but then he considered that she might see through him, as well.

He thought the luckiest thing about Diane's death was that Olivia was no longer in diapers. He wouldn't have known what to do. But that night, he heated up the casserole Rita had left, and he and Olivia sat together at the table. It would be a month or so before Luigi realized that he could cook and began to do so. When their meal was finished, he looked questioningly at Olivia.

"I don't think I need a bath," the girl said.

"No," he agreed. How often was she bathed? He'd have to ask Rita. He didn't know how many times a week she gave him a sweet good-night kiss smelling of talcum and how many times a week she smelled only of herself.

Tidily, Olivia folded her paper napkin and placed it on the table. Then she pushed back her chair and hopped off. He watched her leave the room with a mixture of pride and despair. She would help him; still, his task seemed impossible. He was going to have to figure out what to do with a child, and not just a child, but a girl.

THE ONLY MAJOR DECISION LUIGI HAD MADE ABOUT OLIVIA DURING HER FIRST five years was her name. Diane wanted to name her Rita, for her own mother, or possibly Emma, for somebody in a book she loved. Luigi's mother was Rosalba, an impossible name for an American child. That wasn't what he wanted to call her anyway. There was only one girl's name he would give her.

"If she has your mother's name, it will be confusing," Luigi said, ready with his arguments.

"But you wanted to name her Louis if she was a boy." They'd only discussed boys' names when Diane was pregnant, and they'd quickly agreed on Louis.

"That's different. A son should have his father's name."

"But you would have had the same first and last name. She'll just have my mother's first name. It won't be confusing at all."

"Little Rita? Baby Rita?" Luigi said dismissively. "She'll hate that." He'd only laid eyes on his daughter for a moment, through the glass window of the nursery. He hadn't touched her yet.

"What name were you thinking of, then?" Luigi pictured the Madonna with child that hung over the altar in the church where his mother prayed. Diane exhibited none of that serene quality. She had the exhausted attitude of somebody pulled from a river. Her face had pillow creases on it. Her hair exploded from her head in ratty clumps.

"Olivia," he ventured softly.

"What?"

"Olivia," Luigi repeated.

"But what does it mean?"

"It means peaceful, like olive trees."

"I've never even seen an olive tree." Diane's eyes were closing.

"You lie there and don't think about a thing," Luigi said. He'd heard Rita say it to her earlier, after Doug and Rita had stood worriedly by their daughter's bedside, then hurried back to the nursery, where they pestered the nurses to hold their baby up to the glass.

Diane seemed to catch on to his game. She opened her eyes and fixed them on him. "Rita just makes more sense," she said, rubbing her own forehead.

"But Olivia is a pretty name, and when I saw her, I thought it fit."

"I can't argue right now, Lou," she said.

"Okay, let's not argue."

When the nurse came around to gather the information for the birth certificate, Diane was asleep. Luigi filled it all in. O-L-I-V-I-A. He signed his name with a flourish, using the pen he kept in his pocket for just such occasions. It was his first act as a family man. As he did it, he wondered whether Olivia—he was getting used to the name already, and surely Diane would, too—would make them whole.

IN THE SHED, LUIGI PRIED THE LID OFF A TRASH CAN. IT WAS AWKWARD WORK, because he still held Smudgy draped over one arm. The cat seemed to be gone, but then occasionally it twitched and Luigi jumped in answer. Being in the shed made him edgy anyway. Only once had he conceded to come in and sit while Olivia performed a demonstration for him, and she was so pleased with herself as she made a bowl and then paced around the limited space, pointing out the others that were drying and explaining how her small kiln—as squat as a beer keg—worked.

He tried to be enthusiastic, but the close space made him anxious, and he couldn't stand to see how dirty the whole process was. By the time she'd finished, her shirt was splattered. When he exited into the sun, there was clay around the edges of his shoes, as if he'd been walking along a riverbank. He'd moved to Shaleford for its sanitary sterility, and now his daughter passed time in the backyard in a shed, digging in the mud. He begged her to leave the door open when she threw, but she used a padlock to secure it overnight and left the lock's small, unremarkable key on the kitchen windowsill, next to his car keys. She promised to run the kiln at night only, but he still feared the electrical system was unreliable, and sometimes at work, in the middle of recording the result of a blood test in its honest, straight square, he'd panic at the thought of the shed exploding into flames.

With a pop, Luigi removed the lid from the trash can. He tossed the lid aside and saw that the can was full of bits of clay. Olivia had explained to him on the day of her demonstration that the clay was—what was the word she'd used?—*reconstituted*. (The conversation had made him anxious, too, because it was all in English, which they rarely spoke to each other. Olivia explained apologetically that she didn't know any of the pottery words in Italian.) The second trash can he opened had dinosaur-egg lumps of smooth clay, neatly stacked to fill it halfway. The third, however, was empty except for a splattered baseball bat that sat inside. He placed the bat on the cement floor of the shed and, with Smudgy hanging over his arm like a waiter's towel, rolled the empty trash can out into the light. From the shed, he collected a plastic bag and a heavy round white thing like a flat stone. Olivia had called it a "plaster," he recalled, during her demonstration. There were four of them stacked in a corner. Surely she wouldn't miss one.

Luigi uncoiled the hose from the side of the shed and placed its metallic mouth in the garbage can, then turned on the water. He'd been amazed that the shed had electricity and running water the first time he saw it. In Italy, it would have been a small apartment—the place where a mother might move after she'd given up her own house to her adult son or daughter. In Italy, old people, like lame dogs, had crept away silently in the night to die. He remembered the smell of Ester's grandfather in his wheelchair—the scent of old man never quite disguised by lavender soap. She used that soap, too, but on her it smelled like a promise.

After his father hit him that day, Luigi didn't pass out, but held on in a fog, trying desperately to understand why his father would have done such a thing. Blood trickled out of his ear. His father walked away, but his mother clucked over him and dabbed at the ear with a rag soaked in warm water. A high-pitched whine began deep in his head. What did I do? Luigi wondered. His father had hit him before, but never without a reason.

Eventually, the blood dried into a crust, but the right side of his head sang for weeks. He slept on his left side, because when his right ear touched the pillow, pain shot from his head down through his limbs, branching out like the complex arterial system he'd seen in drawings in his high school anatomy class. He didn't go to Ester's house or to school for several days afterward, and his mother said nothing. Luigi stayed in bed, trying to ignore the pain, trying not to hear the noise. When, three days later, he finally made it out to Ester's in the afternoon, she lifted her face from the book she was reading and began to ask where he'd been, until she saw the purple side of his head—like the inner workings of a sausage—and reached up a hand as if to stroke it. She didn't touch it, though. Her hand hovered in the air for a moment, and then she brought it back down to her lap.

Over the next few weeks, the swelling went down, until his skin was simply flat and bruised. The bruises faded. The shriek in his ear lessened to a dull buzz and then went away completely, so that there was just nothingness. Sometimes he tested his hearing by rubbing two fingers together near that ear, but they were silent. When the draft notice arrived— delivered by a boy in uniform who carried a sheaf of them under his arm—he understood why his father had done it. Luigi rode his father's bicycle to the offices and explained that he would love to march, really he would, for the good of the *patria*, but he was, you see, completely deaf in one ear. He would remain his father's property.

The cat cried. Its fur felt oily and unpleasant in Luigi's hands. It cried again, a soft creak like a door opening, and he came back to the moment. The garbage can had filled with cold water. It was cruel, he worried, not to use warm water, but there was no controlling the temperature of what came out of the hose. Smudgy's skeletal frame reminded him of the game birds his father used to kill and his mother would roast, the painstaking work of detaching shreds of flesh from the spindly bones. He placed the plaster in the bag, then rested the cat on top of it. Smudgy didn't struggle. Luigi felt the cat's pulse, hoping the anesthetic would have done its job, but there was still a faint blip there, like a memory. He knotted the top of the bag, then lowered it into the garbage can. The bag sank with a thud. Water flowed up the sides and splashed onto the brown grass. He placed the lid on the garbage can and hurried back to the house. He'd wait twenty minutes, he decided, before opening it.

"*Assassino*," he hissed to himself.

"It feels good, doesn't it?"

Luigi turned, startled, to see his neighbor, Mrs. Teitel, peering over the fence at him. She'd cultivated bushes on her side, but they were scrawny and anemic and provided no extra privacy.

"Excuse me?"

"It feels good to get things cleaned up, doesn't it?"

"Cleaned up?"

"I didn't mean to intrude, but I saw you throwing out a bag of garbage. I assumed you were cleaning out the shed." Mrs. Teitel tilted her head to one side and squinted as she spoke, although the sun was behind her and shining in his eyes.

"Yes, good," he agreed.

"I only wish I could get Frank to clean ours," she said. "It's so full of rakes and buckets and snow shovels that you can't even see the floor."

Luigi nodded. Her perkiness was intimidating. Since his own wife had died, he'd had little contact with adult women. Once Diane was gone, he'd forgotten about all the housewives cooped up in their homes, or driving around town doing errands in their station wagons. He'd seen something about "women's lib" on TV once, and he gathered that this was what the straight-haired, serious women were talking about—the way that middle-aged women formed a whole army of ghosts who made things function even while they remained invisible.

"Mine is full of pots," Luigi said. He'd picked up the habit from Olivia of referring to any ceramic piece as a pot, whether it was really used as a bowl or a vase or was purely decorative, like the hollow egg she'd presented to him with delight.

"Excuse me?" Mrs. Teitel wrinkled her nose.

"Pottery," he said. What was the word? *Ceramica*. "Ceramics."

"Oh." She fluttered a hand at her throat. "I thought you were growing something."

Luigi had no idea what she meant. "Olivia does pottery."

"What a wonderful hobby."

Luigi glanced at his watch, wondering how long the cat had been under. He hadn't heard a single splash, which was a good sign.

"You probably need to get going," she said.

He nodded. "I must go to work." Even as he said it, he knew it was wrong, maybe not that the grammar was incorrect, but that the phrasing was unnatural. English words were still stiff in his mouth sometimes, like stale bread that scraped his palate as he tried to chew it. Inside the house, he climbed up to the second-floor bathroom and stood at the window, curtain tugged back slightly, to watch until she went inside. Mrs. Teitel brushed something invisible off a lawn chair, glanced again toward his yard, then slid open the glass door at the rear of her house and disappeared.

When he opened the bucket twenty minutes later, the cat was dead, but then it occurred to him that he had a dead cat in a bag and didn't know quite what to do with it. Smudgy's waterlogged body felt like a sponge through the plastic; the weight of the plaster from Olivia's shed stretched one side. He rested the bag on the ground as he hoisted the garbage can and carried it to the edge of the lawn, where he spilled out the water. It ran in a dark river through the dirt, then split into tributaries that ended when they met rocks or pits in the ground. As he did this, he kept an eye out for Mrs. Teitel, but she didn't appear.

Gingerly, he picked up the plastic bag from inside the trash can and carried it down into the woods. This had never been a problem back in Urbino—the kittens in their bags had simply sunk to the bottom of the *fiume*. With his foot, he tried digging a hole through some ground cover, but the pine needles were matted and dense and his shoe lost its shine, although the hole barely penetrated the surface. He had a shovel in the garage, but it was a flimsy snow shovel, which would be no more use than the spade Olivia had taken to the beach when she was little, also still in the garage with its matching yellow plastic bucket.

He trudged back through the woods to the house, holding the dripping bag in front of himself so that he wouldn't get his work clothes dirty. He opened the trunk of the car and placed Smudgy in the back, cradled in the round center of the spare tire that was stored there. Luigi loved the term *spare tire*. He'd gone to driving school right after he moved to Shaleford, and he could feel the lingo of the automobile working its magic, Americanizing him, as he sat and studied the small blue book that New York State provided. A spare tire was a cushion, one more partition between himself and disaster.

At the dump, he placed the bag gently on top of the other garbage. There was no one around except for the man who drove the toy-size bulldozer, turning over the layers, as if plastic and metal and old furniture could be mulched until they broke down. Luigi hurried away and returned to his car, still afraid Smudgy might make a sound. As he went to close the trunk, he saw that wet Smudgy had imprinted a small, perfectly round dark stain in the well. He pressed it with his fingertips. It would dry, he supposed. Olivia wouldn't know—that was the important thing. And then he slammed the gaping lid shut to cover his secret.

✦ TUESDAY ✦

Olivia woke to rain. Thunder rattled the glass and raindrops sprayed the windowsills. She wondered idly whether the rain after so many hot days would solve Urbino's water problem. Yesterday, she'd heard two men in the piazza complaining about the water situation, too. As best she could tell, it was a boondoggle—a consultant paid to fix the system who never did, a town that ran dry every summer afternoon. Their conversation had ended with the same words the woman in the hotel had used: *la politica*.

Olivia was still trying to figure out how there could be so much water at Niagara Falls, where she and Claire had taken a spur-of-the-moment trip once after spotting a fifty-nine-dollar fare in the paper, and so little water here in Urbino. The falls were as big as a mythological dragon, the folds of flowing water as shiny as scales; she and Claire had had to shout to communicate. They rode on *The Maid of the Mist VII* (one of a fleet of twelve) and laughed at each other in the smelly blue slickers the ship's staff provided, their hair plastered to their foreheads. It was one of those moments when she'd wondered whether work she liked and friends she loved might be enough to make a life. It was a question that came to her often as she stood alone in the art room at Coleman in the morning, awaiting the spill of girls that signaled the start of her day. That question had grown more urgent since she'd moved out of Ivan's apartment. Was it him, or was she unable to connect? Was it true, as he insisted, that her sense of obligation to her father was too strong? That she couldn't help but be disappointed in everyone?

Olivia had lived with Ivan for two years, twenty-four months almost to the day. Ivan was an adjunct at CUNY and a graduate student in radical history. Olivia misunderstood it as "radical hysterectomy" the night they met at a noisy party, and it took her several minutes of conversation to catch up. She'd been drawn to his laconic energy, the way he emptied a bottle of beer with a few long draws, the slow movement of his eyes across the scrap of paper as he jotted down her number at the end of the night. At that party, he told her stories—about himself, his friends, his family. She was charmed.

Ivan had spent the first year they lived together trying to unionize the other adjuncts. For her part, Olivia was impressed by his dedication. She readily made photocopies for Ivan on the sly at Coleman and gamely proofread his leaflets. When the unionization project came to an unfruitful end, Ivan found another—seeking a pay raise for cafeteria workers in the public schools. This, too, she supported as best she could. On Saturdays, when she was manning the desk at the pottery studio, she liked to think of him back home, compiling a list of indignities that would inspire hair-netted lunch ladies to rise up. Olivia's father had never told her about his arrival in the United States, except that he'd come to New York, but she'd made up a past for him out of the immigrant clichés she'd seen in movies, and it wasn't pretty: a crowded apartment, refusals to employ a wop, a slick theft of his money in exchange for a bridge that planted one foot in Manhattan and one in Brooklyn, just as he straddled the Old World and the New. She liked to think that fifty years earlier, Ivan might have stood up for her father.

Things with Ivan had started promisingly, but then Olivia's father had become increasingly confused, and she and Ivan had grown progressively more impatient with each other. In retrospect, she could no longer untangle the widening gap between herself and Ivan from her father's slow shift away from reality. A few times when she called her father, he accused her of moving without giving him her new number. She'd gone to Shaleford and programmed her phone number into speed dial on his phone and explained how it worked, but then he began calling during the day, when he should have known she was at work, or, worse, in the middle of the night. "Can you ever forgive me?" he sobbed to her in the dark, but he couldn't explain what he thought he'd done to hurt her so.

"You need to put him in a nursing home," Ivan said, rolling onto his back and pulling the pillow around his ears after one of those late-night phone calls.

"You don't understand my father and that house," she responded. Ivan's parents were smiling Americans who had always owned a home. Italy, for them, was a place one went on vacation. Every year, the daughter of one friend or another took a junior year in Florence, and Ivan's mother was quick to share this news with Olivia when she called to speak to her son and Olivia answered the phone. They would have clucked their tongues in dismay if they'd known where she was now, that she'd blindly come to dig up the past.

The rain blurred the windows. Her hotel room felt private and comforting. The bed hugged her drowsily. After a quick shower (no sense in taking chances with the water situation as long as she was awake anyway), Olivia slipped back into the sheer nightie that Claudia had lent her. Olivia slept in old T-shirts with yellowed armpits, but Claudia's hand-wash-only erotic honeymoon negligee was surprisingly comfortable, especially in the heat. She settled back between the sheets.

The day before, after she'd left Gianfranco's office, she'd visited the ducal palace. It *was* impressive, although Olivia's favorite part had been not the ornate banquet rooms or the duke's study with its wood intarsia of a cunning squirrel and musical instruments, but the basement, a warren of tunnels and fireplaces that had been the kitchen and servants' quarters. The duke (or more likely, some uncredited lackey, Olivia thought) had invented a rudimentary refrigeration system, so there were wells dug into the basement. These had been stacked with snow and layers of hay to keep food fresh before a banquet. The servants had cleverly arranged their bathing area—a dank, close room—so that the stone tub backed up against the cooking fire.

She'd learned this and more by attaching herself to the end of a group of twenty or so high school–age kids from a *colonia estiva*. They made her homesick for Coleman as they swung their knapsacks from shoulder to shoulder and complained to the woman leading them that their feet were tired. Olivia knew intimately the freedom brought on by a field trip. The souvenir money that sat wrinkled in students' pockets and a day outside the confines of school had a liberating effect. Here, one couple with basset hound eyes for each other hung back from the group and made out as they exited each room; a boy with red hair aggressively pushed one of his classmates and narrowly missed toppling him over a rope and onto the duchess's bed. What would it feel like to sleep in a room lined with tapestries and under a canopy of velvet? Like returning to the womb, Olivia decided, or maybe existing in a padded cell. Or like being her father at the end, when nothing could penetrate.

To her disappointment, the famed Piero della Francesca portrait of the duke that had hung on her father's wall was missing from the museum. It was too important a piece to remain in its place of origin, the guide insinuated indignantly. The government had deemed the Uffizi in Florence a more suitable home. The only Raphael painting was *La Muta*, The Silent One, of a woman with her hands pointed, one index finger extended, as though to stop someone from spilling a secret. No one knew who she was, the group's guide explained.

"Thank God for Duke Federico and that palace," Claudia said at dinner when Olivia mentioned that she'd gone. "Without it, there'd be no work at all in Urbino."

But when Olivia began to ask Claudia what she thought of the bedroom and the duchess's bed, her cousin waved at her not to waste her time.

"I haven't been in years," she said. "I went on a *gita* for school. Alex has probably been recently, no, Alex?"

Alex nodded and swallowed what was in his mouth. "Every year," he said. "What a bore."

Now in her hotel room, Olivia dozed, then woke and stretched her legs. She hung in the limbo between wakefulness and sleep. She'd considered visiting Raphael's birthplace yesterday, too, but that and the palace appeared to be Urbino's sole tourist attractions, so she'd decided to save it. She wasn't expected at Claudia's for lunch today, because on Tuesday both Claudia and Alex had *rientro*, which meant that, unlike the other five days (Sunday, as she'd already seen, was an exception), when lunch marked the end of the workday, they came home, ate, and then returned to work and school, respectively, for several hours in the afternoon. She could work in a visit to Raphael's house then, after Gianfranco took her to see "the very ugly part of Urbino," whatever that meant.

A light tap on the door startled Olivia. The maid, she reasoned. Since that encounter with the cleaning woman and her check-in upon arrival, she hadn't met up with another person in the hotel, but somehow, each day when she returned in the evening, her bed was made with fresh, starchy sheets, and the abbreviated towel in the bathroom had been replaced, as well. The room itself was spotless—whoever was doing the cleaning was also folding clothing and lining up toothbrush and toothpaste, which Olivia couldn't help feeling was a reproof. She cracked the door, expecting a middle-aged woman with dishpan hands. Instead, there was Gianfranco.

"Hi," she said, speaking English in surprise. She grabbed her watch. With the dark, rainy weather, she hadn't noticed time passing. It was almost eleven o'clock. She was supposed to have met him an hour ago.

"It's raining," he announced needlessly. Water was pooling on the ground around his shoes. Gianfranco shook his head like a dog, sending water droplets in every direction. A few splattered across Olivia's breastbone, revealed by the low scalloped neckline of Claudia's nightgown. She closed the door.

"Just a minute," she yelled from inside the room. "Let me get dressed."

She grabbed the clothes she'd worn the day before off the floor, then changed her mind, fished her father's key out of the back pocket of the jeans, and stuffed the whole bundle into the wardrobe. She took another of Claudia's outrageous outfits—a pair of white jeans and a Lycra shirt with a giant hot-pink-and-yellow paisley design, like commas from a book three stories tall. Once dressed, she dashed into the bathroom and brushed her teeth hurriedly. Then she raced back to the door to the hallway and opened it.

"Come in," she said.

Gianfranco strode in. His eyes took in the surroundings quickly. He ended by focusing on her, and she grew self-conscious about the tightness of Claudia's jeans. The denim chafed, reminding her of the rumor that had raced around Coleman the year before that Tracy Carson, a sophomore girl, had worn such tight jeans that she needed to be treated for what the students termed crotch rot. In the back pocket, her father's key clamped to her skin as if it were attached with Super Glue.

"They're not my clothes," she explained.

She handed him the hotel towel. He ruffled it through his hair, then blotted his neck.

"I think something happened," Gianfranco said.

Olivia picked up her watch again. It was 11:02.

"I'm sorry if I wasted your whole morning," she said.

Gianfranco shook his head. "There's not much work now. As I tell you, it's August." He looked stern. When Olivia had asked Claudia about this Gianfranco at dinner the night before, Claudia had said, *"È un tipo serio."* Olivia remained unsure whether being a serious guy was a good thing or a bad thing in Claudia's mind.

"I fell back to sleep," Olivia said. She pulled the formfitting shirt away from her stomach, but it snapped back.

When she'd pushed Claudia on the issue of Gianfranco, she'd said only, "He's not dangerous, at least not the way you mean."

"I think maybe you've changed your mind," Gianfranco said calmly. He stepped into the bathroom and neatly hung the square of cloth on the rack, tugging on each side so that all the corners met exactly. The rain was tapering to a few pit-pats on the windows. When he turned around, he studied her outfit again with a quick up-and-down zip of his head. The room was hot and close, and it occurred to her that being in her hotel room alone with a strange man when there were no other guests around was dangerous, but after her conversation with Claudia, he didn't frighten her.

"How did you meet him?" Claudia had asked after Olivia inquired about Gianfranco, and instinctively, Olivia lied.

"In the piazza," she said. "We were both having coffee." As she said it, she rubbed her thumb and forefinger together under the table, as if she had the deed in her hand and were testing its strength. She felt bad lying to Claudia, but her cousin seemed so delighted at her presence. She couldn't bear to disappoint her, to admit that she'd come to Urbino over something as tawdry as money, and she didn't want to damage their growing friendship. Her mother's family had been small, and her grandparents had died soon after her mother. Claudia was her only shot at closeness with a relative.

"No, no. Still interested," Olivia said now to Gianfranco. Trying to be discreet, she pulled up her jeans by their empty belt loops. They were meant to sit low on the hips, like all Claudia's pants, but she couldn't banish the feeling that they were falling. The rain had stopped almost completely and water rushed through the gutters.

"Why do you not wear your clothes?" Gianfranco asked. When he asked a question, Gianfranco wrinkled his nose, as if he were taxing his brain to come up with a plausible answer to save her the trouble.

"My suitcase." Olivia sighed. "The airline lost it."

"When?"

"I arrived Saturday," she said.

"And still no suitcase?" Gianfranco looked puzzled.

"I called on Sunday, but there was no answer. Monday, I got a recording that I couldn't understand. What's a *sciopero*?"

"It is a—how do you say?—a strike. On Monday, there was a strike of the airport workers."

"And they're back today?"

Gianfranco slipped a small cell phone from his breast pocket. "Do you have your paper?" he asked.

Olivia reached into her book bag and brought out the deed. "Here."

He glanced at it. As in his office, he seemed reluctant even to touch it. He pinched one corner and handed it back. "The paper for your suitcase."

Olivia went into the side pocket of her book bag and drew out the slender folder that held her airline tickets. The green baggage claim check for her suitcase was stapled to the inside. She handed it to him, along with the copy of the form from the lost-luggage office. The phone beeped quickly as Gianfranco dialed a series of numbers. He repeated her name, patiently spelled it out using the names of cities for each letter (*B* like Bologna, *O* like Orvieto), then punched in some more numbers.

"*Sì*," he said. "*Sì, sì, sì*."

Olivia tried to look at him inquiringly, but he was half-turned from her, with his face pointing down. His curly hair was drying and springing away from his scalp, revealing that mysterious lopped-off ear. It was all she could do not to reach out and touch the tender, warped edge. She imagined it would feel like the strips of chamois she used to soften the lips of bowls and teacups.

"*Mille grazie,*" Gianfranco said in an ungrateful tone. He snapped the phone shut.

"What was that about?"

"The suitcase is in Ancona. At the airport. They have it since Saturday evening."

"Well, when are they going to bring it to me?" Olivia had wanted her clothes back, of course, but now that she knew they were nearby, she longed for her things. She couldn't wait to pull on a sweatshirt two sizes too big. The thought of the oversized T-shirts she slept in almost made her swoon.

Gianfranco looked skeptical. "Bring it to you? You have to go. There is a small airport in Ancona. The office for the suitcases is open from nine to one."

"I just thought . . ." Olivia remembered the time she'd flown to Chicago with Claire and her suitcase had shown up late. When they'd awakened the next morning, they'd found it sitting on the back porch of Claire's parents' house, slick with dew. "In the United States, they bring it to your house."

"This is Italy."

Olivia studied him. "Where's Ancona? How do I get there?"

Gianfranco shook the car keys in his hand. "I can take you." He stared at her and held perfectly still, waiting for her answer. She wished she had a camera so that she could photograph him like that, as open to her as a low, wide serving bowl.

"But you were going to show me something. The ugly part of Urbino."

Throughout the conversation, Olivia had struggled to read his expression. Mostly, he had kept his face flat, affectless. Now he smiled, and though afterward she'd chide herself for romanticizing the moment, she noticed that outside, the sun suddenly shone brilliantly through the foggy clouds.

"Now you are interested in the ugly?"

"You made it sound interesting," she replied. She was growing impatient to uncover the mystery of the deed. Besides, she was only here for a week, and a couple of days had already passed. She wasn't sure, though, that Gianfranco had anything to offer. He seemed more intent on supplying an inverted tourist jaunt—the lowlights of Urbino.

Gianfranco waved a hand at her. "It's waited almost fifty years. It can wait for tomorrow." He handed the ticket folder back to her, holding it for just a second too long, so that when she tried to take it, they played a brief game of tug-of-war. He smiled at her again, looking pleased that she'd gotten the joke, although she wasn't sure she had. "Bring your passport," he added. "They need to identify you."

"I WENT TO THE DUCAL PALACE YESTERDAY," OLIVIA WAS SAYING AS THEY SPED along the highway. *"Bello."*

Gianfranco's car, it turned out when they got to the parking lot, was a tinny red Fiat. It looked fine, if small and boxy, from the outside, but now that they were moving along the still-damp road, Olivia was sure she could hear every movement of the machinery of its hardworking engine. If there had been something printed in braille on the asphalt, she thought, she could have made that out, too, the chassis sat so low. The windshield wipers creaked like old bones; the radio hung from the dashboard by a few threads of wire, like a tooth ready to be yanked.

"Beauty built with dirty money," Gianfranco said. He shifted and sped up. He was driving fast. Olivia watched as the quivering needle on the speedometer moved up steadily. She held on to the door handle and kept her eyes facing front.

"Dirty?"

"He was a mercenary," Gianfranco said. "He fought for money, not *principio.* That is the beautiful story of Urbino." He looked away from the road to deliver that last sentence to her, then faced front in time to avoid the back end of a truck that had pulled into their lane. Maybe this was the way in which he would turn out to be dangerous, although judging from what was going on in the other lanes, Italian driving-school instructors told their pupils to move as quickly as possible and never, never to give in.

"So the people didn't love him?" The guide had insisted that Duke Federico was the most popular duke ever. He was such a bold and jovial personality, she claimed, that his poor overshadowed son, Guidobaldo—depicted in one portrait as a girlish child with a strange topknot—never had a chance. After so many museum field trips, Olivia knew better than to take at face value the words of a guide, but she was still surprised at what Gianfranco was saying.

"The people love anyone who oppresses them. Hundreds of people died building the palace, and today we all go and say, '*Ooo, che bello.*'"

Olivia was a little insulted. *Bello* had been her word.

"Can't something be beautiful and popular?" she asked. "Does that automatically make it bad?"

"He is a *mito*, a myth." He pronounced it like baseball mitt. "Like the Popes, or God. You know the story of the duke's nose, no?"

"No."

"He is missing this part." Gianfranco lifted both hands off the wheel to pinch the bridge of his nose. "They say that his eye was injured in a war, so he take out part of his nose with his own sword to see." He made a swooping motion with an index finger to indicate shaving away bone and skin.

"Ouch," Olivia said.

"*Stronzo,*" Gianfranco muttered under his breath as a Mercedes loomed behind them, then passed in a silvery blur.

"The pyramids are beautiful," she said, "and they were built by slaves."

"The *palazzo ducale* is worse. The slaves who built the *piramidi* had no choice. Here, the people *want* to be told what to do. If the duke came back tomorrow—or Il Duce himself—they'd be ready to do anything he asked."

"So, you're interested in history?"

"I am trying to keep the history of Urbino. I have research. But nobody is interested. This is Italy: We want only to be modern."

Gianfranco shifted again and pulled up alongside an identical Fiat in the next lane, this one white. He and the other driver glanced at each other for a moment, then pushed forward.

After a few teeth-rattling moments, he downshifted. "Italians learned nothing from the war. Worse, they create a new history to look good."

Olivia thought of the Gulf War a few years earlier, when television commentators had stood in front of exploding bombs as though they were a July Fourth backdrop. Ivan had seethed. Her father, who had still been lucid then, had refused to watch or even discuss it. She'd wondered at the time if it brought back memories of the war in Italy, another topic he wouldn't go near. Why did he leave after? she'd always wondered. Why not get out before?

"You ask somebody now, they were all partisans during the war," Gianfranco continued. "Where are the Fascists? They all disappeared?"

"History is written by the winners," Olivia said.

"Italians did not win, but they write their own private history anyway. And then their sons and daughters write it again.

"*Eccoci qua,*" he called out happily, downshifting. And indeed, there they were. He crossed three lanes and pulled onto an exit, splashing madly through a large puddle. With a quick yank of the emergency brake, he parked in the lot out front.

In the office marked LOST LUGGAGE, a dour man in a gray uniform sat smoking a cigarette behind the desk.

Gianfranco stepped forward, so Olivia did, too. She pulled out her passport and the ticket folder and opened it. Before she could gather the words in Italian, Gianfranco spoke for her.

"*Buongiorno,*" he began.

"*Buongiorno.*" The man behind the desk took the baggage-claim ticket and without saying another word rapidly punched some numbers into a computer. He flipped open her passport and glanced at her to make sure she matched the picture. Then, still not speaking, he stepped into the storage area behind his desk, where a multicolored jumble of suitcases filled four large shelves. Carelessly, he tossed a few on the floor, then yanked a black wheelie bag off the third shelf and placed it on the counter.

"That's not it," Olivia said, speaking in English to Gianfranco. "*È verde,*" she added. "It's green."

"*No, non quella,*" Gianfranco told the man. He shook a finger at him. The man checked the ticket number and tossed the black wheelie bag back onto the shelves.

"*La riconosce?*" he asked Gianfranco, wanting to know if she recognized it. He indicated Olivia with his chin and the shelves with a sweep of his hand.

"*Parlo benissimo italiano,*" Olivia said, irritated at being ignored. Her father had grown furious when, at the end of his doctor visits, he was sent out of the room so the grown-ups could talk. Olivia had learned a whole new vocabulary: *gerontologist, plaques, apolipoprotein E.* At his first doctor's appointment, she'd read a brochure in the waiting room. "We all forget where we've put our keys," it said in squared-off black type, "but those with Alzheimer's forget how to use a key."

The airport worker continued to address Gianfranco. "Maybe it's better if you look for it."

Gingerly, Olivia rounded the corner of the desk. Gianfranco followed. Nothing on the shelves looked familiar. In fact, it was hard to distinguish individual suitcases at all.

"Let's do this systematically," Olivia suggested. "We should start either at the top or the bottom, take them all down, and go through them one by one. That way, we'll be sure we're not missing anything."

Gianfranco said nothing. He stood back, studying the shelves.

Not only was she invisible to the airport worker—who stood off to the side, staring out the plate-glass window at the parking lot—but Gianfranco seemed deaf to her, as well.

"Did you hear me?" she asked. "Should we start at the top or the bottom?"

Gianfranco reached up to the third shelf and moved aside two bags. One teetered precariously but didn't fall. He reached an arm toward the back of the shelf, then with both hands grasped a green suitcase and brought it slowly to the ground.

"It is this one?" he asked.

The suitcase was battered. When she'd packed it, the front had bulged out like a pregnant stomach, but after days of pressure from other bags, first in the plane's luggage compartment and now here, it was concave and anorexic-looking. There were several pieces of black duct tape stuck to one corner. Olivia picked them off with a fingernail, revealing a long gash. Someone had made an X on the back of the bag with a black Magic · Marker. Even the green color looked faded and blotchy. She stared at it for a long time before speaking, wondering at how presciently he'd gone right to it when she hadn't seen it herself.

"That's me," she said finally, and Gianfranco smiled again.

ONCE OLIVIA'S OWN CLOTHES WERE AT HAND, SHE WAS SO EAGER TO GET OUT of Claudia's that she took the suitcase into the airport bathroom, hauled it into a stall, and squatted by the seatless toilet to pick out an outfit. It was surprising how she'd forgotten her own clothes during the three-day period she'd been without them. She couldn't believe, either, when she thought about it, that she'd only been away from New York since Friday. New York felt like something she'd dreamed up, a fantasy that her Italian self might have had. As she took out shirts and pants and shoes, she sighed with pleasure. Nothing seemed to be missing or ruined by the damage to her suitcase, just flat, as compressed as the clay wall of a large bowl after she squeezed it hard between two sponges to make it strong.

Finally, she chose a T-shirt that said PROPERTY OF COLEMAN ATHLETIC DEPARTMENT in a faded arc across the chest, not because it was nice or even because it was on top, but because it felt most specifically hers. The T-shirt had been a welcoming gift from the headmaster when she'd started teaching at Coleman ten years earlier, after a brief period trying to cobble together a living by giving classes at various Ys and craft studios and even one disastrous three-week course at a paint-your-own-pottery place that had resulted in a few unattractive mugs for the participants and a note from the owner letting Olivia know that she wouldn't be invited back, as she "took things a little too seriously for our clientele." Every Coleman teacher had a similar T-shirt, seniority indicated by how faded it was. Olivia was secretly pleased by a pinprick of a hole starting to unravel in the left armpit. She pulled on a faded pair of jeans, as well. These weren't clothes she'd brought to make an impression; they were what she'd pictured herself wearing on the plane going home.

Sitting in Gianfranco's car in those jeans, with a clean bra—the underwire only slightly warped from its journey—under her T-shirt, Olivia had never been more comfortable.

Gianfranco shifted, then glanced at her. *"Di che anno sei?"* he asked abruptly.

"What?"

"What year are you from? I mean, what year are you born?"

"Oh. Sixty-one," she said.

"Like me."

He sped into another lane and she gasped at the motion, then laughed.

"You are happy?" The air had begun to heat up, and with the remains of the rain still sizzling around them, it was growing very humid again. They both had their windows open to keep cool, making it hard to maintain a conversation.

Olivia nodded. "It feels good to wear my own clothes."

"*Fai la maschietta.*"

"What?"

"Your look," he said, waving his hand up and down. "*La maschietta.* How do you say? Like a little boy. A girl-boy."

"I don't know about that," Olivia said. Was he insulting her? Did he think she looked better in Claudia's clothes? She'd stuffed Claudia's things into the suitcase, which was now in Gianfranco's backseat. She'd return everything—the thong, the nightgown—tonight, or maybe tomorrow, as that would give her time to wash it all out. Then she was flooded by a recent memory: She stood at the sink in the Shaleford bathroom, scrubbing vainly to wash the brown streaks out of a pair of her father's pale blue boxers. He'd worn the same kind as long as she could remember—she'd see a stack of them, the blue of a milky marble, folded neatly whenever he did laundry. The nurses would throw his things into the washing machine, but they wouldn't scrub, and she couldn't blame them. Everyone had to draw the line somewhere. She'd stood at that sink for what felt like hours, palpating the two halves against each other, hoping that they'd have enough strength to wipe each other clean. Then she'd soaked the boxers in bleach, but a faint scrim remained, like the ghostly clay splotches she so often found on her own clothing.

Gianfranco's driving seemed less scary now, because it was less of a surprise, and because they were no longer on the highway. By the time she'd changed her clothes, it was almost one o'clock, and he asked whether she'd like to eat lunch in a place he knew. The ride so far had taken them past several ugly shopping centers with an architectural style that smacked of preglasnost–Eastern Europe meets Miami Beach: bare cement structures with the occasional pastel storefront with shiny trim. It had also taken them past fields of sunflowers, their heads pointing upward in unison, and vineyards, the craggy arms of grapevines reaching for one another. As they sped by more than one farm, the smell of manure filled the Fiat, then faded just as quickly. At one point along the curvy road, a pig trotted across in front of the car. Without losing control, Gianfranco swerved to avoid it. Olivia watched it shrink to a tiny pale pink dot in the side-view mirror. She'd seen horses, several herds of sheep (from far away, they looked like clouds that had fallen from the sky and now dotted the hillsides), three mangy dogs, a yard full of goats, and a chicken coop with one proud rooster perched on its roof, crowing.

"He doesn't know the hour," Gianfranco laughed. "He lose his watch."

Twenty minutes later, after slow progress down an ever-narrowing strip of road piled on top of itself like a piece of ribbon candy, they pulled in front of what appeared to be another old farmhouse. Gianfranco maneuvered carefully, then shot his car down a narrow gravel driveway to a parking area in back. There was one other car there.

"*Hai fame?*" he asked as the Fiat shuddered to a stop. Olivia feared it would never start up again, like a horse in a Western that gets run too hard. She *was* hungry. She hadn't eaten since dinner the evening before at Claudia's. The rain and oversleeping this morning had kept her from breakfast.

She nodded. "Starved. But are we near what you wanted to show me? Should we do that first?"

"It will be there in two hours."

The restaurant—if that was what it was, because it seemed more like a cross between a private residence and a speakeasy—had four tables, each one robed in a white tablecloth. Two tables were littered with the remains of someone's lunch—ashtrays overflowing with butts, dirty espresso cups, wineglasses rimmed with lipstick. She and Gianfranco were still standing at the entrance when what she had taken to be a cupboard slid open and someone peeked out from a kitchen tiled in brilliant white.

"*Talpettino!*" A voice cried out from the other side. A door swung open, and a man dressed in checkered chef's pants and a white coat blooming with stains clomped out in a pair of clogs. He rushed to their side and kissed Gianfranco once on each cheek. "*Talpettino, come stai?*"

"*Ciao, Leo,*" Gianfranco replied, looking sheepish. He'd taken off his sunglasses and was squinting at the restaurant. "*Ti presento Olivia.*"

"Olivia?" Leo lifted his eyebrows in surprise. "*Piacere.*"

"*Ciao,*" Olivia said, taking the hand he offered her.

In the center of the table Gianfranco led her to sat an unmarked green glass bottle of wine—red, she saw as he poured it—and a bottle of mineral water. Soon, Leo returned from the kitchen with a plate holding four slices of bread, two topped with something brown and two topped with something black.

"*Buon appetito*," he said seriously as he set it down. Then he turned and raced back to the kitchen.

Olivia picked up one of the brown slices and nibbled at it. Gianfranco was watching her closely. It was earthy and sweet—something she couldn't identify. She set it down on her plate.

"What is it?"

He picked up the other piece and took a healthy bite, then chewed thoughtfully. Finally, he tossed it back with a gulp of red wine.

"*Fegatino*," he said. "*Fegato di pollo.*"

"*Fegato?*" Olivia nibbled some more. It was tasty, but still unidentifiable.

"*Fegato* is . . ." Gianfranco looked up at the ceiling, as if there might be a dictionary hidden among the rough-hewn beams. "Not heart," he said, placing his hand over the left side of his chest and forgetting to stress the *h*, so that it sounded like *art*. "Not *reni*." He rested his hands on his waist.

"*Reni* must be kidneys," Olivia said. Her father's doctor had warned on more than one occasion of possible renal failure.

"Yes, kidney," said Gianfranco.

"Spleen?" Olivia asked. She didn't know if spleen was edible. Did chickens have spleens?

"What is spleen?"

Olivia shrugged. That was as far as high school biology took her. She flashed on her father drawing the chambers of the heart, trying to instill in her how important it was to know the parts of the body. She'd sat sullenly and shaded in the aorta but refused to learn.

Gianfranco took the other piece of bread. "This is *olive*," he said.

"Olives," she agreed, biting the fourth piece. The topping was thick and oily. Her stomach growled in anticipation.

"This is where your name is from, I believe."

She nodded. "Peaceful, like an olive branch. That's what my name means."

"But *fegato?*" Gianfranco popped the last piece of the brown toast into his mouth. "*Fegato* is bad if you drink," he said when he had finished chewing.

"Liver, of course."

"Like the verb *to leave*?"

"*Live.*"

Olivia had eaten chicken liver only once before, at the Second Avenue Deli, where it was heavy with onion and served thickly packed into a metal bowl. "Chicken liver is Jewish food in New York, not Italian."

"Jewish?"

"The religion?" She traced a six-pointed star on the tablecloth with her finger.

"*Ebrei*," he said sadly. "The Hebrews. They are problem."

"Jews *have* problems," she said, correcting him. Several faces came to mind: her friend Rachel, a science teacher at Coleman, her childhood neighbor, Jared Teitel, Ivan.

"He is a Jew?" Olivia's father had asked when she brought Ivan home to Shaleford the first time. Ivan was upstairs in her bedroom, lying down with a headache. Before sinking onto the single bed, he'd surveyed her childhood room with its rose-covered wallpaper, then smiled at her. "Very you," he said. Ivan's own parents had transformed his room into a gym with a cross-country ski machine and a set of gleaming dumbbells as soon as he moved out.

"*Babbo!*" Olivia admonished her father, horrified. "Don't use that word."

"Why not? This is what he is, no?"

"*Sì, ma non si dice,*" Olivia said. "Say Jewish."

"He is a Jewish?" Luigi frowned, as if he knew that wasn't right, either.

"Yes, he is Jewish," Olivia said. She waited one, two, three beats for her father to say something else, but he didn't. "Does that bother you?" Her father hadn't gone to church, and she'd never heard him say anything she would have classified as Catholic, unless you counted his shouts of "*Dio santo*" when he stubbed a toe or broke a glass.

Her father turned from the sink, where he was washing the dishes from lunch. "There were *vongole* in the pasta."

Olivia laughed with relief. Ivan always joked that he was so nonreligious that the Ethical Culture Society was too Jewish for him. His favorite take-out dish was mu shu pork. "He doesn't keep kosher, Babbo," she said. "Hardly anybody does that anymore." Sometimes her father was alarmingly innocent.

"There are many Jews in Urbino," Gianfranco continued. "Or there were many Jews in Urbino. Duke Federico was good to Jews—a mercenary, but good to Jews. So many came." He set down his wineglass.

"So there were a lot of Jews in Urbino during the Renaissance?"

"After, too. There is a long history of Jews in the city. Many families. A big ghetto, with a synagogue."

"Still?"

Gianfranco sighed. "Do you know about 1938, the *leggi razziali*?"

She shook her head.

"In 1938, there were laws that we do not study in *la scuola di giurisprudenza* today."

"Like what?"

"Like no Jews can go to school. Like Christians cannot work for Jews in their home."

Leo swept out of the kitchen holding two soup bowls full of pasta.

"*Ravioli burro e salvia,*" he said proudly as he set them on the table.

Gianfranco and Olivia were quiet again, almost reverent, as they sprinkled cheese on their pasta and began to eat. The ravioli skins were thin and eggy; the ricotta and spinach filling mild. Melted butter glistened on top. Olivia had observed that Italians were like children, or at least ate like children. They loved to be coddled and fed; they suckled cappuccino like mother's milk in the morning and preferred food soft enough that it could be gummed down rather than chewed, flavorful versions of the grainy purees that were the last foods her father ate. Leo stood off to the side, waiting for their reaction.

"*Buonissimi,*" Gianfranco said.

"*Sì,*" Olivia added. She could feel her chin growing shiny with melted butter, and a fleck of sage leaf had lodged in her teeth. She wiped her face with the cloth napkin. It had a cigarette burn hole in one corner.

"*Grazie, talpettino,*" Leo said.

When he had left the table, Olivia asked, "What is it he calls you?"

"*Talpettino.* It's a little animal that lives underground. A *talpa.* How do you say this?"

"A lizard?"

"No, not *lucertola*. It is blind."

"A mole?"

"Yes, that is right. A mole."

Olivia studied him but could find nothing molelike about him. She could see an earnest dogginess in his eyes, maybe something vaguely feline in his honest mouth and the way he doled out smiles sparingly. At home, lawyers were often tagged sharks or snakes, but Gianfranco didn't have any of those qualities, at least not so far as she could tell. But a mole?

"And why does he call you a little mole?"

"We go to school together, Leo and I, and when it was time to—how do you say, when you copy answers on an exam?"

"Cheat?"

"Yes, cheat. When it was time to cheat, I could never see the answers on other papers. So I did not cheat. Everybody make fun of me for this." He looked satisfied with his explanation, as if cheating were the norm and it were to be expected that friends would tease him for not joining in and conforming. Olivia shook her head, not sure she'd understood correctly.

"Also," he continued, not seeming to notice her confusion, "I am blind to other things."

He sounded so sad that she didn't want to pry. Olivia took a deep sip of wine.

Gianfranco set down his fork. One square ravioli remained in the center of his bowl. "I must ask you something."

"Go ahead." Olivia speared her last piece of pasta with the fork and let it fill her mouth.

"Fix me," he said.

"Fix you?" She thought of Smudgy coming home from the vet after she had been spayed, a red line down the middle of her belly, which healed to pink and then faded in days.

"Yes, when I make errors, in the English, I want you to fix me."

"Correct me," she said, complying.

He smiled. "See, I know I make errors."

"Mistakes. We say 'mistakes.' It's more natural."

"Which language is *mistakes*, English or American?"

"There's only one language," Olivia said. "English. I have an American accent, but I speak English."

He shook his head. "This is not right. In school, I have learned that they are two languages."

She laughed. "You learned wrong. I should know, shouldn't I?"

He looked doubtful and changed the subject.

"What is the life like in New York?"

"Busy," she said. Without asking, he refilled her wineglass halfway. As she drank, she wondered whether that was true. Saturday afternoons doing desk duty at the pottery studio and regular Tuesday-evening dinners with Claire, Rachel, and middle school guidance counselor Veronica made her life full, but hardly varied. And those dinners often left her feeling deprived. She sat quietly as her three friends complained about their siblings, who demanded more than their fair share of parents' attention, or the antics of parents themselves. Olivia couldn't bear to make fun of her father, and she didn't know any stories.

"Not like Urbino," Gianfranco said dismissively. "Here the life is very boring. Always the same. The only interesting thing in Urbino is its story."

"History," she said.

"Okay, what is the difference between *story* and *history*? It is all one word in Italian."

"History is far in the past," she said, thinking as she did that she wasn't sure of the difference herself. "And it's bigger and involves more people— like the history of a country, or a war, or a revolution. Story is smaller. Your personal history is your story."

"So I tell you my story, but I tell you the history of Urbino?"

She tilted her head. "I guess so."

"Okay. In history, Urbino was very important. Now it is nothing."

"Would you like to leave?" she asked. "Why don't you leave?"

"It is very difficult in Italy. You only get things, a job, a house, because you know someone, and you only know someone because you have grown up together in the same city. In another city, in Rome or Milan, I am a *straniero*, just like you."

"My father left."

Gianfranco looked into the distance, past her shoulder. "That was different."

"What was so different about it?"

"He was—" Leo swooped up on them, balancing oval dishes, one with spinach glistening with olive oil, another loaded with puffy brown potatoes, and a glass bowl that contained a green salad topped with a tuft of grated carrots, like a clown's wig. He reached over to another table and lifted a little metal holder that contained a bottle of oil, a bottle of vinegar, a shaker of salt, and a scattering of toothpicks. Then he dashed back to the window to the kitchen and lifted two plates off the sill. Each plate was filled almost completely with a slab of beef still pink in the center.

"*Buon appetito*," he recited again, and he withdrew from the table quickly.

Olivia wanted to know what Gianfranco had started to say about her father. He seemed poised to clear away the secrecy. But the smell from her plate distracted her. Gianfranco lifted the spinach and the potatoes and generously spooned some of each onto her plate.

How many years had it been since she'd eaten red meat? Probably twenty. It had become almost a joke among Claire, Veronica, Rachel, and her when they went out on Tuesdays. Olivia was the least picky of the bunch, as she didn't eat red meat, but she didn't mind chicken or fish. The only fish Claire would touch were shrimp—they looked more like a vegetable than most vegetables, she was fond of saying. Due to some vestige of her kosher grandparents, Rachel wouldn't eat any pork products or shellfish, although she was fine with cheeseburgers and roast beef sandwiches with mayonnaise, and Veronica was on a low-carbohydrate kick, so she ordered no-bun hamburgers, soup without noodles, and western omelets, hold the toast and home fries.

Gianfranco picked up his knife and fork, shaved off a corner of his steak, and chewed it contentedly.

"I don't eat red meat," Olivia said.

"Not cooked enough?" He looked puzzled.

"No, I just don't eat steak. You know, cholesterol and everything." It was a health issue, or at least it had been at the start, but eventually steak had come to seem decadent, something an investment banker would choose, as male as cigars and cognac. In college, she'd been the only non-vegetarian among her friends. The most common lunch for the girls at Coleman consisted of a container of yogurt and a diet soda. When seniors left during free period and went to the deli next door, they described eating candy bars or potato chips as "being bad."

"You don't like?" Gianfranco looked stricken.

"It's not that."

Gianfranco cut off a piece and began to chew. "It's good," he said.

Tentatively, she lifted her knife and fork. A trickle of blood squeezed out as she cut a piece of steak, and she balked for a moment, but then she put it in her mouth and closed her eyes. How was it possible that she had forgotten the taste of meat? But clearly she had, because its vital, metallic essence in her mouth felt new. She chewed vigorously and followed it with a swallow of wine, not to wash it down, but to keep it company. For the first time, the pairing of red wine and meat made harmonious sense. Greedily, she stabbed three potato pieces onto her fork and crunched them, her cheeks full, her eyes wide. The spinach was smooth, distilled to its basic state, but still slightly grassy.

"You're right. It's good. Really good." She dabbed her mouth with her napkin, leaving a lip print of brown juices.

When they had finished the meat, Gianfranco tossed the salad with oil and salt, scattering the carrot shavings over the white tablecloth. Olivia wasn't hungry anymore. She held out her plate for a few leaves of pale lettuce, just to be polite. He deposited a tomato wedge in the center. Around his wrists grew fine hairs, not nearly as coarse as those farther up his arms. Their table was a round one, meant for four people, but they were sitting close to each other. She hadn't noticed him moving his chair during lunch, but he must have been shifting toward her, because now his right arm almost brushed her left. He handed her the bread basket and let her pick a piece.

Olivia ate two bites of salad, then put down her fork. Gianfranco smiled complicitly. He hadn't served himself any salad at all. "Leo always does too much," he said.

She nodded.

Gianfranco tapped the rim of the glass ashtray that sat in front of him. "You don't smoke?" he asked.

She was growing used to the smell of stale smoke everywhere, even here in the restaurant. It underlay the smell of food in kitchens, the odor of exhaust fumes on the street, and even the strong aroma of coffee in bars.

"No. You?"

He shook his head. "Even when we don't smoke, we are smoking in Italy, right? *Il fumo passivo.*"

She smiled. "In English, we say 'secondhand smoke'—*il fumo a secondamano.*"

"You are a good teacher," he said.

"It's what I do."

"What?"

"I'm a teacher. I teach art."

"And do you . . ." He flicked his wrist in the air to mime painting.

"Faccio la ceramica."

"Part of a long *urbinate* tradition."

She shook her head. "Not really. I don't like majolica. It's fussy."

"Fussy?"

"Fancy. Tricky. Busy. Too many things to look at." She was feeling the wine now.

"Fussy," he repeated, banking the word.

She covered her mouth to hide a yawn.

"Caffè?" he asked.

"Please."

"Leo, *due caffè!*" Gianfranco called out without rising from his chair.

"Subito," came the muffled reply from the kitchen. Moments later, Leo appeared with two espressos and placed them on the table. Gianfranco picked up a sugar packet and poured half into his own cup.

"Sugar?" She nodded. He poured the rest of the packet into hers. "Like this?"

"Yes." She stirred the coffee idly with her spoon to dissolve the sugar. Then they drank in identical swift motions. Olivia dabbed her lips with her napkin and placed it on the table.

"Leo makes good coffee, no?"

"It was all delicious," she said. They sat in silence for a moment, recalling the meal. Then Gianfranco spoke.

"You were asking about your father," he said. In the pleasure of the meal, the fullness of the moment, she'd almost forgotten about her father for the first time since her arrival in Urbino.

"Do you know something?" She remembered the way he'd handled the deed.

He exhaled and sat back in his chair. She leaned toward him. He looked so serious that it frightened her—maybe this was what Claudia had meant, that he treated even the simplest facts with close attention. What could be such terrible news about her father? He was already dead—it was hard to go downhill from there.

"I know some things," he said. "In Urbino, some things we all know."

"So tell me."

Later, she would regret those words, and she'd realize how difficult it was to recognize the moment before something was destroyed. She could remember the beginning of her father's Alzheimer's, but not the last time she'd seen him normal. All the cranky small moments that had led to the end of her relationship with Ivan were recorded indelibly, but she had never woken in their railroad apartment and considered that she was beginning the morning of the last good day. And just the same, she said those words now blithely, easily, completely unaware that what Gianfranco had to tell her was the start of a loss.

"Okay," he said, placing one hand on her wrist. "Here is the history."

✦ WEDNESDAY ✦

Olivia opened her eyes to harsh sunlight. She hadn't closed the shutters. She'd been too stunned for even that most normal of motions in her hotel room. The events of the day before came back to her like a slide show of Hieronymous Bosch paintings: the constant spray of gravel battering the underside of the car during the white-knuckle drive to the airport, the unexpected and unsettling meat and potatoes lunch, and finally Gianfranco's face as he told her about her father.

Tuesday would have seemed a bad dream, but when she glanced down, she noted that she was still wearing the PROPERTY OF COLEMAN ATHLETIC DEPARTMENT T-shirt she'd changed into at the airport. Below the final letter in DEPARTMENT was a small stain—a drop of oil that had seeped in and left its mark during her lunch with Gianfranco. She'd slept in her clothes.

Olivia uncurled and got out of bed. She opened her suitcase and fished out her toilet kit. A small tube of moisturizer was puffed like a pimple ready to pop from the pressure on the plane. She loosened the cap and it released air with a sigh. She unpacked nail scissors, tweezers, a small bottle of Tylenol. These anonymous items lined up on the bathroom shelf made her feel at home. At the bottom of the toilet kit sat her diaphragm in its beige case. She left that alone.

Then she began to pick absentmindedly through the compressed mass of clothing for something to wear. The choice was almost overwhelming after three days masquerading as Claudia. Here were comfortable shirts that wouldn't bite into her armpits; pants that wouldn't announce every panty line to the world. Relieved, she made a small pile of Claudia's things on the bed and set her cousin's painful-looking red thong on top, like a maraschino cherry dotting a sundae.

Going through her clothes was comforting at first, but then—like the sight of her lonely, infrequently used diaphragm—sobering, as the gap between what she'd imagined about Italy and what she'd discovered came clear. She'd brought a skirt and high-heeled pumps, which would never do on Urbino's cobbled streets. She'd brought a white blouse, which was now cobwebbed with wrinkles after being cramped in the suitcase all that time. She'd brought a few things she'd imagined were Italian, at least in spirit: a pair of black sandals, Armani pants purchased at the Barneys warehouse sale, and a sleeveless black shell that always reminded her of Audrey Hepburn. Now that she was here, though, none of them seemed quite right. After what she'd learned yesterday, she doubted anything would feel comfortable again. She slipped on a faded green T-shirt and a pair of khaki pants. After hesitating for a moment, she took the key from the pocket of her jeans and slid it into the back pocket of her pants.

Unpacking was making her melancholy, forcing her to think of what she'd expected to find here. She withdrew the deed from her book bag. What had been the purpose of all this? Had she imagined she'd come here and magically make sense of her father's mumblings? That she'd find him alive, some parallel version of him as he would have been had he stayed, like the fantasy Italian version of herself she'd been picturing— working at the university and wearing tight clothing and enjoying a carefree existence? That he'd be standing in the piazza in a hat and long sleeves, his breath heavy with espresso, his thighs strong from years walking up and down these hills?

Olivia stared at the deed and then tore off a blank corner, a tiny triangle of paper, and placed it on her tongue. When it had dissolved to pulp, she swallowed hard. She considered ripping up the whole thing, but instead, she simply folded it and returned it to her book bag.

"Your father did something to the Jews," Gianfranco had started by saying the day before in the restaurant.

Olivia smiled nervously. "What do you mean?"

"How much do you know about the war?"

"I know there was a war," she said.

"*I fascisti?*"

"Fascists, Mussolini, Hitler. The Allies and the Axis. I know that much."

"So it is true, what they say about Americans. All black and all white."

"Like I said, history is written by the winners."

Gianfranco said, "Really, history is written by the survivors. Who is left tells the history."

"You were saying, about the Jews and my father?"

"There was a family, the Levis. A Jewish family."

"The name on the deed?"

Gianfranco nodded. "When the Germans were coming, the Hebrew families had to leave. They gave their things to Italians to keep safe."

"So my father wasn't the real owner? They just loaned him the house while they were out of the country?"

"Not exactly."

Olivia poked her finger through the burn hole in her napkin and wiggled it, making the empty space bigger. "What, then?"

"Not a loan. They had to sign the house over. And then the problems started."

"What do you mean?"

"He did not return the house. He did not want to return the house."

Olivia shook her head. "Do these people want the house back? If my father did something wrong—which I find hard to imagine—if they can prove that the house is theirs, I'll give it back to them." Her vision of selling the house, achieving solvency after his death, had never been real. Besides, what could a house in Urbino be worth? She'd be happy to salvage her father's reputation.

Gianfranco blurted out a bitter laugh. "That would be—how do you say?—a good trick, to sell a house from one *morto* to another."

"Doesn't this Ottavio Levi have any descendants? I'll give the house to them. They gave it to my father, and I'll give it back. He probably would have given it to them before he left if he could have." This was a misunderstanding, obviously. Her father had departed quickly after the war. He hadn't had time.

Gianfranco lifted his spoon and tapped it against his espresso cup as if checking whether it was tuned or not. "You do not understand. You believe your father had the house by accident, yes?"

"It sounds like, you know, it was wartime, and things were confusing, so they gave him the house for safekeeping, and he didn't have a chance to give it back before he left for America."

"You loved your father?"

"Of course I did. He was my father."

"Why must you know this? Why not just love him?"

Olivia rested her chin in her right hand. "I'm here now. I've started to unravel it."

"Unravel?"

"Take it apart, like when there's a piece of yarn hanging from your sweater, and you pull, and then you've got a whole ball of yarn and no more sweater." She tugged gently at one of the threads that hadn't been cauterized by the cigarette burn and pulled loose a quarter of an inch more of it. The tip of the thread was black, but the newly exposed area was white.

Gianfranco nodded. "I think I understand this."

"What were you saying about the Fascists?"

"In America, it is all black and all white, good and bad, right? Your father, he was not on the good side."

"He was a Fascist? He told me he was never in the army." Olivia rested the napkin on the table. She forced herself to keep her hands still, not to fiddle anymore with the napkin. Gianfranco didn't know what to do with his eyes, she noticed. He kept looking away and glancing back to her. Was a person with such a shifty gaze to be trusted?

"Your father did not wear a uniform. Perhaps he did not believe in fascism, but he helped them the same."

"What did he do? Deliver messages? What?"

If her father had simply been following orders, there must have been thousands like him.

"The Levis. The reason there is no one from the Levis today in Urbino is all the Levis—mother, father, two children—died in a *campo di concentramento*. You know what this is, right? We had one right here in Italy, in Trieste. Italian Hebrews did not need to go all the way to Auschwitz."

"My father helped deport the Levis?"

"Your father told the Germans where the Levis were, so he could keep the house. We call it still *la casa degli ebrei*."

"That's not possible." Olivia shook her head. Her father had been a good man. She was the daughter of a good man.

Gianfranco cleared his throat and looked away from her. There was no sound from the kitchen, as if Leo had gone home and left them alone. "The house is always problem in Italian family."

She thought of her father and the house in Shaleford, how he'd made her promise to let him die there. Gianfranco looked ready to cry, but Olivia was too stunned to form tears. She jammed her thumb through the hole in her napkin, and it ripped with an angry sound. This story was too specific to be made up, too cruel to be a joke. Despite herself, she believed it. The steak roiled in her stomach.

"My father," she said with amazement, "did something to the Jews."

"It's what happened," Gianfranco answered. "*È successo così.* Every-body knows."

"HISTORICALLY, THE KITCHEN WAS THE CENTER OF THE *CASA*," THE OLD GUIDE at Raphael's house was saying. As he finished each of his memorized speeches, he smiled, showing a vast hole on the right side of his mouth where three—or was it four?—teeth were missing. This grizzled guide, Olivia thought, didn't look as though he had the least interest in art or art history. He looked more like a survivalist who should be out in the woods, spearing wild boar for meat and digging his own well. Yet he was official and wore a plastic badge with his photograph around his neck on a beaded metal chain. The second man, who sat behind a table just inside the front door to Raphael's house, would not allow her to visit the house without the guide. He explained this as he smoothed Olivia's money and deposited it in a gray metal lockbox. She'd had to get out of her hotel room, so she'd come here, to the house where Raphael had been born. Museums usually had a soothing effect on her. Cool, pale walls calmed her; innocuous facts pacified her.

"*Parla italiano, sì?*" the guide to Raphael's house had asked nervously when she entered, and when she nodded, he sighed with relief. "I thought you were German," he told her, giving a disapproving glance at her outfit.

What had she inherited? Olivia had wondered as she sorted her father's things in Shaleford, weighing each item in her hand. Now, at the guide's words, she asked herself the same question. Was there some mark on her? Did she look German because of what her father had done? She peered at her pale, blurry reflection in the glass covering a framed drawing on the wall and sighed. Here she was in a mecca of art history. She should have been breathing the air that fed Raphael, studying the sights that informed his artistic vision, and instead, all she could do was try, unsuccessfully, to see herself.

"This is the spot where Raffaello Sanzio was born in 1483," the toothless guide continued, pointing to a paving stone in front of the enormous fireplace. "And this is a Madonna attributed to him." He pointed to a framed portrait on the wall. The figure looked sallow and unhappy. She lacked the penetrating stare of Raphael's women, Olivia thought. The attribution seemed like something made up to promote the artist's birthplace.

"How has this been dated?" she asked. "What's the source?"

The man shrugged. One jagged tooth snagged on his chapped lower lip and pulled off a flake of skin as he spoke. "I have no idea."

"How many people lived here?"

"His mother died in 1491. His father in 1494."

An orphan, thought Olivia, like me.

After her father's death, she'd been relieved that her memories of him began moving backward. For the first few days, she could remember him only as he was at the end—addled and incomprehensible. The blank stare he gave her when she entered the room. At the end of the week, after the funeral, she shifted to memories of him during the worst time, when he was paranoid and unpredictable. He'd never hit her when she was younger, but she couldn't help wondering as he lashed out in those days whether he'd wanted to.

The gerontologist had promised that his true personality remained unchanged. By the time she left for Urbino, in her mind he was still sick, but speaking in complete, if meaningless, sentences. His skin had seemed transparent then. And during her first days in Italy, she'd started to recall how he'd been when she was newly an adult. She remembered the two times he'd come to New York to take her to lunch, how he looked around nervously on the street, as if he were afraid he'd be mugged, and she'd thought that he was finally and thoroughly American. He used to call her and ask her to come out to Shaleford on the weekends, to keep him company, and a few times she went. He was still standing on his own power then.

Now she pictured him as he'd been when she was a child—taller (or maybe it was just that she'd been shorter then) and straighter and more imposing. He wasn't violent, didn't spank or threaten, but when she was bad, he went stone-faced and silent, the worst punishment of all. And earlier? Before she was born? Before he left Italy? She wasn't sure now that she wanted to know.

Raphael's father had been an artist, the guide had told her at the beginning of the tour, and, as was the tradition in those days, son followed father. The stones in the house's floor were so smooth—worn by five hundred years of footsteps—that they were slippery. Olivia caught herself about to offer the guide her arm as he climbed up the three stairs into the next room. Her father never liked it when she supported him that way, but toward the end, when he forgot everything, he forgot, too, to resent her help. Then he forgot how to put one foot in front of the other.

The next room was empty of furniture except for a large pewlike wooden bench against one wall.

"This is from the fifteenth century," the man said quietly. The room was dark, with only a few small windows. As Olivia's eyes adjusted, she saw that the walls were lined with drawings. In the center stood a Plexiglas display case.

"Is the bench original to the house?" she asked.

"No, but it's from the same period." He motioned for her to come to the center of the room. Under the Plexiglas was a dark, smudged piece of wood.

"The father's palette," he said. "The artist's first experience was mixing his father's colors."

"But his father died when he was"—Olivia did the math slowly—"eleven."

The man shrugged again, but he looked amused by her. "They were put to work early then. By the time he was twelve, he was an apprentice, working in Perugia." He let out a funny giggle that whistled through the empty spot in his mouth.

"I guess life was short."

The man smiled, delighted with his pupil. "He was thirty-seven when he died. Not even particularly young for the time."

"So he never really worked in Urbino?" Olivia thought of *La Muta*, the woman's slender fingers silencing someone, maybe herself.

"He probably never returned to Urbino," the guide said. "From Perugia to Florence, from Florence to Rome."

Those would have been long, difficult trips. Olivia pictured harnessed mules pulling carts up the winding road she and Gianfranco had taken from Leo's restaurant back to Urbino the day before. With each curve, her stomach had sloshed, the unfamiliar meat and tannic wine mixing unwillingly. When Gianfranco parked in the lot where buses idled, without saying a word she'd opened her door and made a dash to the hotel. The hill was steep, and she was breathing hard by the time she reached the lobby, collected her key from the cubbies behind the desk, then jabbed the elevator button until the little car shuddered to a stop in front of her. Once inside her hotel room, she'd knelt over the toilet and vomited, turning all the food that Leo had lovingly prepared for them into hot, acid bile.

Half an hour later, Gianfranco showed up with her suitcase. He remained in the hallway and shouted his apology through the door as she stood resolutely on the other side. He'd made a mistake, he said. He realized that now. He, of all people, should have known how hurtful such things could be. And how important was it anyway? Her father was dead. The war was a long time ago. Forget the house. He would take her around, show her Urbino for the rest of her time here. She should come with him now, out into the light. It was early, too soon to retire to her hotel room.

"*Lasciami*," she whispered through the door. Then she repeated, more loudly, that he should leave her.

"*Merda*," he said in the hallway, and a fist or forehead hit the wall hard, sending reverberations through to her. She leaned against the inside of the door, her heart in her ears like the lockstep march of hundreds of soldiers. Then, finally, she heard his shuffling feet as he walked away. Ten minutes later, she opened the door and found her suitcase in the hallway. Rather than pick it up, she kicked it into her room, where it collapsed on its side like roadkill, and she shut the door.

At Raphael's house, Olivia examined the artwork that hung on the walls. There were some not very practiced charcoal drawings, a rendition of the ducal palace, clearly executed in modern times, as it included a couple on a moped climbing the hill in front. There were a few freehand versions of Raphael's Madonnas. One of the largest pieces was an amateurish sketch of his *Transfiguration*.

"Isn't there anything by Raphael?" she asked.

"There's the Madonna."

"But nothing that's definitely his."

"No. It's all been stolen by the church or the state."

"So who did these?"

The guide raised his palms. "Most are by local artists, or students at the *accademia*."

"So these aren't even from the *cinquecento*?"

"Some are. A few here and there." He pointed to a murky depiction of a gathering of figures. "This is by his father, Giovanni Santi."

The guide turned the corner and was walking back around to the front desk. Olivia followed.

"Eccoci qua," he said.

"The tour's finished?"

"There are more rooms upstairs, but they are not for visiting. Offices."

Olivia sagged with disappointment. Two almost empty rooms and some bad art—it would take more than that to stop her from replaying yesterday's conversation.

"Was Raphael's father an important artist?" she asked.

The man behind the table in front looked up. Both he and the guide wore navy blue sweater vests with little patches sewn on, like the merit badges that Olivia had proudly applied to her sash when she was a Brownie. But these bore the legend ASSESSORATO AL TURISMO—COMUNE DI URBINO, rather than cunning depictions of flowers or pots and pans.

The guide said, "He was a court painter."

"And a poet," said the man at the table. "He wrote a famous *rima*."

The guide turned away from them and wandered over to the kitchen area, then stuck his head into the hearth and peeked into the heavy iron pot hanging there (a reproduction—Olivia had glimpsed the words MADE IN CHINA stamped on the inside) as if he were checking whether an imaginary stew had finished cooking. With a sudden pang, Olivia thought of her father standing at the bottom of the stairs in Shaleford, sending his notice, *"Butto giù,"* in her direction.

"Chi sei?" the man at the table asked abruptly. "Are you a journalist?"

Olivia laughed bitterly. How wonderful it would be to be a journalist, an objective observer. "No."

"Sei sicura?"

"Just a curious tourist." It felt funny not to relate her status in the usual way—"I'm American, but my father was from Urbino." Today, though, she didn't relish saying her last name and seeing those looks of astonishment. They—the cleaning woman at the hotel, Gianfranco, Claudia, the man who made her cappuccino in the morning—were surprised, she realized now, that she'd dared to come back.

"There are a few pieces," the man said. "Paintings, sketches. Have you been to the ducal palace?"

Olivia nodded.

"You saw some of his work, then, but you probably didn't notice it."

"So not much survived?"

The man looked ashamed. "We have it. We just don't show it. Some paintings are hung in corners. Most of them are stored in the basement. He wasn't particularly good. The painting in there is about the best one."

Olivia turned and looked back to the last room, where Giovanni Santi's work hung. It was a religious scene of some sort, men in robes grouped together. The heads were out of proportion to the bodies.

"Rescued from the dustbin of history," Olivia murmured in English.

"Scusi?"

"Nothing."

The man sighed and put his hands together on the table as if he were praying. He was silent for a minute. "Urbino is a small city, *una città d'arte,"* he said. "There isn't much here. We have the ducal palace, we have Raffaello. This is a place that can be charming, but never important."

"So you're promoting second-class artwork for the sake of the city?"

"Raphael is our icon. We have to present him in the best light possible. The story is beautiful, no? The son of a well-known artist from a small town who travels to the big city and becomes one of the most famous painters of his time? We love this story of a father who teaches his son. It's *commovente,* no?"

"Yes." Olivia agreed that it was moving.

"But what if the father was not good?"

What if indeed? Olivia's throat closed, as if she were having an allergic reaction. The foundation she'd rested on—the concept that her father was a good person—had been yanked out from underneath her.

But this man was talking about Raphael's father, about artistic ability, she supposed. "Not good in what sense?" she asked.

The man made a face, as if he'd cracked a peanut shell and found a musty, dried nut inside. "You saw that painting."

Olivia thought about saying, Those who can't do, teach. But she didn't know the parallel expression in Italian. It wasn't a phrase she liked anyway, for obvious self-incriminating reasons. "Does it matter?"

"If you're trying to build tourist business, it does."

A group of two dozen or so middle-aged tourists speaking a Scandinavian language entered, and the man with the lockbox began taking their money and tearing tickets out of a little book. Olivia didn't know whether to stay or leave. She hovered in the doorway to the house, shaded from the sun. The steeply slanted street was filled with people, and occasionally a small car tootled by, its wheels grumbling over the uneven cobblestones. Across the street was a bakery, and a steady stream of customers entered with empty arms and exited with brown paper bags. Next to that stood a Swatch store, brightly lighted and empty. On the corner was a store that appeared to offer thirty years' worth of unsold cheap Chinatown merchandise; the display window was crammed with nylon stockings and umbrellas, board games and kazoos, plastic headbands and collapsible drinking cups. A woman, probably the owner, stood outside with a small white dog tucked under her arm and watched the pedestrian traffic. It was a breed of dog that looked like it had walked into a brick wall.

She remembered what Gianfranco had told her the day before, the words landing with a sickening thud on top of all that they'd eaten. "Your father did something to the Jews."

If only she could erase those words, all Gianfranco's words, from her mind. If only she could erase this trip. When she was little, spurred on by too many episodes of *Bewitched* and C. S. Lewis books, she believed in magic, not silly tricks with coins and rubber bands, but real magic. She'd close her eyes and concentrate hard on what it was that she wanted to happen, but when she opened them again, she was inevitably in her room in Shaleford, facing that rose-covered trellis wallpaper that reminded her of prison bars. Last night in her hotel room, she'd squeezed her eyes shut. I'm in a hotel in California, she thought. I'm on a bike trip with Claire and we're staying in a hotel. She imagined cycling past vineyards and goat farms. There would be wine tastings and rustic picnics of cheese and bread. She'd opened her eyes, though, and was still in Urbino. Across the street, the shop owner's dog sneezed and shook its head violently.

When the tourists had moved on, she went in to say good-bye to the man who took the money.

"Delusa?" he asked when she came back. He wanted to know whether she was disappointed. He smiled.

"I'm not disappointed. It just seems silly to go to such lengths to create a history for the town that's not true."

"Protecting the reputation of the town is a very good reason."

"That seems, I don't know, *superficiale.*" She remembered what Gianfranco had said the day before, that people would be happy to see a duke take over, because then they wouldn't have to think for themselves.

The man marked something in pencil on a piece of paper that sat on the table, then straightened the seven-thousand-lire guidebooks in five languages—all with the same cherry red cover—that were fanned near his elbow.

"In Urbino," he said, "our reputation is all we have. If that becomes ruined, we have nothing."

"ESAGERATO!" CLAUDIA REPRIMANDED ALEX AS HE REACHED OVER AND TOOK another pastry off the small gilt cardboard tray.

"Is it Sunday already?" Giovanni had sneered when he opened the door and found Olivia standing there with the daintily wrapped package, a gold ribbon tied in a bow on top. The waxy white paper that covered the pastries proclaimed the shop at the top of the hill LA PASTICCERIA DELLA DUCHESSA and was printed with the profile of the duchess of Urbino, her hooked nose and high forehead unmistakable. Giovanni thought she was pushy, or perhaps an *ambiziosa* show-off, or both. But Olivia did feel she owed Claudia something for feeding her. Plus, it never hurt to bring a gift when you were looking for something in return.

After dinner, Claudia picked up an index finger–size *cornetto* piped with chocolate and ate it in one bite. The pastries were miniature versions of local favorites—meringue disks sandwiched around whipped cream, fruit tarts topped with kiwi and strawberries, and beignets filled with coffee cream.

"*Che buono,*" Claudia said. "It's not right to save pastries just for Sundays anyway."

They'd eaten another of Claudia's effusive meals—penne with peas in tomato sauce, followed by cod topped with olives and capers, eggplant tongues coated with herbs and garlic, green salad, and tomato slices glossy with olive oil. To top it off, Claudia had unloaded the contents of the refrigerator onto the surface of the table, offering three kinds of cheese, prosciutto, bresaola, and mortadella to any takers. Olivia had picked at the pasta and ate only a small piece of fish, but her stomach now seemed fine. They'd eaten for a long time. Still, she hadn't found the right moment to ask what she wanted to ask.

"*Caffè?*" Claudia offered.

Olivia nodded.

Of course, there was no guarantee that Claudia had the answers, either. After all, Claudia hadn't been alive during the war. On the other hand, Gianfranco seemed sure that everyone in Urbino knew the same things—as if they drew on a collective memory that hovered over the city.

Olivia worked up her courage, and by the time the coffee bubbled, she was ready. Claudia set down three small cups in three equally small saucers. Then she added sugar to her own cup, to Giovanni's, and, without asking, to Olivia's.

"*Grazie,*" Olivia said, stirring it lazily with the stunted spoon.

"Thank you for the pastries," Claudia said. Alex, without speaking, stood from his chair and went to his bedroom in the back of the apartment.

"I need to ask you something," Olivia said. She'd wanted to speak to Claudia alone, but Giovanni showed no sign of moving. He cleared his throat and blew briskly on his coffee. "It's about my father."

"*Sì?*" Claudia said absentmindedly, rubbing at a wet spot on the tablecloth.

"Well, it has to do with a house."

Claudia looked at her but said nothing. Then she shifted her gaze to Giovanni and raised her eyebrows as if to say, See? I told you so.

"And Gianfranco told me some things yesterday." She wanted to say unpleasant things, but didn't know how to word it.

"Gianfranco Diotallevi?" Giovanni said.

"Yes," Olivia replied without looking at him.

"*Quel ladro,*" Giovanni said.

"*Ladro?* Gianfranco's a thief?"

"Ignore him," Claudia said. "*Sta' zitto,*" she commanded her husband.

"He said my father obtained a house illegally."

"Not illegally," Giovanni said.

"*Sta' zitto,*" Claudia repeated. She placed a finger over her lips to shush him.

"So you know about the house? What do you know?" Olivia asked.

"I know Gianfranco Diotallevi is a thief," Giovanni said.

Was that what Claudia had meant when she said Gianfranco was dangerous? That he stole?

"What do you know about the house?" Olivia asked.

Claudia rested a hand on Olivia's wrist. "You see," she said, "this is what happens when people live too close together in the same place." She glared at her husband. "We know this, we know that, little pieces, but never the whole story."

"If someone has been in *prigione*, I think that is enough of the story," Giovanni mumbled.

"Gianfranco's been in prison?" Olivia tried to picture him behind bars but failed.

"When he was very young," said Claudia. "And for a very short time."

"What did he do?"

"*Giochi da ragazzi,*" Claudia said. "Kids' stuff."

"Ask him yourself," said Giovanni, agitated. "Ask him about his ear."

"I don't want to talk to him," Olivia said. "I'm done with him."

"What did Gianfranco do?" Claudia turned her head three-quarters as she spoke, looking at Olivia out of the corner of her right eye, as if she couldn't face what came next head-on.

"He said my father stole a house. That he killed a family during the war."

"*Ma no*," Claudia insisted. "That's not how it happened. *Esagerato*. Gianfranco gets very excited over things. You shouldn't listen to him."

"Or at least you shouldn't believe him," added Giovanni. He threw back his coffee and wiped his lips with the back of his hand.

"Then who were the Levis?" Olivia asked.

"The Levis were a family in Urbino. They owned a lot of land. And of course they were *ebrei*," Claudia said.

Giovanni nodded. "The Jews owned everything before the war." Claudia batted at his hand to get him to stop talking, and for once he obeyed.

"During the war, they put their property into other people's hands, to save it. That's all. Your father was no *ladro*."

"Gianfranco Diotallevi is the *ladro*," Giovanni mumbled. "With a name like that, what do you expect?"

"A name like what? Gianfranco?" Olivia asked.

"Diotallevi."

"I don't get it," Olivia said.

"*Dio ti allevi*," Claudia said slowly. "God lifts you up."

"The name of a *ladro*," said Giovanni. "*Sì, certo*. God lifted him." Claudia raised her hand to tap her husband again, then changed her mind and lowered it. Instead, she stood and began wrapping the pastries back in their paper. She slid the tray into the refrigerator.

"So you knew about my father and the house?" Olivia asked.

Claudia returned to her seat. She looked at Olivia and sighed. "Everybody knows," she said. Olivia remembered Claudia in her hotel room that first day, when she'd tried to argue that Shaleford was a small town, too, and Claudia had said, "Not like Urbino. You'll see."

"What about after the war?" Olivia asked.

"*O Dio*, I forgot to offer you fruit," Claudia said, looking around as if the food police might break down the door. "Do you want an apple? A banana? A kiwi?"

Giovanni stood from the table as if he'd seen something resolved.

"What about after the war?" Olivia repeated.

Giovanni walked toward the back of the apartment. She could hear his boots clomping onto the bathroom tile. He closed the door and turned the key.

"Are you sure you don't want any fruit?" Claudia asked.

Olivia shook her head brusquely. She didn't want food filling the table and their mouths. "What happened after the war?"

Claudia sank into Alex's chair and put her hands on the table. "After the war, it was a huge *casino*, a big mess here. So disorganized. At the end, Italians didn't know what side they were on. American tanks came through the piazza. If you look at San Francesco, you can see where they replaced bricks on the corner, because the tank knocked into it."

Olivia leaned forward and spoke loudly. "But what happened with the house?"

"It was really a villa," Claudia said, "out by the new hospital."

"But what happened?" Olivia wanted to knock her knuckles against Claudia's skull and shake loose the information.

"You are going to ruin your *vacanza* with all this old stuff. It's *roba vecchia*. What do you care about some old house? It's not as though it's worth anything."

"I'd like to know what happened with it."

"It's falling to pieces, that's what happened. It's too dangerous even to go inside."

"No, you don't understand. I want to know about my father and the house. What happened?"

"I don't know." Claudia looked directly into Olivia's eyes when she said it. "I don't know," she repeated, and Olivia was about to believe her. She wanted so badly to believe her cousin. She wanted them to be friends. But she remembered something Claire had told her once—that the way you could tell if someone was lying was not by whether they looked you in the eye or not, because everyone had learned that one from cop shows on TV, but by whether they held still when they spoke. Claudia's eyes locked onto hers as she claimed not to have any knowledge of what had happened with the house after the war, but her fingers, with their long, manicured cherry red nails, performed a dance on the tabletop. Up, then down went the pinkie, and when it was halfway through with its step, her ring finger rose and then lowered. Claudia stopped and stood abruptly. She took a pack of cigarettes out of the purse that hung on the coatrack in the hallway, then opened the door to the terrace.

"Giovanni doesn't let me smoke at home." Claudia shook the cigarette pack at Olivia. "This is our secret."

"OLIVIA!"

She turned toward the other side of the piazza, facing the clock and the Benetton store, but then she saw who was calling her name. Of course it was him, because no one else knew her. Instinctively, she turned and began walking quickly in the direction of the hotel. Her New York pace came back. She was almost trotting compared to the slow, rolling walk of those around her.

"Olivia!"

He was still yelling behind her. She sped up a little, her pace going from hustling to the subway after work to just remembered the coffeemaker is still on.

"Olivia!"

His hand landed on her shoulder, and she was forced to stop.

"Olivia."

She turned.

"Olivia."

She didn't speak. They stood for a moment, taking each other's measure. He pushed his hair behind his ear and she saw the ridged top again. "Ask him about his ear," Giovanni had said. She suppressed an urge to reach up and touch it.

"*Scusami,*" he said, taking one of her hands in his. "*Perdonami. Ti prego.*"

"There's nothing to forgive you for," she said. "Not if you were telling the truth. It's my father I have to forgive."

"I shouldn't have said anything. I thought you knew."

Olivia struggled to keep her face from crumpling. She cried when angry or frustrated, although she couldn't have said which of those emotions was stronger now. Since that conversation in Leo's restaurant, when her insides had crumpled, when she'd realized that what Gianfranco was saying made sense, she'd been unable to detect anything beyond the shame that burned like a cool fire in her stomach.

"*Non è colpa tua*," she said. And it wasn't his fault.

He switched to English.

"But it is my guilt. I should know not to say such a thing to the daughter of a man."

"I prefer to know." Her voice cracked on the last word and she looked away, irritated with herself for crumpling like this, here. An old woman walked by with a shopping bag on her arm and stared. They were standing in front of the entrance to an *alimentari*. Gianfranco took her hand and guided her toward the piazza.

"Come with me. I know a place to talk," he said.

She hesitated. Giovanni and Claudia, Giovanni especially, had frightened her, talking about Gianfranco. But his eyes were soft and imploring. He was the closest thing she had to a friend in this place. She trusted him more than she did Claudia, her own cousin.

Silently, he led her through the piazza and down under the portico, then up a flight of stairs to the ducal palace. Halfway up, the stairs divided. To the right was a path up the road and around to the front. To the left, another led to a dark arch through the center of the building. Gianfranco took her left and settled down to the ground, his back against the wall. She did the same, right next to him, so that their knees were touching. They were hidden from view but could still hear the sounds of the street below.

As if they'd known each other for years, he put an arm around her shoulder in comfort. The only thing odd about it was that it didn't feel strange at all. She lowered her head to his shoulder, where it fit perfectly between the sinew of his neck and the bump of bone. She remembered a pot that she'd thrown back in Shaleford, in her old shed, the week before her father died—a shapely vase with one bubble resting atop the other, in a Japanese style that she'd been trying to achieve for years. With the corner of a rib, she'd created a perfect, definite line between the two parts, so that they were joined yet distinct. With no hookup for the kiln or chemicals to make glaze, she'd had to sacrifice it once it was bone-dry, but she'd done so with regret, chipping off dime-size pieces and letting them fall into the bucket. She'd thrown a lot as he was dying; she'd bought a ten-pound bag of clay and reconstituted it continuously. But that vase was the only thing from those weeks that she would miss.

"*Delusa*," he said, not as a question, the way the man at Raphael's house had posed it, but as fact. Disappointed.

"Claudia, my cousin, says it's not true at all." Even as she said the words, *non è vero*, she could hear how unconvinced her own voice sounded. She thought again of Claudia's fingers galloping across the table like horses let out of a gate at the track.

"It was a shock to hear all of that at once," he said.

"But Claudia said the Levis gave my father the house."

Gianfranco sighed. "In 1938, after the *leggi razziali* were put into place, Jews couldn't own property worth more than twenty thousand lire."

"Twenty thousand lire?" Twenty thousand lire was about fifteen dollars, not even walking-around money.

"Twenty thousand lire was a lot more money back then. Do you know this song?" He whistled a few notes of music. He was a good whistler, his lips steady and firm. The tune was right on key.

She shook her head. "Never heard it."

"The words are 'Mamma, give me a hundred lire, I want to go to America,'" he explained. "That was a lot of money then. Now it doesn't buy an apple."

The lyrics made her imagine her own father leaving this town. Had he asked his mother for money? Had he sneaked off in the middle of the night? Had it been shame and not opportunity that propelled him? Had her whole American life been the result not of the inescapable hand of fate, but of her father's wrongdoing? Behind them on the street, a young woman laughed loudly.

"Claudia says my father was no thief." The word for thief, *ladro*, floated above them, like a balloon that escapes a child's grasp and in seconds is too far away to retrieve. They'd used the same word to describe Gianfranco. "Claudia says the Levis gave him the house."

Gianfranco studied her closely. "What would you like to hear? Tell me what you would like to hear, and I will say it to you."

"The truth."

"There is no one truth. You should know that by now. The past is not a piece of your *ceramica* that you can hold in a hand." He grabbed at the air, grasping nothing in the fist he formed.

"My father was a good person. I'm sure of that."

"If you are sure." Gianfranco shrugged.

"You don't believe me."

"I think . . ." He opened his fist and made a motion as if he were releasing a bird.

"What?"

He sighed. "I think if you were sure, you wouldn't be here right now," he said, "with us thieves."

Olivia had to look away. He knew Giovanni and Claudia had told her he'd been in jail. Perhaps that was why he'd been so kind to her. He was familiar with the weight of what everybody knew. His arm was still around her shoulders, and she reached up and touched the fingertips of his right hand.

Gianfranco said, "I used to come here a lot when I was younger. I liked that you could hear everything but no one could see you."

He was changing the subject, and she didn't mind. She needed time to absorb what had been said about her father—from all angles. She had to decide what she believed, what to keep and what to discard. Her instincts, however, had already voted.

"So you came here with your girlfriends?" Say no, she thought. Say no.

"No," he said. "*Da solo.* It's a long time since I've had a girlfriend."

"Really?"

"You?"

Olivia sighed, thinking of Ivan. "I was with the same man for a couple years. We lived together, but it didn't work out." Saying this, she could hear her footsteps on the wooden floors of the apartment as she moved her boxes to the curb one by one. Ivan had gone out that afternoon; they'd decided mutually that would be easiest—compatible until the end in ways that turned out not to matter.

"It's easier to be alone than with the wrong person," Gianfranco said, and she nodded.

They had been moving closer as they talked, so that now the left side of Olivia's body and the right side of his were pressed against each other, knee to knee, foot to foot, shoulder to shoulder. She liked the pressure, the feeling of being surrounded.

"In Italy, it's normal to marry the person who was your girlfriend when you were fifteen," he said.

"Really?"

"Well, you live with your parents, so you can't have a private life."

"Do you live with your parents now?"

He nodded. "I have my own entrance and my own rooms. Very independent for Urbino." He laughed to show that he knew his little victory was ridiculous.

Olivia thought of the weeks she'd spent waiting for her father to die. "Doesn't that bother you?"

Gianfranco raised his eyes as if he were considering this for the first time. "I owe them a lot. And if you try to talk about moving away, Italian mothers have a *crisi*. It's 'Are you doing drugs? Do you want to do drugs? What do you want to do that you can't do in this house?' You should have heard her when I went to England."

"I'm surprised they let you go."

"There were circumstances."

Olivia let that slide. She didn't feel like hearing any more terrible news about people she liked.

"In India, the parents arrange the marriage," she said instead. A few years earlier at Coleman, a beautiful senior named Meena Pachtel had let slip to Olivia that her parents were going to bring a groom over from India for her. At graduation, a polite-looking young man with dark hair slicked to his forehead sat in the third row with Meena's family. Olivia was horrified, but Claire thought she'd gotten it wrong. "Our parents can't be any worse at picking men for us than we are," she'd insisted.

"It's not like that here," Gianfranco said, "but close. You're together for eight or ten years, and then the girl gets pregnant, so they say, Why not?"

Olivia considered a life decided at fifteen. The fifteen-year-olds she taught had to be reminded, then cajoled, then threatened in order to turn in their work. She had been in love only with pottery when she was fifteen. It was a maxim among teachers that everyone taught the year that had been a turning point for herself—Olivia nodded when she heard this; at fifteen, she'd started throwing.

"So what happened to your girlfriend from when you were fifteen?" she asked.

"She got pregnant."

"And you didn't marry her?"

"It wasn't me."

Olivia took a minute to understand. "Oh, I'm sorry."

He shook his head. "It was a long time ago. She wasn't right for me."

"It's easier to be alone than with the wrong person," Olivia said.

And then he turned, and she almost protested at having the warmth of his right side removed, except that he took her chin in his left hand and, with his lips barely parted, kissed her softly on the mouth. He smelled like cherries and detergent. He smelled both familiar and new, and with her eyes closed, she could hear more clearly the sharp taps of people passing on the cobblestone street below, and sometimes the gentle thud of sneakers. She could hear their voices, but not what they were saying, just the soft murmur of companionship, and a breeze passed through their private tunnel and ruffled their hair, and they both smiled but did not move their lips from each other's, and she reached up a hand to touch his freshly shaved cheek and his soft hair and, finally, his wrinkled ear, and all the while she was kissing him back.

✦ 1945 ✦

"Good morning, Doctor."

Luigi looked into the man's face as he spoke. Pasquale had pointed out that people at the hospital would understand him better if they could see his lips moving, and it was true.

"Good morning," the doctor said. Luigi looked from the doctor's startlingly white coat to his own tired hands, the gray-scummed water bucket, the stringy mop. He longed to go over to the other side—to the cleanliness and precision of the doctors. But he quickly and guiltily tamped down the feeling. The last time he'd longed to rise above his station—in Italy, when he'd believed himself superior to his own family—nothing good had come of it.

Pasquale had told him right away that no Italian—no *guinea*, he said, and he had to explain to Luigi what that meant—was ever going to be a doctor. It wasn't going to happen. His precious *liceo scientifico* diploma was useless here. Medical school cost money. And despite what he'd heard about the land of opportunity, only the rich had the privilege of clean labor. Pasquale had promised to find him a job as a janitor in the hospital where he worked, and he'd been true to his word. That had been only two months ago. Luigi, accustomed to the slow rhythms of Italy, was astonished at the generosity of a stranger and the speed with which he found himself working side by side with Pasquale, although Pasquale was an orderly, a step up from janitor. Pasquale had also been in America "a hell of a lot longer" (he had to translate that into Italian for Luigi) and spoke English and could follow orders. So what if he was from the South and uneducated? Luigi himself took commands mainly in sign language—the head janitor, Len, simply pointed to spots to be cleaned, as if Luigi were a dog that was not yet house-trained and needed to be shown his own mess.

It had never occurred to Luigi before he arrived in America that people would want to keep animals in their houses. At home, only the biggest *cafone*, a rustic hick chewing a piece of straw, would still live the way his grandparents had, with the animals on the first floor and their quarters on the second. Civilized people left their animals outside, in separate buildings. Professionals—teachers, nurses, notaries—lived in the city, in apartments. They didn't go near animals at all, unless they hunted rabbits and game birds for sport on Sundays. Animals were kept in a shed, far from the main house, out where their smell couldn't offend anyone.

Here in New York, though, everything was turned around. Pasquale had a better job than Luigi did. There was special food for cats and dogs. People kept birds in cages to make noise in their houses—on purpose. One morning when a gray sparrow was singing outside their apartment back in Urbino, Luigi's father got up, charged his shotgun, and let fly three rounds. Luigi could still remember the noise, like teeth chattering. His mother had yelled at his father for being wasteful; his sister reprimanded him for killing a bird that could easily have been waved away. His father insisted that he'd only shot to scare it off, but when Luigi went into the garden that afternoon to cut fennel fronds for his mother, he'd seen the little bird, like a bloody pincushion, lying dead among the carrot greens.

"Good morning, nurse," Luigi said as a woman with a white bishop's hat passed him. She didn't bother to turn in his direction. Luigi loved the nurses, dressed in white from head to toe.

"The nurses ain't going to look at you," Pasquale had warned him the first day, but Luigi couldn't help trying. Nurses were the only women he had contact with—the only nice women, at least. They were perfectly groomed, with sleek hair that smelled of shampoo. They were so irresistibly modern and pure and clean, it was hard to believe they were animals, just as he and Pasquale and all men were.

Luigi and Pasquale shared an apartment on the Lower East Side with four other men. There were only three beds, but Luigi and Pasquale and Franco worked day jobs and slept at night, and the other three—Gerardo, who claimed to be Italian but was really from Argentina, Guglielmo, and a third, whom Luigi had yet to see—worked nights and slept days. Luigi, Franco, and Pasquale had the day shift at the hospital. Luigi hated the feeling of sliding into bedsheets still humid with someone else's presence. Some nights, he took the blankets and moved to the floor, just so he wouldn't have to absorb the damp that another body had sunk into the mattress. He tried not to remember the house he'd thought would be his to live in, with its gracious open rooms and substantial furniture. As far as he could tell, they didn't make houses like that in America—only crowded apartments with thin walls and greasy linoleum floors.

Now, Luigi dipped the mop into the bucket, swished it around, then dragged it to the floor of the corridor. He was outside the surgery unit, and he practiced saying the word, the first syllable with its hard *r* (his still rolled), the second with its soft *g*, and the ending like a belch. "Surgery. Surgery," he mumbled under his breath in time to the movement of the mop. Like some English words, it wasn't far from Italian—surgery, *chirurgia*, hospital, *ospedale*. Picking up a bottle with a nipple, he squirted antiseptic liquid into the bucket. It caused a few ripples as it drifted down through the dirty water. That reminded him of hunting with his father in the colder months, how his father would pull his *pisello* from his pants and urinate wherever he was, and steam would rise from the yellow puddle as it melted deeper into the snow.

He tried to erase his parents. He pictured their faces on the tiles as he mopped, dousing them with water from the bucket and smearing their features. *La ragazza è morta.* It was as constant as the whistling in his ear, as automatic as the pumping of his heart. It is lucky, Luigi had thought when studying biology, that we don't have to remind our hearts to beat. The human body is an ingenious mechanism that keeps going on its own. He hadn't considered that there would be thoughts or images that would repeat endlessly, and that he might want to bring them to a halt.

Just then, Pasquale came around the corner holding a bedpan. Luigi saw with relief that it was empty. Pasquale had a habit of standing and conversing while holding a full one, and Luigi was squeamish about the way his friend made stunted gestures with his hands while talking, the contents of the bedpan threatening to spill onto the floor. Inevitably, when they did, they marked a square tile that Luigi had just finished cleaning.

"*Buongiorno, Dottore,*" Pasquale said to Luigi. Pasquale was sarcastic about Luigi's insistence on presenting a *bella figura* as he cleaned floors. Luigi wore a tie to work every day, even though his clothes were covered by his uniform smock. He kept an excellent pen in his shirt pocket—shirts that he ironed every two days on the kitchen table—and he looked forward to the moment when a doctor would be searching for a writing instrument to jot down some notes, and he would triumphantly pull the pen from his pocket and offer it. When Pasquale had brought him in to meet Len, Luigi had to write his name and carefully memorized Social Security number on the application, and he was sure that he'd seen in the rise of the man's eyebrows an appreciation for his excellent pen.

"*Buongiorno*," Luigi replied, continuing to mop. He stopped saying it, but in his head he still heard the word: *sur-ger-y, sur-ger-y.*

"*Come va?*" Pasquale took a cigarette out of his pocket and stuck it between his lips but didn't light it. He claimed that sucking on them for a while before smoking them—as if they were fine cigars—helped a pack last longer.

"*Non mi lamento.*" It was what Luigi's mother said when someone asked how things were going—I'm not complaining. As if to say, I *could* complain if I wanted to—there's plenty to complain about—but I'm not going to do it.

Luigi didn't have complaints about work, except for the occasional backache that dogged him. Working at the hospital was the first real job he'd ever had. Looking after the Levis had been his job, of course, and one he'd failed at miserably. He'd made the rounds with his father when he did odd jobs in people's houses, too. Together, they changed Signora Bruna's lightbulbs and repaired the venetian blinds at the Tozzis' house so that the slats moved as smoothly as lizards crossing a sunny rock. He'd never seen any money from that, though, and while his sister, who was four years younger, cleaned with his mother and the money the two of them earned went into the household, he studied.

He was the special one in his family, allowed the luxury of *liceo*, while his sister left school at thirteen. In return, he promised to care for them with the money he'd earn, although his father complained occasionally that Luigi ate too much for someone who wasn't contributing. In Italy, one gained the right to schooling through a series of heavy-handed *raccomandazioni*. The Easter Luigi was fourteen, when the priest came to bless their house and the basket of four eggs, his mother had given the man an entire leg of prosciutto, the heart-shaped split hoof of the pig still attached to the narrow end, a white cap of fat on the stump. Luigi knew it was more than Christian generosity; it was for his future.

"*Ciao, allora. Ci vediamo dopo,*" Pasquale said, and he turned the corner and headed out of sight.

When Luigi first met Pasquale, he had trouble understanding him. The man who approached him in the coffee shop that day—after he'd tried to bargain with his dozen or so English words over the price of a sandwich—spoke Italian, but he had a southern accent so thick that Luigi could hardly make out what he said. His *c*'s were *g*'s, and his *t*'s were *d*'s. He spoke as if he'd taken a big bite of the dust of southern Italy into his mouth and sucked on it until it turned to sludge. Luigi cocked his left ear toward Pasquale and concentrated hard, and under the table he pulled the rigid leather suitcase closer to his leg, just to be safe.

But when Pasquale offered a place to live, Luigi, just one day out of his miserable quarantine cell with its view of Manhattan like a shiny toy, understood. And when he offered to find him work, he understood that, too. Pasquale was a friend, the guide he needed in this strange place. He was also someone Luigi would never have associated with at home—not only because he was southern, but because he was coarse. He called women *fiche*, which always made Luigi picture figs split down the middle to reveal their fleshy pink insides. Once, Pasquale had gotten a letter from home—he'd left purely for the money, he told Luigi, and sent some to his *adorata mamma* every month—and he handed it to Luigi in the dark of their bedroom.

"Can you make that out?" he asked, and Luigi had read aloud three-quarters of the perfectly legible, if chock-full of misspellings, letter before he realized that it wasn't the handwriting giving Pasquale trouble—the boy didn't know how to read. Luigi admonished himself not to look down on his new friend. After all, he was as good as illiterate himself in America. Conversation buzzed past his ears like the bombers they'd heard going over Urbino at night toward the end of the war. Signs could have been in Chinese. With a grade-school book he found on a park bench, he began to teach himself English. The words in one of the first lessons were *cat* and *dog*, and whenever he saw NO DOGS ALLOWED written outside of a store, he thought of 1938 and the signs that had appeared in windows overnight, freshly painted: VIETATO AGLI EBREI.

Pasquale was *bravo*, Luigi told himself, if not well educated. Their bond transcended the superficial things that separated them. Luigi had no family here. Pasquale looked out for him, and Luigi was grateful.

Luigi was slowly moving down the corridor behind his mop. Today was Friday, payday. The other favor Pasquale had agreed to do for him was to cash his paychecks.

"Le banche qua, sono dei ladri," Pasquale had explained. Banks were thieves, so it didn't make sense for all of them to have separate accounts. He and Franco already shared an account, and they'd be happy to take in Luigi, too, he said.

This sounded plausible to Luigi. Back home, his father kept his cash under the mattress. (Luigi blushed as he remembered the way his heart had pounded that last night as he shoved his hands under his father's mattress and pulled out wads of lire practically made back into paper by inflation.) And real estate was always being transferred from one person to the next for safekeeping, even before the war. Of course, that, too, made him think of the Levis, which gathered a ball of guilt in his stomach as hard as the rinds of cheese he'd wrapped in paper to take to them. He should have been more cautious, but of his own father?

"Va bene," Luigi agreed, and Pasquale shook his hand with a manly grip.

Luigi thought of home often, but he hadn't written to his mother since he'd arrived. The first days, he'd considered informing them that he was safe, but he didn't know where to buy stamps or writing paper— certainly not the fancy stationery stores he lingered outside of, studying the delicate sheets and impressive pens. The longer he went without contacting them, the less inclined he was to do it. Besides, there was nothing good, nothing important to report. What would he say? That he, a good student of the sciences, now slopped already-dirty water onto the floor of a hospital in the name of sanitation? If he'd written, he'd have had to lie. He'd have alluded to a job in a hospital, but not the job he had. He'd have told them he'd found a house, but he'd never have admitted to the hot, close room with its shared beds, even if it was all he deserved.

The months between leaving Urbino and now were a jumble. Naples had been full of uniforms, yet lawless—an economy of cigarettes and chocolate bars and sex. A man grabbed him in a *vicolo* and kissed him on the mouth, hard, and Luigi kicked the man's shins and ran. American soldiers walked the streets. They laughed boisterously and spoke with force; Luigi had to remind himself not to stare at their shiny white teeth. America, he thought, must be a loud, jolly place. Boats could not leave, and then they could, and then the answer was no again. He waited for the port to open, just as he'd waited for the *partigiani* to contact him, and he worried that once again no word would arrive. As the boat pulled out of the embrace of the Bay of Naples, he felt ill, not with seasickness, but with a fever of possibilities. He didn't know what he'd become without a family to restrain him. He didn't know what he might be.

La ragazza è morta. His mother didn't smile ever, so she didn't smile when she said it, but she didn't look sad, either. That was just the way it was. "Life is suffering," his mother used to say, raising one shoulder toward her ear as if she couldn't imagine what else one might expect. She said it as if it were a fact, a precept as much a given as "Jesus is the son of God" or "Walking in the rain will give you pneumonia." Things no sane person would doubt. Things the flicker of doubt would not even bother to go near, as they would never, ever catch fire and burn. The girl is dead. The girl died. In Italian, they were one and the same: *La ragazza è morta.*

He squirted more disinfectant into the bucket, but the nipple at the top of the bottle sputtered loudly. Nothing came out. Luigi headed to the supply closet for a new bottle. Inside, the shelves were lined with rolls and rolls of toilet paper, Ace bandages, plastic drinking cups, and starched sheets folded neatly. He pulled the stepladder out of the corner and climbed to the top shelf, where dozens of bottles of bright pink disinfectant sat in tidy rows. Before pulling one down, he paused for a moment to admire their uniformity. Factory work was for suckers, Pasquale had warned him, but Luigi still liked to imagine the industrial products used at the hospital coming down an assembly line, one after the other, all exactly the same.

The light switch to the supply closet was on the wall in the corridor, and the janitors and orderlies were supposed to leave the door open when they were in there. "*I capi non si fidano,*" Pasquale had explained to him his first day of work, already remembering to mumble into Luigi's good ear. Even though Luigi recalled Pasquale saying the bosses didn't trust them, he always closed the door, as he thought it was sloppy for patients to see into the supply closet, just as it had ruined the magic of the movies for him once he'd learned to turn back toward the cone of light shooting out from a square hole in the wall. Some mysteries were sacred.

As Luigi moved from the shelf toward the door to drag his bucket back into the hallway, someone switched off the light from the outside. He froze, holding the bottle of pink liquid in his left hand. The closet was completely black. The doors in the hospital were all equipped with rubber pads at the bottom to fit them into their frames. He held a hand out on each side and could feel the shelves around him, but he was wildly disoriented.

At night, when he lay on the thin mattress and tried to ignore the deep breathing of the others as they slept, he sometimes tortured himself by imagining how the Levis had died. *La ragazza è morta.* It was said with such finality, but he never knew the method. Had they died together? Were they shot? Or had the life simply leaked out of them until they collapsed? He thought he saw them in the dark now, but when he reached out a hand, he grasped only air. "You can trust me," he'd told Signor Levi. He hadn't considered the part of him that was his father, a part not to be trusted.

Oxygen (number eight on the periodic table, his brain flashed) seemed to be missing from the room. Luigi's breathing grew ragged as he moved in what he was sure was the direction of the door, but he found only more shelves. He set down the bucket and the disinfectant bottle. Once he'd found the door and turned on the light, he could come back. He revolved 180 degrees. The closet was rectangular. If the door wasn't in front of him, he reasoned, it must be behind him. There, too, however, there was no knob, just shelves of something soft that made him pull his hand away, as if he had touched the Levis in the flesh. He turned, attempting to keep track of the directions he'd already tried, and felt along one long wall, but still no door. He turned again, but this time his foot splashed into something wet, and he realized he was standing in his own bucket.

Luigi yelled in frustration and disgust and kicked the bucket across the floor. It hit metal. He reached out an arm and swept a row of supplies off a shelf. They landed with a soft plop—towels. His eyes were adjusting to the dark, and he could make out the faint outline of light in a rectangular shape. He had just reached it and was putting his hand out for the knob, when the door opened and light poured in from the hall.

"Jesus H. Christ!" Len yelled when he took in the scene. Luigi turned and saw what he'd done—a dozen or so clean towels sat in a puddle of dirty water. His bucket dripped slowly from a shelf onto packs of toilet paper. The new bottle of disinfectant had rolled into a corner.

"What the hell happened?" Len asked Luigi. He reached a brawny arm out into the hallway and switched on the closet light.

Only one English word came to Luigi. "Dark."

"You mean it's bad? It sure is. You better clean this shit up now." Len's tough face was so rock-hard that it was difficult to know when he was angry and when he was just looking like himself. Most of the time, Luigi thought, he seemed resigned to working with idiots. He swore constantly, and Luigi admired the way he did it. Italian *parolacce* and *bestemmie* were too long, Luigi had decided, but he hadn't yet learned to swear naturally in English.

Slowly, like the old man he'd be someday, Luigi made his way to the corner of the closet and picked up his bucket and the bottle of disinfectant. He began using the dirty towels on the floor to mop up the mess.

"What the hell are you doing in here with the door closed anyway?" Len asked. "How many fucking times I got to tell you to leave the door open when you're in the supply closet?"

Luigi shrugged. He wasn't sure what Len was saying, but he had an idea that a silent response was best.

Len surveyed a shelf empty of towels. "I better tell the laundry to refill."

"Okay." Luigi tried to make a circle with his index finger and thumb the way he'd seen Pasquale do, but he couldn't keep his three remaining fingers in the air, so it looked as though he were making a fist at Len. Len stared at him, hard.

"This shit better not happen again," he said. *Shit* was one of the first words Luigi had learned at the hospital, not the scientific Latin vocabulary he'd hoped medical work would bring him.

Luigi nodded. His bad ear whined, as it often did when he was humiliated. Even if he could have explained, Len would not have been interested in the least in the story of how he had learned to fear dark, close spaces, the way his head swam when the light went out. There was no one to listen to his story of how he'd come to be here.

They all had stories, some worse than his, and others better. Len's parents were from Poland, he'd told Luigi when they first met. "Immigrants who pulled themselves up by their bootstraps," he'd said. Pasquale explained it later. In the mornings, when Luigi woke up, there was a moment of blankness, and then the memory of what had brought him to this place trickled into his brain. Luigi reached for the bucket and set it on the ground. He was a body here. "*Il figlio di nessuno*, nobody's son," his mother would call a shiftless man back in Urbino. He gathered the dirty towels in his arms and headed toward the laundry. In the corridor, he switched off the light.

"*HAI PRESO IL MIO ASSEGNO?*" LUIGI ASKED PASQUALE ON THE SUBWAY THAT evening.

Pasquale nodded, confirming he'd gotten Luigi's check. "*Certo.*"

Each Thursday, Pasquale picked up their paychecks, and the next morning, after they'd been endorsed, he deposited them. In the top dresser drawer, next to Pasquale's bankbook, Luigi kept a tidy ledger in which he marked down the amount deposited each week. Then he subtracted his payments for rent and food. On Monday mornings, as they descended the cement stairs into the station, Pasquale gave him subway money for the week. He also doled out spending money, which Luigi used to go to the movies, or sometimes, when the column of numbers in his ledger made him feel flush, to buy a sandwich in the hospital cafeteria at lunchtime. The sandwiches were made on a kind of bread called "white." Luigi didn't like it exactly, but he was fascinated by it, as he was by the squishy fillings compressed between the slices. His favorite was egg salad, brilliant yellow, both bland and sulfurous. It felt daring to eat something that smelled so bad, yet the substance had barely any taste at all. Once he entered a *profumeria* and bought a small bottle of lavender water, which he kept in his drawer. He never opened the bottle, but it scented his T-shirts just the same.

The subway car rumbled along the tracks. When he first arrived in New York, he'd been afraid of the subway. Even the elevated trains, swaying high in the sky, were intimidating, but the idea of closing himself voluntarily in a car that would speed underground through a tunnel, like a bullet through the barrel of a gun, was too much. He'd walked to work at first, but finally Franco had convinced him, and gone with him when he'd bought a paper ticket, and sat next to him as, wide-eyed, Luigi saw that there were ways of being underground that weren't threatening at all. It was not so different from the times he'd ridden his father's bicycle through the woods outside Urbino, the branches forming a canopy over his head, and the wheels bumping over the uneven ground. Of course, those trips had ended badly, but on the subway, he was merely going to work.

At their stop, he and Pasquale and Franco got off the train. Franco had black hair and a permanent five o'clock shadow. A crush of people surged around them as they climbed the stairs. Sweat stains like sunbursts were forming in Luigi's armpits. His shirt was white, with blue pinstripes. He'd brought it from Italy, like all of his clothes, and it was close to fraying at the collar and cuffs. He could imagine the day in the future when everything he'd brought with him—the black socks, the shirts, two pairs of trousers—would wear through, and then there'd be no memory of the country left in his wardrobe. There was a spot on the heel of one pair of socks that his mother had darned after he'd snagged a hole in it. Every time he put on that pair, he ran his thumb over the heels to locate that little bump. Sometimes he rubbed it on his cheek and felt, in relief, everything he'd left behind.

At the top of the steps, they turned right. Without ever discussing it, on Fridays Luigi, Pasquale, and Franco went to a bar in their neighborhood for a beer. It was not a nice place, not anywhere women would have entered. The beer was cheap, though, and the bar's most important quality was that it was not their workplace or their crowded rooms.

Luigi took a pickled egg off the plate on the bar and sucked on it. His cheeks reached for each other across the sourness. It was funny how eggs here tasted like so many different things, but they never tasted of just plain egg. He'd tried cooking an egg once, frying it in a pan with a little salt and pepper, but it tasted of nothing more than the oil he'd used. Being so far from chickens, he figured, was the cause.

"Three beers," Pasquale said, ordering for all of them as he held up three fingers the American way. Luigi had tried and tried, but he could not bend his hand into an American three. He still used his thumb and index finger and middle finger. The American way hurt.

"Tomorrow it'll be warm enough to go to the beach," Pasquale said.

From the first hot day to the cool end of September, Pasquale planned to go out to Coney Island when he wasn't working. By the end of summer, he would be as brown as a piece of cooked meat, Luigi thought, but he said nothing. Franco passed his free time playing solitaire at the rickety table in their half kitchen, with its two burners and no stove. On his days off, Luigi walked until his feet ached, but he spoke to no one. There were sights, however, that he kept in his head—still and fresh and real. He could picture the lights of Times Square at night, blinking like all the fireflies in Italy put together. He remembered a day when, on West Forty-fourth Street, he'd seen a woman wearing a white fur stole and smoking a cigarette, and only when she put out the cigarette with her heel did he realize that one end of the fur was the dead head of the animal the fur had once belonged to, but the other was the face of a tiny dog, tucked under her arm like a purse. In his own neighborhood, on a Friday, he'd witnessed a stream of men with long curls and black wool coats and fur hats entering what he recognized as a *sinagoga*. As he walked, he marveled at the number of people who could fit on an island. On the boat, a seasick Neapolitan woman had refused to believe that New York was an island, and then, when he'd convinced her, she'd shrugged and said, "I'm going to someplace called New Jersey anyway."

For the first week or so, he often thought he saw a familiar face in the crowds. Instinctively, he'd start to turn away and hide, only to realize that he was in the wrong place to run into Alberto Tozzi or Riccardo Diotallevi or anyone else he knew. Once, he spotted a fair-skinned, dark-haired girl wearing a deep purple cloche, and she took his breath away. He ran toward her, but when he got close and touched her arm, and she looked up expectantly, he saw she was nothing like the person he'd been thinking of, and then he remembered he'd never see Ester again.

He wished, more than anything, that he might lose his memory.

"*Figli maschi*," Pasquale called out as they clinked three heavy beer glasses together. It was an old toast: "May you have male children." Luigi felt funny saying it now, not only because he didn't like to speak Italian too loudly—once Americans knew you were an immigrant, they ripped you off—but also because his parents had had one of each, and his sister was still taking care of them, while he was far away. His parents had allowed him to study for the return it would bring, and now he was shirking his duty. But he hated his father, too, for what he'd done.

On Sundays, he pictured his family gathered around the table. Since it was a fantasy, he added his dead grandmother in her black shawl, both crabby and sweet. His sister's dark eyes squinting as she served the pasta. His father with his cane and his resentment. His mother would be apologizing for the food—too salty, overcooked, not enough—before anyone had had a chance to take a bite. He'd hated Sundays when he was a boy—they were long days that stretched out, empty and dull. He overate out of boredom, then had to lie down with a stomachache. Now that they were out of reach, though, those days had taken on a sheen of loveliness. Even when he'd walked so much that his feet pulsed and his chest was tired from breathing, he never shook the ache of being familyless. Without his father to claim him, he belonged to no one. *Il figlio di nessuno.*

"*Figli maschi,*" Pasquale repeated more softly between sips.

"Shaleford," Luigi said, savoring the name on his tongue.

"*Cosa?*" Pasquale stared at him, then shook his head with derision. Like Luigi's father, Pasquale thought Luigi was too tender and dreamy to survive. Luigi knew this was an insult from both of them, but he ignored it. Without *fantasia*—that and opposable thumbs—men were animals.

"*Niente,*" Luigi said.

That morning, the chief of radiology, Dr. Nesmith, had spilled a cup of coffee, and Len had sent Luigi to his basement office to clean up the mess. Luigi knocked timidly on the door, which was ajar when he arrived, but nobody answered, so he went in and began mopping up. The coffee had spilled on the desk and then dripped onto the floor. Papers on the desk had been blotted. Still, where coffee had soaked into them, they'd turned brown and curled around the edges, instantly aged. With a rag, Luigi removed a puddle of coffee that had dripped between the papers.

On Dr. Nesmith's desk sat a photograph of what had to be his family—Dr. Nesmith stood in front of a white villa with columns, as big as the house Luigi had owned. In the photograph, Dr. Nesmith smiled, but he also blocked the front door. Luigi thought of the ducal palace back in Urbino. He'd learned in school that the duke had wanted the facade that faced the approaching road to look friendly and accessible with its decorative towers. Only on closer inspection would you notice the gun ports in the brick wall that pigeons now used as a roost. Dr. Nesmith had his arm around a woman with curly light-colored hair. They both wore hats. In front of them stood two matching children, a girl and a boy the same height. The boy was missing his two front teeth. The girl wore a white jacket that was cut round at the bottom rather than straight across. The image stirred a question in Luigi: Could a man be a man without a family? Family was dangerous, of course, a closed system of like organisms that could turn against itself. But what was he without one?

"Excuse me," Dr. Nesmith said just then as he came into the office and caught Luigi holding the picture.

"Sorry." Luigi set the frame on the desk. He looked down in embarrassment and went back to blotting the surface.

He had told no one here that he, too, had once owned a house. He'd never considered the house his, and although his English was improving, he still didn't have the vocabulary to tell the story of what had happened in Italy. He kept the deed between the last page of his ledger and its back cover, as if that, too, were money in the bank.

"No need to apologize," Dr. Nesmith said. He took a step closer and picked up the photograph himself. "Can't help but admire a family like that, can you? Certainly understandable." He looked satisfied with himself and his perfect American family, but not, Luigi thought, in an offensive, boastful way.

"Beautiful," Luigi said simply. For a moment, they both stood and looked at the picture. "Where is?" Luigi finally asked. He pointed to the image for emphasis.

"We live in a small town outside the city," said Dr. Nesmith. "It's a great little place. None of the dirt and crime you've got here."

Luigi could almost smell the grass and trees where Dr. Nesmith lived. He'd been to Coney Island once with Pasquale on an unseasonably hot day, but the place barely qualified as nature, the water crowded with bodies, the sand crowded with more bodies. At least Pasquale claimed there was sand under the layer of towels and skin that stretched as far as Luigi could see in both directions. There was none of the languid charm of a hot Saturday afternoon by the river in Urbino. After an hour, he'd longed to be back in Manhattan, where at least there was respite from the sun.

"I like," Luigi said. It was one of his first conversations in English with a stranger, and he was struggling to create dialogue.

"Anyone would like it," Dr. Nesmith said, and he clapped Luigi on the shoulder as if they were friends. "Have to be crazy not to like a place like Shaleford."

"Shaleford?" Luigi had never heard of it. Desperate to continue their connection, he struggled to fit his hand under his smock and into his shirt pocket, where he located his pen. "Write?" he asked, miming the action in the air.

Dr. Nesmith took a prescription pad off his desk and printed "SHALE-FORD" in big block letters. Luigi recognized it as the handwriting someone would use for a child. The doctor hadn't noticed his pen.

"Shal-e-ford," he repeated, making it three syllables. "I like Shaleford."

"We all like it," Dr. Nesmith said. Then he set down the picture and ripped the page from the prescription pad into small pieces, as if he were afraid of Luigi knowing where he lived. Suddenly, he and Luigi were not friends anymore, but a doctor and a janitor. "Think you'll have this mess cleaned up in five minutes?" he asked, tapping the glass on his watch.

Luigi nodded. "Five minutes." He held up his hand, fingers spread.

"I'm counting on you," Dr. Nesmith said, and he left the room quickly.

"Shaleford," Luigi responded, rather than *good-bye* or *okay* or any of the other words Pasquale had taught him. "Shaleford," he repeated when Dr. Nesmith was out of earshot. It was a word he'd tuck inside and keep close to him, like the key he stored below his underwear in a bureau drawer. When he had mopped Dr. Nesmith's floor clean and was ready to go, he turned one last time to look at the picture. Only then did he realize that Dr. Nesmith had slipped Luigi's pen into his own pocket. Someone used to having fine things, Luigi realized, couldn't understand how much a pen or a few words could mean.

"Shaleford," Luigi whispered with longing, staring at the happy foursome and their neat home. A place where nothing happened. A place where neighbors shared no walls. A place where houses contained their inhabitants and didn't let them go. "Shaleford," he repeated. Then he turned out the light and stepped into the hallway.

✦ THURSDAY ✦

Before pulling out of the parking lot, Gianfranco leaned over and kissed Olivia lightly on the mouth, and then he pulled back and studied her.

"*Come sei bella,*" he said. Her stomach dropped to her knees and rose in her throat. She could feel her cheeks flaming. *Ciliegie*—cherries—her father had termed the two spots that burst there when she was embarrassed. She stared down at her lap.

"I can't be the first man to tell you this," he said.

Olivia thought of Ivan, their shared ironic view of love, the inevitable deflation of romance. They would avoid disappointment, they'd agreed, by being honest and not pretending to find each other perfect. This led to a lot of list making and discussion, but not to a lot of sex or passion. She liked compliments, Olivia had decided the day before as Gianfranco cooed over her soft skin, her perfect mouth, her strong legs, and she didn't mind risking disappointment to hear them.

They were in Gianfranco's car, heading, finally, to the house. Olivia bent her right arm and rested it on the open window. Her elbows hurt—not the bone, but the skin—from rubbing against the starched sheets in her hotel room. She had sneaked Gianfranco upstairs—for once, there was someone behind the desk in the lobby—and they had nuzzled in the rickety shoe-box elevator. Gianfranco had easily turned the skeletal key in the lock, and once inside the room, they'd fallen onto the bed without removing their hands from each other. She'd run her palms down the side of his torso over and over, the way she would have caressed a pot with a particularly pleasing form. Now her elbows were chapped from the rough touch of the sheets.

He'd only pulled away from her once. They were still standing, clothed, by the bed when he ran his hands down her back and came to rest on her pocket. "What is this?" he asked, tapping the key.

"I found it in my father's things. I've had it with me ever since."

Now, in the car, with the easy familiarity gained only through sex, she rested her hand on top of Gianfranco's on the gearshift. He grabbed her fingers so that they were intertwined with his.

"You are sure?" he asked.

It was the same thing he'd asked repeatedly the day before as they'd lain tangled in the sheets. She'd asked him if he would take her, finally, to the address on the deed, and he'd promised to do it, if she was sure it was what she wanted.

"I'm sure," she said.

Gianfranco was driving around the long way, outside the city walls. He'd explained to her the day before that traffic through the *centro storico* was, in theory, restricted, but truly it was restricted only to visitors, as anyone from Urbino simply stopped at the little guardhouse at the arched Santa Lucia gate and requested a permit, which the *vigile urbano*, or traffic cop, on duty automatically wrote up and handed over. It was the same with handicapped parking, he said. Anyone who wanted to park in a handicapped area simply told the person on duty that his foot hurt, and then he wouldn't receive a fine. As a matter of principle, however, Gianfranco tried to park outside the walls. He was, after all, supposed to be upholding the law.

"My father was a good person," Olivia said again.

"You said this, and I believe you."

"He raised me by himself after my mother died."

"I know you are true," he said.

They rose up the hill and turned down a street shaded by pine trees.

"This is *la pineta*," Gianfranco said. "You know it?"

"No."

"It means a place with pine trees, but in Urbino it is the—how do you say?—the place where lovers go with the car."

"Lovers' lane," she said. "Makeout point."

"Exactly." He smiled, satisfied. "In Urbino if a boy asks you, 'Do you want to see the lights of Urbino?' he take you here."

"I'll remember that," she said.

"Where do you go in New York to 'see the lights'?"

Olivia thought about this. "To really see the lights, you go to the Empire State Building," she said, "but to fuck, you go home, to your bed."

"Fuck," he repeated.

"What's wrong?"

"Nothing. I like this word. It is good, like a hit." He made a fist.

"Punch."

"Yes, punch."

"Why, what do you say in Italian?" The night before, he'd murmured in her ear, "*Voglio fare l'amore con te.*" She blushed now, remembering.

"*Scopare.* Sometimes *chiavare*, like a key." He made a motion with his hand, turning his fist as if he were fitting a key into a lock, then opening a door.

"*Chiavare.* I like that," she said.

"I like it, too." He slipped his hand out from under hers and rested it on top, his palm pressing hard on her knuckles each time he shifted. She could feel the tremor of the engine rise up through her hand.

The afternoon before, she'd used his cell phone to call Claudia—relieved when Alex answered and didn't ask any questions—and say she wouldn't be coming for dinner, and then Gianfranco had gone out and come back with two cans of *aranciata*, a wedge of sheep's cheese, and a greasy packet of *cresce sfogliate*, flaky flatbreads cut into quarters. They'd picnicked on the bed, their faces shiny. It felt to Olivia like Gianfranco never took his eyes off of her, even when he drank, even when he left the room.

After eating, they'd talked for hours, lying in the crumb-filled bed. Olivia still hadn't dressed; she'd eaten with the sheet pulled over her chest. She felt as happy as she did each year on the first Monday of summer when she woke up, glanced at the clock, then remembered the day was hers. They leaned against the wall side by side as they ate. Catching their reflection in the mirror over the dresser, Olivia thought of Michelangelo's *Pietà Rondanini*, the sculpture that had haunted him. The one he'd left unfinished when he died. Michelangelo had pounded off the original Jesus head and carved another from Mary's shoulder. He kept chipping away at the image. Jesus and Mary were fused together out of necessity as the marble grew smaller and smaller.

Gianfranco was an only child, he'd told her yesterday. Before him, there'd been a girl who drowned when she was seven, and his parents had then had him late in life. He was, he claimed, a consolation prize. His father was a lawyer, and his father before him, and practicing law in Urbino wasn't the track he would have picked. When she asked what he would have chosen instead, he'd looked shy for the first time.

"*Archeologia,*" he said.

"Like digs?" She mimed shoveling.

He nodded happily. "It is fascinating, no?"

"Yes."

"I would be happy working in Pompeii, or Turkey, or Greece, removing the dirt from history."

"I can see you," she said. "I can see you doing that perfectly."

"But," he shrugged, "my father was a lawyer. I have his *studio.* And there is no archaeology at the university."

"They must teach archaeology somewhere in Italy, no?"

He shrugged again. "Of course, other cities, but here, we say we are lucky if we don't have to go away. We are too *mammoni.*"

"*Mammoni?*"

"There is this expression in English, too: mama's boy. You understand?"

She laughed. "I understand perfectly. But you don't seem like a *mammone.*" Olivia glanced at her watch. "It's eight-thirty at night and you haven't spoken to your mother all day."

He patted her leg. "I saw her for a minute when I went to buy this." He pointed to the remaining cheese sitting on the nightstand in its wax paper.

"You saw your mother?" Olivia, who was protected only by the sheet, sat up and covered her chest with one arm, as though his mother were in the room with them. "What did you say?"

"Nothing. We say hello, and I tell her that I am not coming home for dinner. She is buying some *sott'aceti*—you know, eggplant and peppers."

"And that was it?"

"That is how it works. That is the only way it can work. We live together, but we do not know each other."

In the car, she slipped her hand out from under his on the gearshift and moved it to his thigh.

"What did your mother say to you this morning?"

He sighed. *"Mi ha rotto le palle."*

"What does that mean?"

"You understand *rotto*, no? Past tense of *break*. She break my *palle*." As he said the last word, he slipped his left hand off the wheel for a second and grabbed at his crotch.

After they'd talked for a couple hours the night before, they'd started kissing again, their mouths pleasantly salty, with a glaze of sweetness from the soda. They'd made love more slowly the second time around. Olivia thought of clay on a wheel. The best part of throwing was when the piece was perfectly centered, and then she could drop in her thumbs to open it and begin to shape what had existed only in her mind the moment before.

Afterward, he murmured, *"Non c'è due senza tre.* Do you know this?"

She shook her head lazily.

"We say, 'There is no two without three.' If something happens two times, it happens three times."

He'd stayed until she'd fallen asleep. When she woke, it was 6:30 in the morning, and she had no idea when he'd left. There was a note in the ashtray on the nightstand, the hotel room key and its saturnian ball resting on top of the paper.

> Sorry to go. If you want to see the house,
> meet me at 10.30 tomorrow in piazza. You
> don't must go. I had a beautiful day. I hope
> history is okay with you.
> P.S. When you read this, lock the door.

Olivia locked the door and started to throw the note away, but then she took it and folded it into a square, and then another, until it was the size of her thumbnail. She tucked it into the side pocket of her suitcase, right next to the deed. Seeing the paper there made her think how distant Shaleford was, and how far she'd come, only to look back.

✦ ✦ ✦

THEY PULLED UP TO AN UGLY HOUSING DEVELOPMENT, NOT TALL APARTMENT buildings, but squat town houses. They were the same pastel colors—baby aspirin orange, Necco wafer green—as the shopping centers they'd passed on their way to lunch on Tuesday. Maybe Italians liked to pretend they lived in Miami Beach. Maybe they didn't realize those Art Deco buildings were full of old men wearing black socks and shorts.

Gianfranco parked. "You are sure?" he asked again.

Olivia looked around at the ugly buildings with their cast-iron detailing. What could be so damaging here? From the looks of these houses, they hadn't even been built when her father lived in Urbino.

"Positive."

He pushed his hair behind his ear and looked concerned. "I could take you somewhere for the day—Gubbio or Perugia. We drive there, eat lunch. You have hardly done any *turismo* while you are here."

"I said I want to see it. I feel like I won't understand until I do."

He nodded, then pushed back his hair.

She'd finally asked him last night, after they'd eaten, what had happened to his ear.

"I had a fight with somebody," he said.

"And he cut off your ear?"

"She," he replied. "Well, not exactly. Truly, I did it to myself."

"Like van Gogh?" Olivia tried to imagine Gianfranco's gentle hands carving off a piece of his own flesh, but she couldn't.

"Not a very decided van Gogh," he said. "I only lost a little—how do you say?—cartilage."

"Who was it? The person you had the fight with, I mean. Your girlfriend?"

Gianfranco nodded.

"The one who got pregnant?"

He nodded again.

"But aren't you glad now?" Olivia asked. "I mean, you'd have a son the age of, I don't know, my cousin's kid, Alex. Wouldn't that be weird?"

He held very still and studied her. She thought she might have something stuck in her teeth, but when she discreetly ran her tongue over the inside of her mouth, she felt nothing.

"I didn't want it to be my baby. I just wanted her not to sleep with another man," he said.

"Okay, that makes sense. And you were so sad, you cut off your ear?"

He shook his head. "I do not like to talk about this very much."

"Sleeping with someone gives you the right to ask three questions and have them answered truthfully." It was a line of Claire's, one Olivia had always scoffed at, but Gianfranco appeared to buy it.

"Okay," he said solemnly. "You have asked about my ear and about the law. What else?"

She didn't think that was fair. She hadn't asked about the law specifically; it had just come up in a getting-to-know-you postcoital conversation. He'd explained that in Italy possession was not nine-tenths of the law as it was said to be in the United States; instead, it was everything. There had been cases in which tenants gained control of their rental properties after they lived there long enough, a rent-paying squatters' arrangement, as Olivia understood it.

"Well . . ." she began, formulating her third question. Her voice shook, and she started over. "Well, Giovanni said you'd been in prison. Is that true?"

"Giovanni tells an interesting history." Gianfranco gave her a close-lipped smile she couldn't read.

"Story," she corrected him.

"I think this is history." He crossed his arms over his chest and moved up the bed so that his back pressed against the wall. He was still dressed from his trip outside to buy dinner. He lodged his hands in his armpits. "It is far in the past, and there are a lot of people."

"I think it's pretty simple," Olivia said, annoyed. "Were you in prison or weren't you?"

"Well, officially, in the documents, no. You cannot be a lawyer in Italy if you have been in such an institute."

"Institution."

"Institution. So it is cleaned from my papers. But, yes, when I was young and very stupid and I was very serious, I was in love with this girl, and like I told you, she slept with another boy, and she got pregnant, and to show how I loved her, loved her more than he did, I steal some money from a store. I was always good boy. As you know, from Leo, I could not even steal answers in school. This is true: I could see the papers of others. I just didn't want to steal answers."

"And you got caught?"

"I was very, very stupid. I entered a store at night, late, but the *padrone* lives upstairs. He hears the noise, comes down with a kitchen knife. I am moving slowly along the wall, like this." Gianfranco pressed his back against the wall and turned his head briskly to the left and then to the right, affecting a wide-eyed, frightened expression. His curly hair framed his face like the backlit halos of Jesus in Renaissance paintings. "And, *zak*, he puts knife through my ear, like a piercing, but not in a good place."

"Ow." Olivia reached forward and moved his hair off of his ear to get a better look. "But it's so straight across," she said, thumbing the tender skin.

"Later, at the hospital, they try to make it look good." He laughed. "Or better at least."

"So you were just stuck to the wall like that? What did you do?"

"I cried," Gianfranco said simply. "And then I tried to get away, which only made it worse. Have you seen the pig when they make prosciutto?"

Olivia shook her head.

"The blood must be removed. It is so much. You cannot believe that a small animal has this much blood. I was like that."

"And the girl, what happened to the girl? Was she impressed?"

"Not at all. She was not interested in me, and soon I became not interested in her. When someone does not love you anymore, it is easy not to love them, no? It happens very quickly. The love dies."

Olivia thought of the dismay she'd experienced coming home at night to the apartment she shared with Ivan, the way her heart felt like an apricot pit sucked of all the fruit's flesh. She'd started staying at the pottery studio later and later, grabbing containers of yogurt at the deli in lieu of dinner and hoping that in her absence he'd change, just as she hoped her father would go back to the way he'd been. But inevitably, she returned to a sink full of dirty dishes and Ivan just the same as ever, and her father kept getting worse. *It's easier to be alone than with the wrong person.* When Gianfranco had said that, she'd felt again the clattering loneliness of living with Ivan, heard the harsh tone she used with him near the end, before she'd realized that she'd have to be the one to leave.

"But what happened to her?" she asked. Her veins felt cool, as if they'd filled with mercury. She was jealous, she realized with a flush of embarrassment.

Gianfranco looked at her wide-eyed. "You really do not know, *vero*?"

"How would I know?" Olivia asked.

Gianfranco snorted. "I thought you know. I thought they tell you."

"Who?"

"The girl lives in Urbino. She had the baby, *un maschio*, Alex. She married Giovanni."

Olivia's toes went cold. She pulled her caressing hand away from Gianfranco's ear. "You and Claudia?"

"The girl was Claudia. A big—how do you say?—a big deal in Urbino. *Una vergogna*, for her and for me. Our families, who think for a long time we will be one family, are angry at each other. Everybody takes one part or another part. The whole city."

"Claudia," Olivia said.

"I go to prison for two nights. My father is so angry, he doesn't come to get me. They release me, and I walk home, and my father doesn't speak to me for a year. Then he gets my documents cleaned. I go to England. I come back and go to university. And finally, when I am a lawyer like him, he forgives me."

"Claudia," Olivia said again.

"This bothers you?" Gianfranco rested a hand on her leg. Through the sheet she could feel the gentle heat of his palm. "This is a long time ago."

"But everybody knows."

"It's just *pettegolezzi*. How do you say this word?"

"Gossip," Olivia said, dazed.

"I wish I could clean this like my documents get cleaned of prison," he said. "It bothers you."

Olivia thought for a moment. She'd complained about Ivan's lack of passion for her. His endless lectures about Carlo Tresca or Emma Goldman hardly required her presence at all. It was ironic that he specialized in activists, Claire had pointed out once, when he himself was so passive. "I love Ivan," she'd said to Claire on so many occasions, "but I want someone who's going to chase me halfway around the world, not someone who's going to sit on the couch while I go down to the deli for a pint of ice cream." Gianfranco had been willing, at least when he was young, to make a fool of himself for love.

"It doesn't make me happy," she said.

"I cannot change the past, just as you cannot change the past of your father."

"I know," she said, relaxing. At least Claudia's mysterious pronouncements on Gianfranco were clarified now. She didn't like the thought of him with her cousin, but she didn't like the thought of him with anyone. She placed a proprietary hand on his leg, and he smiled.

"You have heard a lot of bad stories these days," he said.

During the whole time they'd been in bed—which was stretching into hours—she'd forgotten about her father. Now his face popped before her. She heard again the awful croak that he'd issued as he died; she saw the painfully chapped skin that ringed his lips. She closed her eyes and shook her head to get rid of the image. Claudia she could take, but thinking of her father when she was naked in bed with a man was too much.

"Actually, it's a beautiful story in some ways," she said. "Very *Romeo and Juliet*."

"Shakespeare is English, but he place *Romeo e Giulietta* in Italy, no? There is a reason."

Olivia reached over and ran a finger across the top of his ear, then down the bridge of his nose, the spot where the duke's chunk had been taken out.

"You're just part of a long tradition of *urbinati* with missing body parts, no?" she said, rocking her fingertip back and forth over the bone.

"*Credimi*," he replied, pulling her head close to his chest, so she heard his heart's solid beat, "all the important things I have."

"YOU ARE SURE?" HE ASKED YET AGAIN AS HE CLOSED THE DOOR ON THE DRIVer's side. He'd parked his Fiat in a large lot that ran down the middle of the development like a black tar sternum.

Olivia sighed. His concern was distastefully condescending. She'd noticed, even in the short time she'd been here, how Italian women were. They huddled under the heavy arms of their boyfriends and husbands, and if they spoke, they spoke in quiet voices. And the few times they laughed, they covered their mouths with manicured hands.

"Cut it out," she said. "I'm not some delicate flower."

He wrinkled his brow.

"Anyway, it's a question, so it should be 'Are you sure?' "

"Oh. Are you sure?"

She nodded. "I am."

"This is the very ugly part of Urbino," Gianfranco said, waving an arm as if he were introducing the conductor at a concert.

"I can see that." It really was hideous. The countryside around Urbino was uniformly beautiful, and off in the distance were hills planted with crops or inhabited by groves of trees, but the immediate surroundings, with their garish colors and knockoff architecture, were the worst of human impact on nature. Hundreds of cars squatted on the blacktop parking lot, and there were large cement garages like honeycombs. The development, which stretched in both directions, was built onto a hill, so the top row of houses looked down on the row below, and so on, obliterating any hope of privacy. The two of them stood above the lowest level of houses, boxy orange-yellow structures. Olivia thought sadly of the painting of the ideal city in the ducal palace, attributed to Piero della Francesca on its tag, but with a polite question mark. The painting was a little cold for her taste, with its perfectly perpendicular buildings and ruler-straight streets. Still, how had it gone from that to this? How had balanced elements surrounding a circular building and a piazza with a patterned floor led to this screaming bastardization of the American suburbs? Like houses in Levittown, the dwellings here were all identical; Olivia spotted a few welcome mats on the ground and wondered if they served to help residents recognize their own front doors when they came home at night.

"It's this way," Gianfranco said, motioning for her to follow to the right.

They walked the equivalent of two city blocks. Gianfranco took her hand.

"Nervous?" he asked.

She nodded.

"This way." He pulled her down the lowest street. Hanging on the wall of one of the houses was a sign, VIA XXIII SETTEMBRE.

Olivia pointed. "That's not the address on the deed."

"The names of the streets changed many times. This was Via del Rinascimento, then Via Mussolini. Now this is what it's called."

"What about the name of the street where my father grew up, Giro dei Debitori? That's such a strange name."

Gianfranco smiled. "During the Renaissance, the Jewish ghetto was in town. It was the street from the Mercatale, where the *parcheggio* is now, to the piazza. When people owed money to the *ebrei*, they went around the long way." He drew a large circle with one hand. "They made the *giro*."

Gianfranco stopped and turned, and she followed. Squeezed in between the pastel rectangles was an enormous house. It was bigger than the mansions of the richest families in Shaleford, the homes she'd envied as a child, and it dwarfed the tacky town houses on either side. It was three stories high, built of stone and brick. The slate roof was a deep burnt orange color, like the roofs of the oldest houses in the center of Urbino. A long green yard the size of half a football field stretched from an iron gate up to the house. Several enormous trees grew in front of the house, their topmost branches higher than the roof itself. The house was beautiful but also dark, and, now that she was looking more closely, run-down. One window was cracked, and it glittered like a spiderweb dotted with dew. The lawn was chaotic, with tufts of tall green plants and patches of brown. The stones in the path leading to the front door had grass sprouting between them like the hair that had grown wildly from her father's ears and nostrils; he must have been plucking it all those years, she'd realized at the end when it sprang up freely.

Olivia and Gianfranco rested their hands on the fence, wrapping their fingers around the iron posts.

"It's beautiful," she said.

Olivia noticed the gate with its imposing lock, like something on a treasure chest or a chastity belt. She patted the rear pocket of her pants and took out the key she'd found in her father's nightstand.

The key clanged into the lock, but she couldn't turn it. She withdrew it and tried again. Still nothing. She handed it to Gianfranco.

"You try," she said. He, too, inserted the key into the lock, but even with a grunt of effort, he couldn't turn the key.

"*Non funziona,*" Gianfranco said sadly.

What had she expected anyway? That she'd open the gate with her key and the years would fall away and her father would come waltzing out, arms spread for a hug, to explain it all? Yes, she realized now, that was what she'd pictured. Her father a friendly ghost. It had all been a big misunderstanding, he'd tell her. He'd want to know how she could believe such horrible things about him.

"It doesn't matter," she said.

Gianfranco nodded but said nothing.

"Do you want to enter?" he asked.

"Yes, but how?"

Gianfranco motioned for her to follow him around the side of the house. There was a wooden plank leaning against the fence. He moved the plank, and behind it was a space with some of the bars removed. The two of them turned sideways and shimmied through the gate.

"We came here when we were young," Gianfranco explained. "It was another *pineta.*"

The ground was marshy and overgrown with weeds that reached up to Olivia's waist. There were a few large stones with some planks set on top of them to form a walkway, but the planks had rotted in parts and were unsteady. As Olivia stepped on one, it cracked. She leaped back to the stone behind her.

"*Sta' attenta dove metti i piedi,*" he said. "Be careful where you put your feet."

The plank walkway ended around the back of the house. Olivia pointed to a used condom in the grass and a few cigarette butts tossed nearby.

"I guess it still is like the *pineta,*" she said.

Gianfranco smiled and led her to a stone patio by the back door.

"Do you want to try the key?" he asked, pointing to the lock, but it was a new padlock and her key wouldn't fit.

"How are we going to get inside?"

He fetched a stone from the ground and, with one sharp blow, broke the lock.

"I ask myself who puts the lock," he said. "Don't you ask?"

Right now, she could only think about her father, in this house, the way the weight of its ownership had fallen on his thin young shoulders, and the way he'd run from it. If it hadn't been for this building, he'd have been a different man, and she might not have existed at all.

Gianfranco swung open the door. There were no curtains on the windows, so the room they entered was lighted well enough. It was a kitchen, not so unlike the kitchen she'd seen in Raphael's house, but more modern. A giant stone hearth took up one wall. In the middle of the room stood a long table made of wood worn smooth. It was large enough to seat two dozen people, maybe more if they didn't mind being crowded. The thick film of dust on the table's surface was broken here and there by fingerprints. At one end sat a pack of rolling papers and a newspaper dated *12 gennaio 1982*.

"What happened to the rest of the furniture?" Olivia asked, gesturing.

"People come to these houses out in the country and take the old things," said Gianfranco. "Some are very beautiful."

"Out in the country?"

"Until ten years ago, there was nothing here," Gianfranco said. "This was considered deep *campagna*. My father hunted here when he was younger. Probably yours, too. They built *capanne* up in the trees and sat there to kill birds. My father's got a bad back because of it."

"Because he killed birds?"

"From sitting like this." Gianfranco hunched into a gorilla position, then straightened just as quickly.

"I don't think my father hunted," she said. "He didn't seem like the kind of man who could have killed an animal."

Gianfranco looked at her skeptically. "During the war, everybody hunted. They needed to eat."

"So what happened ten years ago?"

"The university increased the number of students. Anybody can go. And families started renting out their homes to students from other cities. They wanted new houses for themselves. Families moved out of the *centro storico* and came to live here."

With three fingers, Olivia drew a curvy wake through the sea of dust on the hulking table. "This table's amazing."

"Probably too large for the door, or they would take this, too."

"Was it a big family?"

"The Levis were four. The grandfather died before the war. They would have had big lunches, lots of people. All the *ebrei* of Urbino could eat here."

Olivia imagined the room filled with light and guests, large overloaded platters passed back and forth, children amused and coddled the way she'd seen people do here with babies—jangling key rings in front of them or tickling their naked feet. And then what? Her father entering with the Gestapo, or leading a charge of Fascist soldiers through the door? She'd thought that seeing the place, being inside it, would set off a genetic memory, that the episode would play across her mind as if it were a movie screen.

"We want to continue?" Gianfranco offered, and before she could answer, he was carefully testing and then mounting the ladder stairs in the corner.

"Have you been here before?" Olivia called to Gianfranco's disappearing back as he climbed ahead of her to the next floor. She was disturbed by an image of Gianfranco and Claudia in a tight embrace. He turned and offered her a hand, and just as quickly as it had come, the image was gone.

"*Nella cucina.* Never up here," he said.

The kitchen was well-preserved compared to the room they entered—the living room, Olivia guessed. The furniture had been removed. The walls sagged; the floor buckled. The room seemed to feel the weight of the other floors of the house resting on its shoulders and to suffer from it.

"It's terrible," Olivia said. In the corner was a crumpled shape. Gianfranco poked at it with his toe. She stood back, afraid of what might scurry out, but it was no animal. He picked it up and held it out for her to touch.

"*Velluto.*" It was a long strip of velvet, crusty but still recognizable. He shook it, and a dry, dusty mist gathered in the air, then fell.

The wall they stood near was lined with bookshelves. A few books were still there, leaning crazily against the others for support. Olivia picked up one at random. The outside felt like canvas or burlap—rough and thick with dust. When she opened it and turned a page, the paper crumbled in her hand like bone-dry clay that had yet to be fired. It was too dark to see the titles, but the bindings reminded her of the series of American classics her father had once ordered from an ad at the back of a magazine—all hardback editions with blue or maroon covers and the titles (*The Grapes of Wrath, The Sun Also Rises,* and, oddly, *Goodbye, Columbus*) lettered in gold. They had sat, their spines uncracked, on his shelves. The few times she'd been assigned those books in English class, she hadn't wanted to take in new hardcovers that smelled of glue; it would have looked like she was trying. Instead, she read the used paperbacks that were made available at school—covers defaced, crude penises drawn on the flaps, 85 percent of the text highlighted.

"Depressing," she said to Gianfranco.

He looked surprised. "What did you wait for?"

"What do you mean? To go upstairs?"

"*No, no. Cosa ti aspettavi?*"

"What did I expect?" She paused. "I expected to feel something."

He put an arm around her shoulders.

"Maybe you expect too much," he said.

"I know, I know." She set the book back on the shelf. "I don't even know if my father was ever in this house. I don't know anything."

Gianfranco sighed. "What would make you more happy? That he was here, or that he wasn't?"

Olivia's throat constricted from the dust in the room. A tickle was building in her nose. How could it be so dark in here with the sun shining outside? The trees, she supposed. They'd been left to grow unchecked for so long.

"I want him to still be alive," she said.

Gianfranco didn't reply. He simply folded his arms around her and held her. They stood like that a long time. Gianfranco's chest was wide and welcoming, protective, and she'd noticed last night when they'd been naked that he had just the right amount of hair. Not sparse like Ivan's, Gianfranco's was closer to the soft oval that had sat on her father's chest like a gray throw rug. She'd never seen her father's chest hair until he was dying and unable to take care of himself. For the first time, she'd seen him naked, too, and she'd looked away as quickly as possible from his poor penis, as unmanly as a child's soft bath toy.

"But in a way, I don't want him to still be alive," she mumbled against Gianfranco's shoulder. "Not if he has to be like he was at the end." One day, he'd tried to hit her, lashing out in a grotesque frenzy. The caregiver (how Olivia hated that word, as if these people baby-sat for her father because they cared and not because they were paid) on duty caught his arm and held it firmly. Afterward, when he slumped into sleep, the caregiver offered to restrain him, but Olivia refused, and shortly after that, he'd grown too frail to act on his impulses, good or bad.

"Of course not." He combed her hair with his hand.

"It was terrible," she said. "It was terrible." And then she was sobbing hard, ugly crying, her mouth filling with saliva, her nose with snot. She mashed her face into his shoulder and let her body shake.

"My father is dead," she whispered into Gianfranco's shoulder between sobs. *"Mio babbo è morto."*

"I know," he said, and held her tighter.

Another of Claire's axioms about men: They could be judged by the way they reacted to your tears. The weak turned away, or they got weepy themselves, so that you had to focus on them. Bullies insisted that you cease the childish behavior immediately. Ivan had always seemed slightly bemused when she cried, as though she'd learned to tap-dance and, while admiring her skill, he couldn't see what benefit it had. Gianfranco held her tightly. The strong, wide band of his arms gripped her until the sobs dulled and turned to hiccups, then stopped. His arms loosened, and she turned and wiped down her face with the back of one hand, grateful that the room was dark.

"Andiamo?" he said quietly. "Or you do want to see more?"

The house had nothing for her. Its history was held tight between the walls, written in a language she couldn't read.

"No, no," she said. "I've seen enough. Let's go."

"Andiamo allora." He reached out and took her hand in his, and she followed him blindly to the stairs in the corner and out of the darkness.

BACK OUTSIDE, THEY BLINKED AT EACH OTHER LIKE CARS FLASHING THEIR headlights. The air smelled almost unbearably fresh compared with the stale air inside that house. Olivia inhaled deeply. All these years of pottery, working to keep clean and free of silicosis, fearing dust as if it were syphilis, and here she was traipsing around an abandoned house that was probably filling her lungs with fifty-year-old particles and worse.

From the back, the house was again mismatched with its neighbors. It looked like a real structure, while the town houses looked fake, like stage sets, or the poster-board model of the Louvre a student had turned in as a final project the year before, complete with a Saran Wrap and toothpick I. M. Pei pyramid. Stretched out in front of them, behind the house, was a swath of open land.

"I suppose they'll just keep building until there's no green left," Olivia said sadly, gesturing in that direction.

"They can't," Gianfranco said. "This land belongs to the house. Also, it's not *costruibile* below here."

"Why?"

"Too wet. Too . . . how do you say?" He held one hand at a slant. He gripped her left hand with the other.

"Too steep. But wasn't it steep above here? It looks like the whole development is going to come sliding down the hill."

Gianfranco said, "Do you understand how things happen in Italy?" He rubbed his thumb against his index and middle finger.

"Bribes? But that's so dangerous."

"Not bribes exactly, more like *benzina*. Without gas, the automobile does not go, right?"

"I guess." Olivia felt as she had when he explained about cheating in school—that here there was a different idea of what was normal and that she was always lagging a few steps behind as she tried to figure it out.

She shielded her eyes from the sun with her right hand and looked over the valley below. In the far distance was a house; a winding road like a rubber band twisted its way through the fields and led up to it. To the right were acres and acres of green, blocked in different shades. To the left were woods. At the edge of the woods, right at the border between mucky brown and intense green, maybe four hundred yards from where they stood, sat a small building. It was too far away to be an outhouse (Gianfranco had pointed out that the small wooden structures in town that hung over the stone stairways and paths were all bathrooms added onto buildings dating back to the Renaissance and earlier) and too modest to be a house. The building had no windows. It was a gray wooden box.

"What's that?" she asked.

Gianfranco followed her pointing finger. "Probably for animals or equipment." He dropped her hand and touched his own chin.

"What animals?"

"Nothing today. I told you, this was *campagna* one time." He shaded his own eyes, but he didn't look at the building she was studying. Instead, he gazed toward the hills behind it.

"So what's the story with the house? I mean, with everything built around it like that. Why didn't they just knock it down?"

"The people who owned the other land, who had houses here, sold to the *comune*. They destroyed everything and sold the land to *costruttori*, who did these *condomini*. They're *cooperative*. People put in money and get a house when it's done."

"So why didn't they knock down this house, the Levis' house?" Olivia swallowed hard. It was the first time she'd said their name. She couldn't bring herself to refer to it, as Gianfranco had, as *la casa degli ebrei*, as if Jews lived there still.

"They couldn't," he said. "They could not buy it. Remember I explained to you about the fifty years? For fifty years, they cannot touch it."

As they spoke, they walked around the side of the house and slipped through the hole in the fence. Gianfranco lifted up the board they'd moved to get in and put it back into place.

"Let's go there," Olivia suggested, pointing to the field below the house.

"Why?"

"Why not?"

"You'll ruin your shoes." They both looked down. She was wearing sneakers.

"I don't care about my shoes."

"What do you want to see? It's nothing. Where a few goats lived once."

"I want to see everything."

Gianfranco was holding her hand. He lifted it to his mouth and kissed her knuckles. "What you wish," he said.

Olivia stumbled in the tall grass. The mud underneath was as soft as fresh clay. It grabbed at the soles of her sneakers. She was glad she hadn't worn her black sandals. When she'd been packing that suitcase, she hadn't pictured this.

"The first day I came to your office, when you told me the house was going to revert to the *comune*, did you know about my father?"

He nodded slowly. "It is one of the things that everybody knows. Luigi Bonocchio got *la casa degli ebrei*, and then he went." He left unsaid what he'd told her at lunch the other day—that her father had led Nazis to the Levis, that he'd done it to keep the house that had been signed over to him.

Olivia studied Gianfranco. He'd let her hand drop and was helping her down the steep incline with his palm on her back. He was focusing hard on not sinking his feet into the wet spots. Her sneakers could be tossed in the washing machine, but he had on lightweight suede driving shoes that were soft and delicate and could easily be ruined. They looked expensive. He'd been too polite to point that out.

Suddenly, something occurred to her. "I owe you money, don't I? I mean, you did act as my lawyer."

He laughed. "I could not take your money."

"But if we prove the house is mine, that my father was the last registered owner, I can sell it. I'll give you some of that money."

He touched her back lightly, and she felt the electric thrill of his fingertips. "I could not take that money, either. You could let the *comune* have the house."

"And you think that's best?"

"I think it is easiest." He looked around. "Of course, there is the risk that they will build here, too. But I think not. The time for building has finished."

"And all I have to do is nothing and the *comune* will get it?"

"Probably that will happen."

"Probably?" She stopped and stood unsteadily on the hillside. Her toes were cold and damp. "What's the other option?"

"The nearest relative can try to have the property."

"But I'm the nearest relative."

"Not according to the *comune*," Gianfranco said. "According to the *comune*, you do not exist. Your birth was never registered."

"So who's the closest relative?" she asked, and then she got it. "Claudia? Claudia wants the house."

"It's too dangerous even to go inside," Claudia had said. "What do you care about some old house?"

Gianfranco nodded. "The *ufficio anagrafe* with the records is closed for the holiday, but I know the *capo*. I call her, after you come to my office, and she is still at home. Claudia and Giovanni have a lawyer. They ask for the records to demonstrate Claudia is your father's relative. They are to try to take it."

"But they've been so kind, so welcoming."

"Family is family," said Gianfranco, "but money is something else." So much made sense now. Claudia's fingers dancing on the table while she assured Olivia the house was worthless. Her rush to the terrace for a calming cigarette.

They stood in silence a little longer, and then in unison began to walk again. In thirty more steps, they had arrived at the shed. It was a nondescript building made of wood, about the same size as her pottery shed back home. There were no windows. She and Gianfranco were almost, but not quite, tall enough to see up onto the roof. There was a peculiar smell coming from it, one she couldn't identify. Something sickly sweet, like talcum powder or daisies.

He tried the door, but it was locked.

"I think they hide," he said.

"Hide what?"

"The Levis. During the war, some *ebrei* were—how do you say?— *battezzati*?" He mimed pouring water over his head.

"Baptized."

"Yes, baptized. But that was good only for a brief time. Then, some left. Others were hiding."

"And the Levis were hiding," Olivia said, prompting him. She sniffed again. What was that smell? Something artificial, like Nilla wafers or Wonder bread.

"I think the Levis were hiding here." He smacked a hand against the side of the shed.

"You think or you know?"

"They were arrested here," he said.

"So you knew and you weren't going to tell me?" Her voice cracked on the last word.

"I do not want any more ugly history for you. If you want, we go away right now."

"Stop babying me," she said angrily. "I told you I want to know everything." The smell was distracting. Was it coming from the fields? A certain plant?

He held out his hands, palms up. "I think I am protecting you."

"Well don't. Why can't you understand that I want to know?"

"You are right." He pulled her close for a hug. He rubbed his hands over her back. He kissed her forehead. She wasn't crying; her head felt empty of liquid, her eyes scratchy and sore. He rubbed her back some more, and then his hand sank lower, toward her rear pocket, and at the same moment they knew.

She reached into her pocket and withdrew the key. Gianfranco rested his hand over her smaller one as she slid it into the lock. With him guiding her, she turned the key slowly and heard the satisfying click of one part fitting into another.

"Don't be angry with me for asking, but you are sure?" he said.

"Yes." She dragged the word out to two syllables, the way her students did if she gave the same instructions too many times. In teaching, you had to account for the lowest common denominator, the girl who was staring out the window or doodling in her notebook. But she was no such girl.

She nodded.

"Don't keep any more secrets from me," she said. "I can't stand it."

"Never."

"My father was a good man, but he kept me in the dark, and that was wrong." She swallowed hard. Even standing here, even learning what she'd learned, it was difficult to criticize her father out loud.

Gianfranco's thumb rubbed her wrist, and he leaned over again and kissed her on the forehead. They were still for a moment, his lips soft against her hairline, the divider between pale, tender skin and the roots of her dark, smooth hair. Then they turned to the door at the same time, and their hands moved in unison, and Olivia was grateful not to be alone as they pressed forward together and swung the door open, revealing a close, unlighted dirt-floored room that smelled, she now understood, like despair trapped for close to fifty years, with no way out.

❖ 1943 ❖

As he'd done every afternoon except Sunday for four weeks, in the gray light of a November afternoon, Luigi removed a large square of brown paper from the kitchen cupboard. His mother saved every piece of string and rubber band, any glass jars that came her way. She paid for the paper around a cut of meat from the butcher just as she paid for the meat itself, and she'd never toss a piece of meat, so why waste its wrapper? Instead, she wiped each one with a damp cloth and let it dry on the kitchen table. The butcher in Urbino had been closed for months, but the shelf was still stacked with brown sheets that smelled faintly of dried blood.

Luigi placed cold food in the center of the paper—bread, cheese, one of the turnips resting on the counter, dirt sunk into its creases. He knew it was skimpy; his own family couldn't get eggs or milk. On Sundays, his mother made pasta using warm water in place of the egg, her arm muscles straining as she worked the dough extra hard to roll it out. He turned the faucet and let the water run into one of the glass bottles that his father used to make wine when there were grapes.

Luigi had never told either of his parents what he was doing. The day after the Germans arrived in Urbino and set up offices in the *municipio*, the city hall in the piazza, Luigi simply went into the kitchen and began to collect food. The arrival of the Germans had been long anticipated, but it was still jarring. Their phlegmy words whizzed through the thin fall air like bullets. They were intimidating physically, too. It was one thing to see Fascist soldiers, still recognizably Italian in their uniforms. When they weren't marching, they walked languidly and spoke with their hands. Mostly, they seemed like children playing dress-up. But the German soldiers were the same on or off duty. They spoke sternly to blackshirts and ignored everyone else. They were, to the people of Urbino, more foreign than the Jews had ever been.

Luigi's mother knew immediately that something was amiss in the kitchen, her realm. That first evening, she stood at the counter and ran her fingers through the dandelion leaves she'd gathered from the perimeter of the garden; the plot itself was picked almost clean. Luigi had taken half to the Levis, although he didn't know if they could stand the bitterness of eating them raw.

"I've heard of greens shrinking after they're cooked, but not before," she'd said, shrugging. Both Luigi's parents knew he had spent his afternoons with Ester; it didn't take much to piece together the rest. While the town of Urbino had always operated like one giant brain, with information shared instantly and simultaneously, the war seemed to have intensified that phenomenon. Rumors spread like kerosene on fire. When Signor Levi signed the house over to Luigi, Luigi's father knew about it before he got home. He greeted Luigi with a nod and said, "*Adesso tu sei il padrone.* Now you're the owner." Then he smiled, baring his yellow teeth, to let Luigi know who was really in charge.

Usually, while Luigi prepared his bundles, his father stood to the side, leaning heavily on his walking stick, and grumbled words of disapproval. Today, though, the old man sat serenely in a kitchen chair, tapping the stick on the ground in a slow march and smiling.

Luigi couldn't figure out his father and didn't try anymore, but if he had a defining characteristic, it was cheapness. Like everyone in Urbino, except for those seventeen families that included the Levis, Luigi's father had been baptized with a sprinkling of holy water. He'd opened his mouth wide to receive his first Communion wafer and even served as an altar boy at the Duomo. He was so good at making the most of his money, however, that his friends had nicknamed him *"l'ebreo"*—"the Jew."

Secretly, Luigi admired the Jews. They were bookish, while his own family marinated in surly silence with no purpose. Ester complained about her own mother, but on the surface at least, her family was placid. A misspoken word, an elbow that reached too far—in his home, these engendered days of silence, followed by recriminations. Nothing he and his sister did wrong was ever forgotten.

"*Stai diventando ebreo anche te,*" his sister accused him one evening when he reached for the final bit of salad. He wanted to slap her sneering face, but not because he was insulted at being told he was turning into a Jew.

Yet his family was his family, as firmly bound to one another as the bricks his father connected with cement, one by one. There was no question of loyalty; it was more than assumed. As much as his sister irritated him, he would have punched anyone who spoke ill of her. His father was brusque, even mean, but Luigi would have stood between him and a bullet with no hesitation.

Then there was school. He'd struggled with his parents to be allowed to study. They saw no point to education when he could be earning money alongside his father. He convinced them only by promising to support them with the money he could earn with a degree. *Lire* were the only mathematical concept they could understand. LA GLORIA DELLA PATRIA STA NEL LAVORO E NELLA DISCIPLINA declared a banner that had been strung across Via Raffaello soon after the Fascists came to power, but Luigi thought Mussolini—whose name appeared in the lower right corner of that banner—had omitted *lo studio*. Luigi had managed to finish high school on time at nineteen, but now he was twenty-one and they were in the thick of the war. There was neither work nor school, and with the damage to his right ear—his war injury, as he thought of it—there was no marching for Luigi, either. He passed time with his father, searching the woods for something they could eat.

After his father had hit his ear, Luigi waited for an apology, and when none ever came, he began to imagine one. I couldn't do without you, Luigi pictured his father saying. You're my son. Then he rationalized that his father, a man of few words, couldn't be expected to express his reasoning. Family hardly needed to be mentioned anyway, just as one would never bother in describing his own body to state that he had two arms and two legs. They had created him, and he belonged to them. In fact, he was them. The blow was a sign of love, Luigi decided, as natural for his father as clipping his hard, thick toenails or hooking his finger on the trigger of his hunting shotgun.

Now, as Luigi turned to pass his father, the old man pounded his walking stick hard against the floor. The sharp noise made Luigi jump, but he wouldn't give his father the satisfaction of glancing in his direction. He arranged the papers with their hidden contents in his pockets and walked out the door. Behind him, his father laughed, pleased with himself.

Luigi understood that deprivation made his father cruel. It made Luigi anxious. He hadn't eaten anything truly good—a piece of chocolate, or *torrone* at Christmas, or carefully folded cappelletti bobbing in delicious broth with winking eyes of fat scattered across the top—since before the war. The *mercato delle bestie* that had once filled the Piazza Mercatale with the lowing of cows and the stench of manure had disappeared. No one had animals to sell. He wasn't sure he remembered what real coffee tasted like, he'd grown so used to the bitter chicory his mother brewed.

War had taught him that no one wanted to leave home, no matter how bad things got. This included the Levis. They made other sacrifices, of course. They knew hunger. They wouldn't have eaten prosciutto before the war—not ordinary pork prosciutto, at least—but now they'd take anything, even the fatty, stringy end pieces that had to be chewed forever, even the *culo* of a loaf of bread, as bland and thick as tripe. Like all of Urbino's Jews, the Levis had purchased special goose salami and visited a separate butcher. They had a house full of fine things and embroidery; the few times he'd found himself alone in the Levis' living room, he'd moved his hands over a velvet runner that sprawled across the dining room table, marveling at the softness.

What did they feel, shivering in the corner of that shed? How long could they survive without sunlight? Their existence reminded him of the experiments he'd performed in high school, measuring seedlings and the effects of light deprivation. He longed to chart the Levis' decline on a grid, to test their endurance. He never saw them, except in shadow, but he guessed their skin must be scaly and flaking now, the way his was at the end of the summer, when his tan faded and his body resigned itself to the coming winter. Their skeletons would be shrinking ever so slightly; their excrement had likely dwindled to short, sharp pebbles, if they were able to move their bowels at all.

Out of curiosity, he had helped himself to their food one day. He stopped halfway to them, in the woods, and drew out the packet. The dry bread scraped the roof of his mouth to rawness; the cheese tasted of mold. He finished it all—he was hungry himself—and after dropping the rind from the cheese to the ground, he got on his bicycle and headed for home.

They didn't eat in front of him, although sometimes they couldn't wait to drink, swigging water from the glass bottles cloudy with his fingerprints. From a boys' adventure book about explorers, he had learned that humans could survive for weeks without food, but only a matter of days without water. He had learned, too, that those lost at sea or in the desert were forced to drink their own urine to survive, but he could not suggest such a thing to the Levis.

After each delivery, Luigi cut through the piazza on his way home. He wanted to be seen in public, in case the *partigiani*, the partisans Signor Levi had promised, needed to find him and free him from his duty to the Levis. They'd shear away from him, finally, when that happened, like elements dividing through a chemical reaction, each part lighter and safer on its own.

He bumped his father's bicycle over the cobblestones; it would have been difficult to ride into the piazza, harder still to ride out, as that would have entailed pedaling up one of two steep hills. Friends teased him about the sad state of his father's bike, with its patched tires and cracked leather seat. They called him "Bici," or "Coppi," after the last winner of the Giro d'Italia. When he stopped to talk, they inserted twigs between the spokes, and when he started up again, the twigs snapped. As he stood there, one eye wandering in search of a nod or other signal from a *partigiano*, he wondered if his friends could smell on him what he'd been up to.

Once, as he'd passed under the portico, bicycle by his side, he'd heard a man say that the Jews of Urbino, with their stuck-up outsider ways, had gotten what they'd deserved.

"They brought the Germans," another replied.

The two men fell silent and looked at Luigi as he passed. Luigi could feel his color rising and the tips of his ears turning red. To stay out of sight, so that they wouldn't see the effect they'd had on him, he ducked into the doorway of the barbershop in the piazza and waited to cool down. He rested one sweaty palm on the seat of the bike and held the handlebars with the other. *Uno, idrogeno*, he thought to himself.

At number seven, nitrogen, he could feel the blood draining from his face. By the time he reached number twelve, magnesium, Luigi was ready to go home. He scanned the piazza as he always did, hoping to spot a *partigiano* flagging him down. As each day passed, he wondered what was taking so long, and imagined a time when he would be free of them. Love groaned under responsibility, he'd realized. For the first time, he understood his own parents and their mix of love and resentment toward him and his sister. He'd loved Ester, but when he thought of her now, he felt only the weight of duty. To the right under the portico stood an old man smoking a cigarette. The center of the piazza was empty of people. The two men whose conversation had upset him were walking companionably up the *monte*—what everyone in Urbino called the steep hill of Via Raffaello, as though it were a biblical mountain and not just a precipitous incline.

Luigi took a breath and stepped onto the cobblestones of the piazza, and then he looked directly in front of him, and there, coming out of the *municipio*, was his father. Luigi's father blinked in the light, the expression on his face as impassive as a rabbit's. A German soldier followed close behind him, and for a moment Luigi feared his father had been arrested, although he couldn't imagine for what. But the soldier clapped Luigi's father on the shoulder in a gesture that was both friendly and intimidating. Luigi's father said something brief—his usual curt, nasal "*Ciao*" or "*Allora*," or perhaps a throat-clearing grunt—and then wasted no time getting away. In minutes, he was halfway up the *monte*. His legs pumped in a regular motion; he used his walking stick as a lever.

Now, on that November afternoon, having finished gathering the meager meal he would take to the Levis, Luigi descended to the basement, where his father's bicycle was stored. The first time he'd borrowed it, the tires were so deflated, they felt like the limp pelt his father left behind when he expertly skinned a rabbit. In the basement, each family from the building had its own small cement-lined room. Some made wine there; others stored tools. Luigi's father had filled their room with rusty birdcages, where he kept thrushes that were used as *richiami*. When his father enlisted him to go hunting, it was Luigi's job to climb trees and plant the small birds in their little cages. Their sweet voices then lured other thrushes, and his father easily picked those off with his shotgun. Luigi wondered why the birds didn't learn that they were killing their own kind and change their notes to a warning. He liked it better when his father hunted pheasant, because then he used a wooden whistle. It seemed more fair.

He dragged his father's bicycle up the stairs from the basement. On the street, Luigi tossed one leg over the bicycle and felt for the key in his pants pocket, and it was there, a stiff reminder that would bump his thigh with each *giro* of the pedals. The bottle of water lay submissively in the frayed wicker basket attached to the handlebars. Luigi patted his jacket pockets, checking that the hard piece of pecorino and the tough rusk of bread were in place. It wasn't much. Farmers who lived outside the city managed to eke out meals from what grew in the fields, but here in Urbino—*in città*—they were stuck. Then again, the Levis were only two adults, a child, and Ester, and they were hardly moving at all. There was a minimum number of calories needed to sustain each kilo of body weight, but he couldn't remember the data. He placed his feet on the pedals and began to ride.

Luigi himself could never have stood being cooped up all day like that. He would have fled. He could have outrun the Germans, he was sure. The other Jewish families in Urbino had. Now it was as if they'd never existed, like the faint ring of grappa that evaporated in minutes from the bottom of his father's emptied glass. All except the Levis. He wondered if after dark they came outside and looked up at the house that had been in their family for so long. He wondered what it felt like to live that close to something grand that had once been yours.

It was his now, although it never felt like that. Three years before, in 1940, two years after the racial laws had settled into place, when it was rumored that the Germans would be coming to investigate, the Levis had signed over to him the big house and the land around it. But he always felt the heaviness of a loan and knew someday he'd pay it back; he'd wondered what the interest would be.

The Levis had lived in the house for at least three generations. Luigi remembered the old man, father to the man who now huddled in the shed on the edge of their large property. He'd had watery eyes and a few strands of white hair that laced his skull like the bubbly white of a fried egg. He couldn't walk; he sat in a chair with spindly wheels, a fringed wool blanket spread permanently over his knees. Even outside, Luigi could smell him—like anything left too long in the sun, he reeked. On nice days, he was parked under the tree in the Levis' backyard, where Luigi sat in the shade with Ester. Sometimes a leaf drifted down and perched on his head or his lap, but he couldn't move his shaky hands close enough, so Ester gently removed it. When he'd died in 1940, they'd buried him immediately. Jews did that, the town murmured, because they had something to hide. Jews were spooky, everyone agreed. That man in the piazza had expressed what Luigi felt from all sides—that the Jews were dispensable, even dangerous.

Luigi always came around to the shed the long way, looping past the house, then approaching through the trees where he helped his father hunt. He stopped for a moment and stood straddling the bike, certain he'd heard something. He turned his head in a slow circle, but he saw nothing. The sky was gray, and the trees cast human-looking shadows on the ground. There was a rime of frost on the leaves underneath his feet. If he peeled a thin sheet of ice off of one, it would be delicately lined with the veins of the dry leaf. Suddenly, a rabbit scampered out of the brush and across his path, a blur of gray fur. That explained the rustling. His mouth watered at the thought of brown rabbit flesh streaked with fat, but before he could reach for a stone to stun it, it was gone. He looked around again and then, satisfied, got back on his bike and, with slow, heavy legs, began to pedal.

What Luigi loved best about riding his father's bicycle was taking a sharp curve fast, the way his body tilted to one side and he could almost scrape the ground with his knuckles. That was the thrill of school for him, the balancing act of doing it right. Soon enough, snow would fall, and he'd have to give up the bicycle and begin making the trip in tall boots, tramping through the snow like a child. At first, it had been an adventure, the real-life version of the games he'd played with his friends in the garden. During those endless afternoons of cops and robbers (no one wanted the dull assignment of *sbirro*), Luigi often crawled under the fence to hide in the tall weeds in the field beyond the garden. His friends called this unfair, but he felt that any way you could save yourself ought to fall within the rules of the game.

Now, however, he was tired of games. He was always scraping his head on branches. One day, his hands had grown hot as he'd ridden through the woods, and when he got home, he realized that one of the gloves he'd hurriedly shoved in a pocket had fallen out somewhere along the trail. His wool socks didn't have time to dry between trips, and his mother wouldn't let him hang them in the kitchen, the warmest room in the house. They were always slightly damp and chilly when he pulled them on, the scratchy fibers pressing moisture against his skin, as unpleasant as the touch of his mother's rough hands.

His and Ester's time together—the innocent time—had passed so quickly. It was like eating *tagliatelle*. He'd thought they had abundant days, an almost endless number, and instead a whole portion had been wound up and, with a single swallow, it was gone. As his father was constantly reminding him, he owned the enormous house that had so intimidated him, looming over them as he'd courted her by millimeters in the grass. When she got out of hiding, she'd be a different person; now he could not bear to consider her a person at all. He'd managed to separate shed Ester from the true Ester, the clean, sweet-smelling girl he'd loved. Quietly and with shame, Luigi considered that maybe Ester had been right—maybe she'd have been better off dying young like the Romantics.

Living in the shed wasn't living. The air there was hot and close. It stank of animals. Luigi always ducked in and out quickly. A reverse evolution was taking place. He'd read in his textbooks that men came from monkeys. The Pope might deny it, claiming Adam over apes, but Luigi knew for sure that it was true. Men had been animals once and, without too much impetus, they could become animals again.

What did they do all day? he wondered. The Levis had been readers. Their living room was still lined with books, which by now would be covered in a thick layer of dust. There were books about history and about travel, with long titles that made Luigi's eyes glaze. There were just three with strange letters that looked like they'd tie a tongue in a knot—*la lingua ebraica*, he assumed—and when he ran his hands over the books, tracing trails through the dust, he made sure never to touch those.

Luigi's own father had never read a book. When he and Luigi hunted in the early mornings—one lucky day, they'd discovered a whole family of rabbits huddled together—his father could sit still for hours, not speaking, not moving. His eyes traveled over the brush the way that Ester's moved when she was reading a book. His feet never seemed to grow cold as they squatted for hours, waiting for something to give itself away. Luigi hated hunting. He always wished that he were home, in his warm bed. His father's morning breath, heavy with what had accumulated during the night, made him sick. He tried not to inhale through his nose and hoped both that no animals would show up to be killed and that if one were going to show up to die it would do so soon, so that they could go home.

One day, his father had led him to the very woods where he now rode his bicycle. It was still dark as they built a makeshift platform in the crook of a tree branch. Luigi's father tested it with his feet and grunted. As Luigi climbed up, he said, *"Sta' attento dove metti i piedi."* From his father, it was both reprimand and protection, Luigi thought. He bent his knees and settled into position, then silently began to recite the periodic table, comforting as a lullaby. They sat for thirty minutes and heard and saw nothing.

"I think it's hunted out," Luigi said. "Empty."

His father held a finger over his lips to shush him, then rose on his haunches and pointed his shotgun into the distance. There was the ping of the pellets hitting glass, then the music of glass shattering.

He'd shot out a window in the Levis' house.

"Why did you do that?" Luigi whispered.

His father held up an empty hand in apology. "I thought I saw something moving." Luigi concentrated hard then, not on the elements, but on not turning toward the shed. That would give away the Levis for sure.

Luigi hated these visits to the shed and would have stopped going, but for the thought that the Levis would die. When the war ended, someone would open the shed and find them in the dirt. Or worse, the war would end sooner rather than later, and the Levis would survive, emerging from their hiding place looking like the reassembled skeletons that hung from a hook in his biology classroom, their bones as shiny and yellow as wax. They'd point at him and accuse.

Instead, he skipped a day here and there, once two days in a row. They never asked, and he never offered any reason. Perhaps they assumed he'd been in danger. After his two-day absence, he'd approached the shed carefully, but they were there, the same as ever, shapes in the corner. They were invisible in the dark, but he knew they were there, the same way he knew the earth was revolving, although it felt firm and steady beneath his feet. They didn't ask where he'd been, but it wasn't as though they were engaging in lengthy conversations in any case. There was the swift exchange of parcels, a full glass bottle traded for an empty one, a piece of brown paper fluttering from one hand to the other, and Ester's father's question: "*Hai sentito niente?* Have you heard nothing?" It was a question Luigi's mother might ask—constructed to assume the negative answer. After five days or so, the question was reduced to a single word: "*Niente?*" And Luigi would reply in kind, or, later, simply shake his head.

Now he was sure he heard a man's voice, deep and unfamiliar. He stopped suddenly and turned slowly, ready to raise his hands over his head. The Germans hadn't been violent so far in Urbino, but there were stories. He stood still for several minutes, inspecting the bark on a tree as though he were considering carving it. It was a ridiculous charade on a cold afternoon, but he remained there until he was satisfied that no one was following him. Someone out hunting most likely, trying to get a little more food for his family, although it was too late in the day to catch anything. He leaned the bicycle against the tree. He always went the last few meters, out of the cover of the trees, on foot. Behind him, there was a loud sound as the bicycle slid to the ground. Startled, Luigi placed a hand over his heart, but he didn't go back to right it.

From there, it was a short walk to the shed. He batted branches from his face with gloved hands. Water was odorless, but the frost had a smell, and he wondered whether that had to do with its molecular structure. There was so much he wondered about. He saw the world as a giant experiment, and perhaps that was what it was—a test of various hypotheses set in motion by God: What if I cover most of the earth's surface with water? What if some insects carry death? What if I let the monkeys grow up to be men?

Luigi slipped the glove off his right hand and stuffed it into his jacket. He reached into the pocket of his wool trousers for the key. It was the first key he'd ever owned. His family never locked the door to their apartment; it was rarely empty, since his mother left only to do the grocery shopping and go to Mass. He put the key in the lock, but with the cold, the metal resisted, and then it slid into place. He turned it and began to push, and just as he did—in the moment before the door slid open and revealed the Levis crouched in their corner—he sensed there was someone behind him.

Too late, he tried to pull the door closed. Too late, he tried to extract the key, drop it to the frozen ground, pretend he'd just been leaning on the shed for no particular purpose. Too late, he tried to turn back, run in reverse, throw them off the trail. But it was too late, and they were upon him.

While two of the three German soldiers in their mold green uniforms lunged at him and then held him, the third dashed into the shed, the expression of a winner in a Christmas *lotteria* on his face. The key dangled in the lock like an arm that had come out of its socket—weak and useless and unattached to anything—then fell to the ground with a clink. Instinctively, Luigi dived for it, which must have angered the soldiers, because a shiny black boot came at him, making sharp contact with his chest. The air rushed out of Luigi with a whoosh, and though he remained conscious, he couldn't speak, not even to wheeze out a name.

FOUR WEEKS BEFORE THE LEVIS WERE DISCOVERED, LUIGI SAT AT THEIR DINING room table with an anatomy book open in front of him. The university wouldn't be taking any new enrollments—there was a war on, after all— but at Ester's urging, he continued to study science anyway. The war would end someday, she'd remind him, and if he kept up with his studies, he'd be ready. She didn't understand that he'd had to fight with his parents to attend *liceo*, that university was a dream he could still taste only because of the war.

"What about your own future?" he asked.

Ester smiled sweetly. "I'm preparing myself," she promised. *"Non ti preoccupare."*

Ester and the Levis had remained in the house for the five years following the institution of the racial laws in 1938; meanwhile, the other Jews were leaving town. The Levis went on living in the house that Luigi owned. ("We ought to ask them for rent," Luigi's father grumbled, but of course they did no such thing.) Luigi continued his afternoon visits to Ester as he prepared for his graduation exams from *liceo*. In the quiet of the Levis' house, he studied better than at his own. Ester's mother was not constantly passing under his feet with a broom.

He and Ester sat in the living room, with its rows and rows of bookshelves, and read. She had given up on schoolwork by then and simply read what she liked, mostly the Romantic poets. There had been a time when she recited their work out loud to him, but that always ended in an argument. Ester believed they would all be better off dying young, preserved in beauty. Luigi believed the opposite—that it was a natural human instinct to do anything you could not to die ever. Sometimes as Ester read, she pulled the end of her braid around to the front and chewed on the strawlike hair gathered at the bottom. Luigi glanced up occasionally from his equations. He found the sight of her, her eyes scanning the lines like hands smoothing a bedsheet, incredibly *erotico*.

All that time, as he conquered one exam after the other, always emerging breathless and flushed from the rooms where professors sat across the table and asked stern, complicated questions, the Levis' friends were slipping away in the night. Rumors were wild. After the Coens left, there was a frenzied moment when the town believed they'd buried their gold before departing, and soon the neat garden of their undistinguished house was pockmarked with holes. The Jews didn't take their jewelry and candlesticks and linens with them; instead, they deposited them in the hands of Christian friends for safekeeping. No one, on either side, believed they wouldn't be back.

Urbino had little news from Rome, but occasionally bits and pieces slipped through. Mussolini was allied with Hitler. Mussolini's troops had marched through the center of Rome in the greatest display ever of Italian military might. The Germans decorated the tips of their swords with the heads of babies. Mussolini was dead, poisoned, but no, he was still alive. Hitler was dead and had been replaced by an actor who played the part frighteningly well, grooming his caterpillar mustache and spitting as he spoke. And over and over and over, the Germans were coming. The Germans were coming. They'd marched through Prague, through Paris, through Rome, and soon they'd come to Urbino. They'd kill everybody. They'd bring gifts. They wouldn't dare show their faces. They'd ride through on horses, like Cossacks. They'd drop from the sky, roll over the citizenry with tanks, sneak in over the top of the hill.

In preparation, the city's art was first squirreled away in the basement of the ducal palace, placed in the giant stone troughs that had served as a refrigeration system during the duke's time, then ferried to Rome in taxis. For Luigi and his friends, who gathered to watch, the thrill was not in the spiriting away of their artistic patrimony, but in sighting an automobile with its compact promise of a new and fairer world. The art—paintings of Jesus, with an occasional cameo appearance by the duke or his son— was old news, but cars were a little-known commodity. Luigi and his friends stood and stared at the miraculous contraptions. The drivers wore berets and smoked hand-rolled cigarettes; they couldn't have been more exotic.

The next day, as Luigi sat in the Levis' living room, Signor Levi appeared behind him and placed a firm hand on his right shoulder. Luigi was gripped by both fear and anticipation. His ear buzzed the way it did when it was about to be touched, then fell silent. Ester, as if by pre-arranged signal, closed her book, marking her place with a slender finger, and left the room.

"I trust you," Signor Levi said. It was the same thing he'd said when he signed over the house, so Luigi answered with the same words he'd used then.

"You can trust me." Was he going to be reprimanded for spending too much time with Ester? It wasn't proper, but there were always other people nearby. Their reading was innocent.

"I need to know that, now more than ever."

Was he going to ask for the house to be returned?

"Whatever you need, you can ask me for it," Luigi said. Of course he'd give the house back. He was insulted that Signor Levi would ever doubt that.

"We're going away, so we'll need you."

That made no sense. Why would they need him if they were leaving?

"Tomorrow, we'll no longer be here."

"Tomorrow?"

Signor Levi nodded.

"All of you?"

Signor Levi nodded again. Luigi could see his own reflection in the brass candlesticks at the center of the table. On Fridays, Ester had explained, they lighted candles and said a prayer. On Saturdays, they sat very still in their best clothes. Most of Ester's skirts and dresses were white and beige, appropriately delicate for a young girl—although she was nineteen now, and her breasts strained against their buttons—but she owned a deep purple wool dress the color of a *melanzana*, with a matching hat that he'd seen her wear only once. He pictured her on Saturdays robed in that rich color, her hands enclosed in the fur muff she'd worn to school on the coldest days.

"But where are you going?" he asked her father.

"Andiamo a nasconderici."

So, they were going into hiding. Signor Levi sat in the chair next to Luigi's. He interlaced his fingers and cracked his knuckles, a man getting ready to tell a story.

"It's too late to run. We've waited too long. The Germans are on the road already. We have very little time, and even if we had more time, we couldn't get very far. We're going to stay in the goat shed at the edge of our property. Eventually, when it's possible, the partisans will get us out. But in the meantime, we'll be there, and we need someone—someone we can trust—to bring us food. When it's safe to leave, someone will tell you, and you'll tell us."

"But where would I get food?" Luigi asked.

"There is always something, no? Always a little you can skim off the top?"

Luigi knew the place Signor Levi was talking about, could picture it in his mind—a small pigeon-colored building. They'd installed a lock three years earlier, after a rash of livestock thefts. When he and Ester sat on the back lawn on warm afternoons, the light glinted off the metal.

Luigi saw the Levis down on all fours, with split hooves, pawing at the ground, horns budding from their heads. "But only for a while, right? Soon you'll get away?"

Luigi didn't like the sound of this at all.

Signor Levi rested a hand on Luigi's knee.

"Either, God willing, the war will end and it will all go back as it was before or we'll leave."

He took a key from his vest pocket. Luigi noticed for the first time that Signor Levi's clothes were getting old. His white shirt was graying; the wool of his suit was pilling around the cuffs and collar.

"You'll need this," Signor Levi said. He rested it in Luigi's palm and folded his fingers around it. "We'll lock ourselves in from the inside. Only you have the key."

Luigi slid the cold metal between the pages of his textbook.

Signor Levi raised his eyebrows and said, "I hope you're going to find a safer place for it than that."

ON AUGUST 28, 1944, LESS THAN A YEAR AFTER THE LEVIS WERE DISCOVERED, Urbino was liberated. Bells rang and men kissed one another in the streets, twice, and then three times, and then four, repeating each cheek. Luigi's mother smiled for the first time, or at least the first time he'd ever seen. To the north, Italy remained occupied, but from Urbino down past the slender ankle of the country to Sicily, the war was over.

It turned out, though, that wars didn't end the way they did in books, with a date that chopped them clearly. It wasn't as though the Germans pulled out one day and the next things went back to the way they had been. Months passed. American soldiers came and went; they had little interest in Urbino, which had never been a crucial battle site. Men began to return from the front, after walking for weeks, and they told amazing stories. Alberto Tozzi's brother stole a truck; Renato Gorelli's cousin sneaked back through the woods from Yugoslavia, avoiding all soldiers—German, Italian, American—because he had no idea which side Italy was on anymore.

Jews got word and began to return. They told stories of living in convents and being fearful that someone might ask them to recite a prayer alone. Little boys had hidden their circumcised *piselli* from prying eyes. The adults had taken shelter where they could find it—farmhouses out in the country where Germans wouldn't bother to look. The Tedeschis had lived in a chicken coop for the last six months. Luigi pictured them there, the scent of guano in their nostrils. At night, when they closed their eyes, they probably felt the fluff of feathers on their faces and heard needlelike beaks pecking relentlessly at the dirt. He wondered whether the Tedeschis had envied the birds their access to the outdoors, even when they were taken swiftly to the chopping block. Luigi listened to the stories of people who had been elsewhere, but he couldn't quite believe that there was life outside of Urbino.

By the spring of 1945, all but four of the seventeen Jewish families were accounted for. The Collis and the Levis were missing. Another family was in France, minus the father, and the fourth had had the good fortune to have relatives in America and had made a quota. They were already long gone. The others reclaimed their property. They moved into their old houses. A few wanted to stay. Most wanted to leave again, however. As soon as possible, they were going to the mythical Palestine, where land was available and free. Luigi pictured it as the Wild West in his Buffalo Bill comic books—long, dusty spreads dotted with spiny cacti and rolling tumbleweed. Others turned to America. They were headed anywhere, really, without the sound and stink of memory. Luigi looked for the Levis every day. He kept the deed on his person now, in a pocket. When he saw them, he'd pull it out. *Ecco, la casa è vostra,* he'd say grandly, and then he'd tear it into strips.

His heart pounded at the thought of seeing Ester again, not the animal, but the girl. He'd be brave; he'd tell her father of his intentions. He'd believed he was a man when he turned eighteen, but now, at twenty-three, he knew what a man was. There'd be no need to flip the deed back to the Levis. He could marry Ester, and they would live with her family in the house, luxuriantly reading in the evenings and taking long walks through the *campagna* during the day. She could convert for real—not just a fake baptism—change her name. Or they'd elope if they had to. They were older now. They could make it on their own, couldn't they? He cautioned himself against dreaming, but he was unable to stop.

The *urbinati* were liberated, too. They'd taken the *municipio* back from the Germans. Many had rewritten their history. While during the war it had seemed that everyone was on the side of the Fascists, now they were all partisans. A few weeks earlier, in the piazza, Luigi had seen an American soldier use the butt of his rifle to knock a man's hat off his head. The fierce gun had barely grazed the man's thick hair and hadn't made a sound, but Luigi had seen how that man, only a month or two earlier the blackshirted king of a tiny realm, stood perfectly still until the American walked away.

The convivial buzz of the piazza was lost, however. Before the war, the town's center had always been filled with people. Luigi had always been able to find a friend to talk to, or eavesdrop on a conversation. These days, a single old man stood in the shade of the portico; a group of kids gathered near San Francesco. On a day in late April of 1945, Luigi surveyed this scene.

On the walls of all the surrounding buildings, where before the war there would have been notices of *defunti*, indicating the community's sorrow at individual loss, there were hundreds of pieces of white paper, their unstuck corners fluttering in the wind. Luigi approached. He read one, then tried to tear it down, but just one side came off in a strip like a bandage. It was a list of those who had cooperated: collaborators.

The list had five names, in alphabetical order, and at the top was his father's. Luigi pulled down one paper intact and shoved it into his pocket, but then he fought the urge to remove them all. There were hundreds. He couldn't possibly take care of that many. He forced himself to walk away slowly.

The day the Levis were caught, after they were dragged into the gray winter light, Luigi lay on the frozen ground. One soldier asked something of the other two, indicating him, and Luigi could tell that his fate was being decided. He raised his eyes to look at Ester and her family and saw what four weeks in the shed had done to them, how hunched they were, their hair flat and dull. Ester had taken on the pointy, thin shape of a pencil; her face was streaked with dirt. Then they were gone, and he was still lying there, gasping.

The soldier who had kicked him drew back his boot one more time, ready to deliver another blow. Luigi closed his eyes. He was sure he was going to die. He thought that there must be no word for *love* or *kindness* in German. But the first soldier stopped the second. He rested his hand on the man's arm, and spoke, and then the two of them walked away in silence. Luigi feared they were hiding, waiting to shoot him for sport. He remained on the ground for hours, pretending he was already dead.

Now Luigi walked toward the *monte*, away from the piazza, crushing the paper with his father's name on it in his pocket, and then smoothing it, only to crush it again.

"*Assassino*," someone whispered close to his good ear. Luigi turned quickly, but there was no one there. It was like the old trick of reaching around a friend when you stood to his right and tapping him on his left shoulder to make him turn the wrong way. Luigi started up the *monte* with a slow, steady pace.

Something whizzed by his ear like a bullet. He turned, and behind him was a group of five boys, each one holding a rock, each one with his arm bent back like a catapult ready to be sprung. Luigi turned forward and began walking quickly, but the boys were catching up, and the crowd was larger. A few men came around beside him, crowding him.

"*Collaboratore!*" one shouted. He wanted to explain, only in Urbino there was no difference between what a father did and what a son did. After his encounter with the Germans, his ribs had been bruised, and his mother had nursed him gently and wrapped his torso in a torn bedsheet to hold the bones in place, but she'd never asked what had happened.

"*Fascista!*" came a voice from the crowd.

Luigi said, "I would never have—"

The week he was bruised, there had been meat on the table for three dinners, and his mother had treated him each time to the choicest piece. She felt sorry for him because of his injury, he figured, as she stabbed a juicy flank with her long-handled metal fork and transferred it to the plate in front of him. It was the only time he could remember that he'd been served before his father.

Another rock flew by Luigi's left ear. He heard it pass and hit the ground, hard. And then he broke into a run. To run up the *monte* was almost impossible. It was something he hadn't even tried since he was little. He refused to lift his eyes to see how far he was from the top, and he knew that to look back would just slow his progress. Luigi concentrated on his feet slapping against the stones. His chest burned. His throat felt shredded. As he crested the hill, he allowed himself a glance. The boys were still coming, but they'd fallen behind. The older men had given up and were back in the piazza. From the top of the hill, he could see the spire of the Duomo, the *torricini* of the ducal palace, and the countryside beyond Urbino. He took a deep breath and then began running again, and he didn't stop until he had reached his building and closed himself into the apartment, locking the front door from the inside.

He raced past his mother and sister in the kitchen and went into the bathroom, where he splashed his face with cold water. Then he entered his bedroom. Luigi sat on his bed and tried to think. His ear whistled crazily, like a *tramontana* wind. Something crashed through the window.

His mother called from the hallway in fright. "*Dio santo.* What have you done now?" She came to the doorway, then stopped.

The floor glittered. Luigi moved closer to investigate. The tile was paved with broken glass. Something dark and heavy rested on the floor. Gingerly, he picked it up and shook it. A few shards tinkled off. It was a piece of metal, paper tied to it with string.

"*Cos'è?*" his mother asked, her voice rising.

Luigi didn't answer. He snapped the string and pulled away a paper that said, in capital letters, "*ASSASSINO.*" He held it up so his mother could read it, but she simply squinted. Luigi turned his attention to the metal in his left hand. It was the fender from a bicycle, twisted and mangled. It looked like the drawing of the human heart in his biology textbook—the aorta and arteries that appeared to be a single mass, although Luigi knew they were separate elements closely intertwined, like a family. He dropped both the fender and the paper on his bed and reached into his pocket.

"What does it say?" his mother asked again, leaning over the bed to look.

Luigi didn't answer. Instead, he pulled a piece of paper from his own pocket. "*Maledetto atto,*" he cursed the deed.

"*No!*" his mother protested, understanding what he was about to do. "Your father wants you to sign the house over to him."

"I'm returning it to the Levis," Luigi said. His face burned.

From the doorway, his sister laughed. "Are you really that big an *idiota*?" she asked. "You have the *cervello* to study, but you haven't figured out yet that the Levis aren't coming back. Haven't you heard what happened to the *ebrei*?"

Luigi had heard horrible stories of boxcars full of Jews singing the prayer of mourning on trains in the night. The people who had remained in Urbino both believed this and didn't. They'd suffered, too. Their sons had been injured; some had died. No one, it was agreed, had come through unscathed. When the Jews heard this, they turned their faces away patiently and bit their lips. They didn't go into the piazza the way they had before. The war was over, but they had been separated out and now, like an organism divided in two, they could not work their way back into the town.

"Your father says we'll make it into apartments. We can live on one floor and rent out the rest," his mother said.

His father had been making plans.

Luigi touched the fingers of his left hand to his right palm. There was a light scar at the center now where a patch of sweaty skin had stuck to the frozen key when he'd grasped it, then was torn away when he deposited the key in his pocket.

"*Ti dovremmo uccidere,*" the German with his boot drawn back had murmured to Luigi in a harsh accent. Luigi had wanted to laugh at the way the *r* got stuck in the soldier's throat when he said they ought to kill him.

He didn't know how long he'd lain by the open door of the shed after they had left. His father's bicycle slumped on its side in the distance. He stayed there until dark fell over him. The door to the shed swung back and forth in the wind, its hinges creaking. Finally, when he couldn't see even the barest glint of the bicycle's metal fenders, and he thought the smell of the dirt where he was lying would now live in his nose forever, he crawled to his knees and then to his feet, locked the door to stop it from crying, and limped home. When he looked back, the bicycle still lay on the ground below the trees, its wheels spinning lazily in the wind.

Now his mother said, "They're not coming back." She crossed herself in a quick motion.

"How do you know?" he asked. "You don't know anything."

"Babbo sent me," said his sister. "He sent me to the Tedeschis to ask. She's right. They're not coming back."

He could picture his sister knocking on their door, arrogantly asking Signor Tedeschi the question while she angled to get a look into the house behind him. The Jews who had failed to entrust their houses to Christians had returned to homes stripped of furniture, the windows broken and the doors busted from their frames.

"What did they say?" he asked.

His mother stood still as a tombstone.

"What did they say?" he asked again.

"*La ragazza è morta,*" his mother said.

Luigi's bad ear hissed. The memory of that day he'd glimpsed his father in town—his father never went to the piazza, couldn't stand the thought that people were looking at him or talking about him—created in Luigi a hollow, breathless emptiness. The taste of the tender meat his mother had served him, after a long dry spell of tough, chewy organs and salads of stems and yellowed leaves, now filled his mouth and made him want to retch. To his father, family was everything, but only his own family. No one else's mattered. And even then, he'd been willing to risk Luigi's life for the sake of the deed. The Germans had stood over him; he'd been at their mercy, and his father had placed him there.

The *maledetto* piece of paper was poisoning everything. He held the deed over his head and tore it into strips, then tore the strips into smaller pieces and let them fall to the floor to be swept up along with the broken glass.

"*Che cazzo fai?*" his sister shrieked.

"Your father will beat you to death," his mother said.

He ignored them both. Still dressed in his clothes, he got into bed. He pulled the sheets and blanket over his head and tried to imagine what it would be like to stay like that for days, weeks, cloaked in darkness, half-afraid and half-hoping that nobody would remember he was there. He heard a broom dragging paper and glass across the floor, and then his mother and sister walking out quietly.

He could not be home when his father got there.

The day the Germans pushed past Luigi into the shed, Ester's brother bit the hand of a German soldier, who smacked him so hard across the face that a trickle of blood ran out of one nostril, and Ester's mother shrieked, hugging her son and wiping the blood with a sleeve, and Ester's father angrily shouted, but Ester simply went limp like a piece of string in their hands and let herself be dragged away.

Luigi crawled out from under the covers. He placed his feet on the floor and stood.

And then he was an action that once set in motion stays in motion. In the back of the wardrobe was a small leather suitcase that, as far as he knew, no one had ever used. He rested it on the bed and opened the latches. The bedsheets were rumpled, but there was no time to smooth them. He moved quickly, although efficiently and neatly. The suitcase began to fill with his clothing. He rested the key on top, then his identity card with the clearly marked *razza: italiana*, and then he closed the lid and locked it all inside.

His mother and his sister were still in the kitchen. He could feel them breathing in there. As he crossed the threshold from his bedroom, a stray piece of glass crunched under the sole of his left shoe. To him, it sounded like a landslide, but there was no reaction from the kitchen. With the suitcase in one hand, Luigi padded his way across the short hallway, past the bathroom, and gently pushed open the door to his parents' bedroom. They slept in two twin beds with equally lumpy mattresses stuffed with cotton batting that leaked out the sides when the fabric tore. Luigi's father complained that his bed was uncomfortable, but his mother reminded Luigi and his sister that at their age, she'd slept on a scratchy burlap sack fattened with straw that crinkled loudly whenever she moved. They'd never know, she'd say, shaking her head, what a luxury cotton batting was.

Luigi advanced to his father's bed. He set the suitcase on the floor, then furtively stuck his hand between the mattress and the metal springs below. He looked away as he did this, his eyes trained sharply on the door. With one hand, he gathered the paper, then transferred it to the other. There was too much of it to fit in his pockets. He folded some and tucked it into his pants, behind his belt. Then he buttoned his coat, picked up the suitcase, and moved to the window. He could drop safely into the soft loam of the garden below, he knew from experience. The well-oiled venetian blinds slid up noiselessly. Luigi swung one leg over the sill, then the other, and he jumped without looking back.

Only later, after Luigi had taken off for Naples in the night, mixing easily with the many men on the road, only weeks later, when he was already on a boat, out in the middle of the Atlantic, wondering what on earth he'd done and what could possibly come next, did he realize that he'd torn up the paper he'd peeled from the wall in the piazza. The deed persisted. It was in his jacket pocket, a clean, folded *fazzoletto*. The boat rocked like the wooden board his mother used to roll out the *sfoglia* for pasta, giving under the pressure of the waves. He held the deed in his hand and stared at it as if he didn't read Italian, and then he returned it to his jacket pocket. There was no use in trying to destroy it now. Like a memory revisited so many times that it becomes more real than the present, it would not leave him.

✦ 1994 ✦

Olivia tried the knob to the front door of her father's house in Shaleford, but it was locked.

"You need the key for that," the real estate agent said. "You can't just leave a house unlocked anymore. Even in Shaleford." She opened her purse and fished out a ring of keys like a jailer's, each one marked with tape. After examining and rejecting a dozen, she identified the Slate Street key.

"Here you go." She passed it to Olivia. "You do the honors."

Olivia slipped the key into the lock. It fit with modern-day precision. It had been four weeks since she'd returned from Urbino, and still she was amazed each time she took a shower without the water dying off or used a key to open a door without struggling. On the train to Shaleford for the final walk-through, she'd realized there'd been no jolt this morning when she remembered her father was dead. She hadn't had to remember at all, in fact. He had died, and now he was dead. Without her noticing, that fact had slipped into her brain and taken up residence.

She'd been angry with him at first. Furious. She was angry with her father for turning in the Jews, then for running away, then for hiding it from her, then just for *being*, even though he wasn't anymore. She was angry with herself for being curious enough to go and find out. Why couldn't she leave well enough alone? Why had she picked at her father's memory like a scab?

Back in Urbino, after she and Gianfranco had visited the Levis' house and the shed where the family had hidden, they'd returned to her hotel room. As soon as they entered, she'd yanked the deed from its pocket.

The upper right-hand corner, the one she'd eaten, was missing, but the rest of the paper was intact. And then, staring straight into Gianfranco's eyes just as she had when they'd made love, she ripped the paper in half. He didn't try to stop her, so she kept going, tearing it into quarters, and then eighths, and then sixteenths, and so on, until the pieces were as small as snowflakes. She moved into the bathroom with the shreds in her hands, and he followed, and in the bathroom she let the paper flurry into the toilet. But when she reached up to the clammy chain that hung from the tank and pulled on it, the toilet gurgled, but no water gushed forth. She tried again. The tank hissed air. And then the two of them turned to each other, and in spite of how angry she was, Olivia began to laugh.

"*Manca l'acqua*," she said.

"This is Urbino." Gianfranco was laughing, too. He wiped a salty tear from under his lashes.

"I wanted to be so dramatic."

They stared into the toilet, where the pieces of paper were dissolving in the meager dampness, creating a paste that adhered to the sides of the bowl. Gianfranco plucked something out of Olivia's hair and showed it to her. It was one of the pieces of paper, white with a black mark on it, the body of a now-unidentifiable letter of the alphabet.

She smiled, then quickly became serious again. He dropped the flake of paper into the toilet.

"You know, the *comune* has the record anyway," he said. "What you did is dramatic, but it does not make a change."

Anger returned, filling her veins with hot liquid. "I hate my father."

"So what are you going to make?" he asked.

"Do."

"Sorry?"

"What am I going to do about my father?"

Gianfranco nodded.

She took his hand and led him out of the bathroom and back to the bed.

"I need to think about it," she said. "I need to figure something out. There has to be some way to honor these people. My father killed these people." She studied the backs of her hands. After nearly a week without throwing, the skin was healed to smoothness, and her nails had grown del-

icate white tips. She hardly recognized her own hands, and then she remembered her father, days from death, studying her hand the same way.
He couldn't articulate her name by then, wouldn't have been able to say
she was his daughter, but did he recognize their connection the way an
animal might, by smell? When he touched her skin, did he sense that she
was something of his?

Olivia and Gianfranco settled onto the bed together, their breathing
evenly matched. She wanted to cry, but there was no more liquid to give.
Manca l'acqua, even inside me, she thought wryly, but she didn't share it
with Gianfranco. How much could one person take? Ivan had, at first,
withstood the pressure of her father's illness, but then he'd retracted. Toward the end, during what passed for an argument between them—a long
exchange of complaints delivered in low voices, neither able to look the
other in the eye—Olivia had accused Ivan of caring more about his proj-
ects than he did about her.

"And you care more about your father than you do about me," he'd
replied.

"Of course I do. He's my father," she'd blurted, and then she'd realized
with nauseated insight that she was accusing Ivan of failing to connect, of
not putting in any effort, but really, she was the one.

IN SHALEFORD, HER FATHER'S HOUSE NOW FELT CLAIMED BY SOMEONE ELSE,
even though the Rodriguez family hadn't brought in furniture yet. Shaleford had been white as bone when Olivia was growing up, but in recent
years a substantial Latino population had begun to build. The Rodriguezes had three children, the real estate agent had already informed
Olivia, and she liked the thought of a family so different from the unit
composed of just herself and her father moving in. She was all for difference since she'd returned from Italy. She'd begun the school year with a
stack of new lesson plans and bought a green silk skirt that shimmered
like water and cost twice what she usually spent; she'd even turned the
mattress on her bed, the way you were supposed to do twice a year, a
housekeeping chore she'd previously shirked.

And Gianfranco was scheduled to visit in November. That was new, and potentially interesting, and something she tried not to imbue with too much hope. She'd already had all the disappointment she could bear.

Holding on to the wall, Olivia turned the corner and entered the kitchen. For a second, she couldn't identify what was so strange about the room, and then she noticed it was odorless. The hulking old refrigerator was unplugged and open, exposing the butter holder and the egg cups built into the door. The house no longer smelled like her father. Missing were the odors of garlic and tomatoes and the steam of boiling water. Absentmindedly, she ran her finger along the countertop, then peered into a cupboard. It was empty.

A week after she'd returned from Italy, Olivia had received a postcard from Claudia that read only *"Saluti da Fano"* and showed a generic beach with turquoise sky on the front. Olivia hadn't confronted Claudia. They'd double-kissed and promised to write when Olivia said good-bye, but she suspected that once Claudia returned from the beach and found out about the arrangements she'd made for the house, there would be no more cheery postcards.

On the day of the walk-through, she opened the back door of her father's house and stepped into the yard. Her father had always claimed to smell something distasteful there—not the septic tank or the sweet but skunky scent of the lady's slippers that grew in the woods past the lawn. She inhaled deeply but, as always, smelled only grass and a faint whiff of barbecue. It was mid-September already and the evenings in Shaleford would soon be cool enough for a sweater; in another month, grills would be stowed in garages, and soon after that the night air would fill with wood smoke from fireplaces instead.

Olivia walked to the shed. Tentatively, she pushed the door open. It was as empty as she'd left it after donating the wheel and the kiln to the Y where she'd first learned to throw. She stood in the doorway, glancing from the dirt-streaked window to the ceiling to the cement floor. She wondered whether the new owners would knock it down. If they didn't, no amount of cleaning was going to erase the earthy scent of clay. It filled her nostrils now, even without her stepping inside, years of it ground into the floor and the walls. She loved the smell not because it was beautiful but because it was reliable, much as she had always taken a whiff of

Smudgy's rank food before dumping it from a can into the cat's bowl, just to reassure herself that it was the same.

The shed in Urbino had been filled with a scent that she couldn't identify. She hadn't been able to see anything at first in the pitch-black, where small bursts of daylight as bright as stars leaked in through the spaces between the boards.

"Does anyone come in here—you know, like the *pineta*?" she had asked Gianfranco.

He shook his head. "People believe there are *fantasmi* here."

"Ghosts? Of the Levis?"

"Of the Levis, of your father, a hunter who was killed by accident out in the woods. They say that on *il giorno dei morti*, they come out and walk around the field, crying."

"What are they crying for?"

He laughed again. "It's silly, really. Only a *scemo* would believe in such things. They say the ghosts are banging on the door. There is a fog over the field, and they hear a voice that says *'Fammi entrare.'* 'Let me in.'"

Olivia sniffed the fetid air. "Why would anyone want to get in here? Especially after what you told me."

Gianfranco said, "Do you believe this?"

Olivia thought. "No, I think when you're dead, you're dead." Her father had been dead already when he was still alive.

"Your father was just gone one day, like the Jews when they left. His family didn't speak of him. As if he had never been."

Olivia shivered. Her eyes were adjusting to the darkness, and she spotted the quick slither of a field mouse in the far corner. She turned toward the door. "Let's go," she said. "There's nothing here."

In Shaleford, Olivia rubbed her hand along the door frame to the pottery shed. There was a cobweb hanging from the ceiling. "Memory is a very complex three-dimensional web," one of her father's doctors had explained, and she'd pictured something like this, cotton-candy shreds floating in the wind. It didn't matter, she realized, whether the Rodriguez family knocked down the shed or not. What she had learned here was a part of her. When she started throwing, her pottery teacher had told Olivia the craft would sensitize her fingers, and she'd been right. Even now, Olivia could feel every potential splinter in the door frame, every pockmark dug into the wood by bad weather and clumsiness and time. Her father was a part of her, too, her father as she'd known him, whatever had come before.

"Olivia!" the real estate agent called from the back door of the house.

"Coming," she said, and she shut the door of the shed and turned to go inside for the walk-through and find out whether the Rodriguezes, too, could accept what her father had left behind.

Gianfranco had begun to lock the door of the Urbino shed when they'd left it, but Olivia had stopped him. He removed his hand, and the key stuck in the lock, then clinked to the ground. She bent toward it. The tip of Gianfranco's suede shoe was inches from her fingers. She picked up the key, and he leaned down and offered a hand to help her up. Once on her feet, she returned the key to her back pocket.

"Let's close the door but not lock it," she suggested. Gianfranco pulled the door, but it wasn't fancy enough to have a knob or latch, so it was impossible to close it all the way with his fingers wrapped around the side. She took the key from her pocket and placed it in the lock, then used that to pull it toward them. Instead of locking it, she simply yanked out the key.

"That way, if anyone—ghost or not—wants to get in, they can," she said, satisfied with the results.

"Also," Gianfranco said, "if anybody wants to get out."

"OLIVIA?"

Olivia turned and glanced over her shoulder. With the walk-through successfully completed, she was headed to the Shaleford train station to catch Metro-North back to the city. She'd been looking carefully at the street, thinking this would be her last sight of it.

"I thought that was you."

It was Mrs. Teitel, her father's next-door neighbor.

"Hi, Mrs. Teitel."

Mrs. Teitel smiled. "You can call me Eve. We're both adults."

Olivia walked over to where Mrs. Teitel was standing in her front yard. "The house sold. Today's the walk-through."

Mrs. Teitel blushed. "Your father was a very kind neighbor. I hope they'll be as nice."

Olivia sighed. Here was the thing: How much should she tell people? She'd told Claire the whole story, of course, start to finish, and at dinner the first Tuesday after school started, she'd shared an abbreviated version with Rachel and Veronica, searching for signs of disgust on their faces when she told them, "My father was a collaborator, during the war." She'd longed for so many years to have a story to tell at those dinners, but she hadn't wished for any particular story, and clearly that had been her mistake. Be careful what you wish for, she thought. Should Mrs. Teitel be told? Too far outside of the circle, Olivia decided. Too inconsequential to his life.

"I'm so glad I saw you. I have something of yours, and I didn't want to give it back to you at the funeral," Mrs. Teitel said. She placed a hand on Olivia's arm. "Will you wait here while I run up and get it?"

Olivia nodded, and Mrs. Teitel disappeared into her house. Glancing through the screen door, Olivia could see a staircase identical to the one in her father's house, leading to a second-floor hallway. She'd never entered the Teitels' house, and now she never would.

Mrs. Teitel came down the stairs. She had nice legs for a woman her age, Olivia noticed. Mrs. Teitel bumped open the front door with her hip and handed Olivia a small, hollow ceramic egg glazed off-white. Automatically, she turned it upside down and saw on the bottom her own pottery mark, an O with a bar over the top.

"How did you end up with that?"

Mrs. Teitel shrugged. "Your father and I were quite friendly, you know."

"But why would he have given you this?"

"It was a gift, because of a favor I'd done for him. He thought the world of your work. A piece you'd made was the most valuable thing he could give anybody."

Olivia shook her head. "He wasn't as kind as you think. I just came back from Italy."

Before leaving Urbino, she'd written a letter signing over her claim to the property not to the *comune* but to the local *comunità ebraica*. There were a few Jewish families left in Urbino, Gianfranco had said. He'd even shown her the small synagogue, locked up for the summer. Most of the

Jews went to Ancona for the holidays, he explained, but occasionally they had a rabbi in for a wedding or a funeral.

"You went to Italy?" Mrs. Teitel asked.

"After he died. You wouldn't believe what happened back there."

Gianfranco was a notary in addition to being a lawyer. In his dusty office, he'd applied stamps and seals to her handwritten letter. Then he typed and printed out a statement vouching for her identity and signature. It wasn't a sure thing, he explained. She wasn't registered with the *comune*, so there was a chance Giovanni and Claudia would get the house, but her letter would, at the very least, complicate things for them. In a third letter, she requested that a plaque be embedded somewhere near the shed to commemorate what had happened. It was, she thought, too small a gesture for anyone to object.

"I know what happened," said Mrs. Teitel.

"You do?" What could her father have told Mrs. Teitel? Olivia had barely seen them speak, other than to exchange friendly hellos.

The last thing Gianfranco had done to each of the three pieces of paper was mark them with a wax seal. He'd lighted a match and melted wax from a red stick and let it drip on the paper. The room smelled like a box of Crayolas abandoned on a radiator. Then Gianfranco planted the end of a metal bar into the splotches and pulled it out, forming a three-dimensional red seal in the lower right corner of each letter. When the wax was cool, she ran her hand over the marks and felt their bumpy authenticity.

"He told me the whole sad story," Mrs. Teitel said, as if reading her mind.

"About the Levis?"

Mrs. Teitel nodded slowly. "About the Levis. Your father never got over it."

Olivia palmed the ceramic egg. Fired, it was no longer mutable. It remained the same. She felt like she could crush it, but she knew if she did, the sharp edges of the shards would dig into her palm and make her bleed.

When she'd started to go through the metal detector at the airport and then left the line for one more kiss, Gianfranco had raised a hand and held his palm against her cheek as though he were cradling a tender piece of ripe fruit and didn't want to bruise it. The combination of joy and sorrow was excruciating.

"I don't know if I can get over it, either," Olivia said. "Did you have a good vacation?" everyone would ask at school when the semester started. How to answer that?

"But you can get used to it. That's what I've learned with age: We can get used to anything."

Olivia remembered hurling adult diapers into the trunk of her father's car and the way that, at the end, if he managed to focus his eyes on her rather than gazing fuzzily toward the ceiling, she counted it as a good day. You could get used to anything.

"He thought he was doing the right thing at the time," Mrs. Teitel said.

"The right thing? People were killed."

"I meant he thought he was doing the right thing by not telling you. He was protecting you."

"Maybe, but he failed to protect a lot of other people." When she'd stood in that shed in Urbino, Olivia had known what it would be like to rely on her father and for him to prove unable to sustain her.

Mrs. Teitel put a hand on her shoulder. "You weren't other people. You were his family."

Gianfranco had stayed with her in the hotel her last night in Urbino, and she'd awakened once during the night and remembered what she'd learned, and that she'd be leaving him in the morning. Gianfranco's fist was thrown carelessly onto her breastbone, and she'd wished, briefly, that they might stay closeted together in a single room.

But then she'd considered how claustrophobic a single room could become, the way she used to burst out of her pottery shed in Shaleford into the air and the light. The way when her father was dying she sometimes thought she couldn't stand one more minute with clay, with him, or with her own thoughts. She'd studied Gianfranco's profile in the dark. She could make out, just barely, the ruffled top of his ear. In his sleep, he'd opened his hand and moved it to her stomach.

She and Gianfranco had talked about her remaining in Italy, the two of them going to the beach together for Ferragosto. But ultimately they'd agreed it was best for her to return to New York. Back home, Olivia was slated for desk duty at the pottery studio. Classes at Coleman would be starting in a couple weeks, and she had a full schedule of administrative work to handle prior to that. It would be expensive to change her ticket, if she could change it at all at this late date. As they discussed all these things, she could feel the Italian alter ego she'd pictured during the whole visit fading and stepping back into her, so that she was just herself again—practical and unwilling to take risks. But he'd promised to arrange a visit, and he'd been true to his promise.

"He sure loved his girl," said Mrs. Teitel. "He never forgot her."

A timer rang shrilly inside Mrs. Teitel's house, jolting them both.

"I'm baking cookies," Mrs. Teitel said. "I've got to check on them." Olivia stepped back and out of the doorway so the screen door could come between them, and Mrs. Teitel turned quickly and vanished in the dark of the house.

So, her father had loved his daughter. She had known that well before Mrs. Teitel said so. And Olivia loved him, too. She hadn't, after all, loved her father because he was perfect, but because he was her *babbo*. That hadn't changed.

The timer stilled, and the smell of burned sugar floated through the screen door. Olivia stood for a moment, as unsteady as a tall pot on a wheel. Clay that wobbled could sometimes be coaxed into surviving. But often the best thing you could do for a pot was to leave it alone.

Her father had closed off Italy from her as carefully as she herself had sealed the ceramic egg in her pocket. She heard Gianfranco's voice the day they'd first met: *He did not want that you should know. . . . I respect your father that he did not want this.* Mrs. Teitel had said, "He was protecting you." With the tip of her index finger, Olivia stroked the bottom of the closed form. There she could locate the tiny indent where she'd pricked it to keep it from exploding. Glaze had trickled in to fill it. Only the potter would find that signature nick, the insignificant scar.

There was no knowing other people, not fully, and there was no knowing their stories, or their histories, either. These things shifted every time you thought you'd gotten your hands around them. "You'll never know the whole truth," Claire had insisted when Olivia tearfully told her father's story. And that day, sitting by the ducal palace, Gianfranco had said, "The past is not a piece of your *ceramica* that you can hold in a hand." She'd gotten closer, and that would have to be enough.

Olivia turned and headed down the front walk. She was lifting her foot at the curb when Mrs. Teitel came hurrying after her, carrying a napkin. It was warm, and Olivia took it cautiously, as if it were a baby bird fallen from the nest.

"Something sweet for later, but be careful. They're still too hot to eat."

Olivia flashed on opening a kiln and seeing her first piece ever, a red-and-black-striped cylinder. So, this will be it, she'd thought at the time. Instinctively she'd reached to touch it, but her teacher had grabbed her hand and warned her that, like an ember, it was still bright-hot and would hold that heat inside for hours.

"Thank you," Olivia said. "It's been a difficult few weeks."

"I can imagine. But you understand, don't you, that your father couldn't stay in Italy after what your grandfather had done?"

"My grandfather?"

"Your father was too sad to stay after his father turned in the Levis."

Olivia closed her eyes in a hard, firm blink, then opened them again.

"My grandfather? I thought he—" Olivia indicated her father's house with her chin. "I mean, he's the one who left."

"You didn't think your father could have done something like that, did you? He didn't have a mean bone in his body."

"For the house."

Mrs. Teitel shook her head. "No, for the girl."

Olivia felt as displaced as she had when she'd returned to New York. That first morning, she woke before 5:00 A.M. and stared out the living room window into the flat gray light. The familiar street looked like a foreign country at that hour. A drunk man stumbled down the block, his night overlapping with her morning. A light burned in one apartment across the way. She'd put on sneakers and walked to the river. As she leaned over the railing and watched the water lap against the cement wall, she wondered at how the tides continued on schedule, even when surrounded by so much that was man-made.

"I don't understand," she said now.

Mrs. Teitel rested a hand on her arm. "Maybe you'd better take a later train. I think there's a story you need to hear."

✦ 1939 ✦

Ester was fifteen to Luigi's seventeen, too young for a *fidanzato*. Also, she was Jewish, although she insisted that her father liked Luigi, despite his family's Catholicism, and could identify that he was special, just as she could. Luigi wasn't sure he wanted to be *fidanzato* anyway. Boys and girls who were did physical things together that he couldn't bear to suggest to Ester. Not that he could have thrust a hand up her skirt even if he'd wanted to. She arranged it around herself on the grass as prettily and neatly as a lace doily on the arm of an overstuffed chair. His mother had two such doilies at home, on a chair no one was permitted to use.

There on the back lawn, Ester's grandfather nodded off in his wheelchair. Luigi had kissed her only once, a chaste, dry meeting of their lips as they lay in the shade of the enormous tree whose branches reached past the roof of the house and darkened the rooms on the first floor. Her skin, he noticed close-up, was covered in the finest shimmering coat of soft hairs, like the sweet fuzzy pelt of a muskrat his father had once shot after mistaking it for a rabbit.

He came over almost every day that spring, after school. The first time, he went on the pretense of offering schoolbooks. She was so welcoming—delighted to have the company, she told him, since she was stuck at home with her three-year-old brother and her parents and grandfather—that he began to drop by once and then twice a week with news that had been shut out by an invisible barrier of Jewishness.

Ester began to wait for him. She confided the strangest things as they sat on the grass, books in their laps. Luigi sat cross-legged, but Ester folded her legs beneath her so that they disappeared under her skirt, and she looked like she was sprouting out of the ground, her feet sunk deep into the dirt like roots. Her mother should never have had children, she told Luigi one day. She was lacking in maternal instinct. Luigi didn't think that was possible for a woman, but Ester insisted it was true. At night, she told him, hiding her smile with the thin fingers of her right hand, her mother wore a chin strap that pressed an oval metal plate against her forehead. It was supposed to smooth out the wrinkles while she slept. Childbirth had gobbled her youth as though it were a piece of chocolate, her mother often complained.

"Was she pregnant when she got married?" he asked.

Ester blushed, pink running up her face until it met the border of dark hair, pulled back hard off her forehead.

"Of course not," she said, as if such a thing were impossible.

It was Luigi's turn to blush, and he stared down at his own hands. His fingertips were blotted with ink. He couldn't take notes without staining himself. His own mother had been pregnant with him when his parents got married; she told it as a cautionary tale. His grandmother, before she grew senile and died, had cheerfully admitted that she'd been pregnant with his mother when she married. "We went out to pick fava beans," she'd told him, smiling, "and the next thing I knew I was *gonfia* and wearing a *fede*." Luigi pictured the skin on his grandmother's stomach stretched the way his did after Sunday lunch as it strained to contain his gluttony.

Another time, Ester confessed that she sometimes crossed herself when she lay in bed at night, just in case the Jews turned out to be wrong and Jesus was the son of God after all. He was strangely moved by the thought of her shrouded in a nightshirt, awkwardly touching her forehead and then her navel and then her shoulders.

"*Odio il mio nome*," she told him one day. And then she pronounced it with her mouth squinched in a sour pucker. "Ester."

"It's a fine name," he said.

"No, no. It sounds like *estero*, foreign, or *esterno*."

It *was* foreign. It was a Jewish name. Luigi's sister had four friends named Maria, two named Anna, and two named Franca, but he knew not a single other Ester.

"In the Bible, Ester saves the Jews from death," she said, "but not because she's intelligent. Just because she's beautiful."

"At least she saves them. Does it matter how?"

"It's an old-lady name. It was my great-grandmother's."

He nodded.

"A Jewish tradition," she added. "They give you the name of a dead person."

"What do you wish your name were?"

She looked up at the sky. Clouds were skimming overhead. They reminded Luigi of the ice-skaters who slid across the surface of the river when it froze. Then she looked at the fields behind her parents' house, filled as far as he could see with grapevines and stumpy olive trees.

"Olivia," she said.

"From now on, I'll call you Olivia," he promised.

She blushed and looked down at the book in her lap.

"Only when we're alone." She glanced over her shoulder at her grandfather, who had dozed off in his wheelchair. Although it was warm enough that Luigi had rolled up the sleeves of his button-down shirt, her grandfather wore a cap and had a knitted shawl spread over his shoulders.

"But we're never alone," Luigi said. It wasn't a complaint, just a statement of fact.

"Maybe someday we will be," she said hoarsely. She'd had a sore throat a few days before and was still sucking on barley candies to soothe it.

"Names are strange anyway, aren't they?" Luigi said.

"What do you mean?"

"I can meet another *ragazzo* whose name is also Luigi. We have the same name, but we're two different people."

She considered this for a second. "That's true. There could be a Luigi in China." Ester's father had traveled as far as France and Greece. Luigi had never been outside of Urbino. He wasn't quite sure he believed in the world beyond.

"No one in China has the name Luigi."

Ester wore her long dark hair pulled back with a ribbon, but the fine strands around the peak of her forehead had sprung loose and were moving in the breeze. Tiny freckles dotted the skin across her nose, so that it looked like a speckled brown eggshell.

The afternoon sun glinted off the windows at the back of the house, as if the building were winking at them. Luigi looked down to shade his eyes, then wrapped his fist around a clump of grass and pulled it free of the earth.

She glared at him. "Even plants feel things," she said.

"No they don't." He held the blades of grass in his palm.

"How do you know?"

"Science."

"How can you know plants don't have feelings, though?"

"Observation. Hypothesis. Experimentation."

"But you've never been a plant, so how can you know?" she asked.

He shrugged.

She smiled with satisfaction. "So you admit that there are things your biology can't answer?"

"I admit nothing," he said, and then he took the loose blades of grass and tossed them toward her. Several landed in the open pages of her book, while others stuck to her ecru dress.

"One day," she said, brushing them out of her hair, "you'll have to answer for all these little deaths." She smiled and shook the grass from the book, then tossed it back at him. She closed the book and rested it in her lap.

"So, you believe in *paradiso*?" he asked, mocking her gently.

She shook her head. "I would like to, but no."

"Where, then, will I have to answer for everything?"

She frowned. "On earth. Maybe you won't even know it's happening."

"I believe in heaven," he said, and suddenly, smelling the warm grass, he did. Her grandfather emitted a burbling snore from his wheelchair, then fell silent again. His chin rested against his chest. Old age seemed to Luigi as far away and removed as heaven.

Ester patted the book of poetry on her lap. "Shall I read one to you?" she asked. "It would help us forget about death and biology."

Luigi started to say that death and biology were not two separate things, but one and the same, but then he looked at her, and a tangle of hair danced on her forehead, and he wanted nothing more than to hear her voice.

"Yes, read one." He glanced at her grandfather to be sure he was still sleeping. "Please read one," he said, "Olivia." She fluttered open the pages of the book and rested a finger against the paper, and then she began.

YOUR NEXT GREAT READ IS JUST A CLICK AWAY!

Join St. Martin's Read-It-First E-mail Book Club

★ ★ ★ ★

Be in the know and sample hot *new* releases. Every weekday morning, a taste of the week's featured title will be sent right to your inbox. By Friday you'll have read enough to decide whether it is the right book for you . . . sometimes before it even hits the stores!

And it's all completely *free!*

Sign up and:
- **Sample** books before you buy
- **Discover** new books and new authors
- Be the **first** to read new releases
- **Enter** to win free books

Sign up at www.Read-It-First.com

FIC DANFORD
Danford, Natalie.
Inheritance

05/29/19

CPSIA information can be obtained
at www.ICGtesting.com
Printed in the USA
LVHW040839040419
612951LV00001B/89/P